Jack Easter

The Wichita Kid: A Caddie's Story

By Rob Fisher

For Laura

Prologue

For the summer of 1979 I was the Wichita Kid. I got the nickname the very first day I showed up for work, and it stuck with me all summer. I suppose I spoke a little differently from the other kids, but apart from that I didn't really stand out. I never had a nickname before – you know, something like Lumpy or Jughead or Fonz; a name the guys give you and it becomes such a part of who you are that no one remembers your real first name or where the name came from in the first place. But for a few months, I was the Wichita Kid. It had a gunslinger-type quality to it.

It was a clear August morning when I 'hit' the shot. Not that I had many great athletic moments in my life. Okay, none. But this still was my best.

There was a slight chill to the early morning Cleveland air despite the week-long heat wave. Roll call had just ended, and with little activity on the golf course, we needed something to pass the time. Mouse was the one who came up with the idea of throwing the driving range balls from the caddie yard toward the 9th green.

My first throw – over the fifteen-foot high caddie yard, past a practice green and beyond a line of small trees – came embarrassingly short of my target about 100 yards away. Mouse at least reached the sand trap, short of the elevated green.

We attracted a small crowd on our second attempts.

'Closest to the pin for a buck,' said Mouse.

'Okay; how much if I sink it?'

'You get all of my earnings for the rest of the summer.'

1

I smiled. 'Sounds good.'

'With your arm, I think I'm pretty safe.'

This time I took a couple of steps before heaving it with all the might my 12 year old body could muster. My shoulder nearly popped out of its socket. The ball started off to the left of the green but drifted toward the pin.

'Get right!'

'Get legs! Get legs!'

The ball bounced once on the fringe and then kicked up a trail of morning dew as it rolled twenty feet, hit the pin and dropped into the hole.

I looked at Mouse agape, bug-eyed. Our small crowd erupted. Mouse and I took off in a sprint through the caddie house and around the parking lot to validate the miracle we'd just witnessed. Sure enough, when we reached the 9th green, the red-striped range ball sat comfortably in the cup.

I grabbed it, held it high and jumped up and down like I had just won the Masters. Tom Watson can keep his chip-in on 17 at Pebble Beach; Larry Mize can have his shot to win at Augusta. I'd take my perfect throw that morning at Westwood any day.

And most importantly, I didn't throw up amid all the excitement.

Now that I think about it, Mouse still owes me that money.

Chapter 1

'Did I turn the oven off?' Mom's voice broke an hour long silence.

I unglued my forehead from the passenger door window and turned her way. 'I don't know.'

'Do you think I turned it off?'

'You probably did.' I returned to the thoughts churning in my mind. I tried to get my brain around what was happening, tried to picture myself in a new environment, but I couldn't. I was terrified.

'I probably did,' she parroted.

A sign for the Wichita Mid-Continent Airport passed over her left shoulder. Her hair was a brown mess with gray invaders scattered about. Her piercing hazel eyes had dark circles beneath and burgeoning crows' feet beside.

'What if I didn't?'

'I'm sure you did,' I choked out.

A few more minutes passed in silence. My hands were numb. The left side of my face was tingling. I felt a little dizzy. My stomach was a zoo. I was on the verge of passing out.

'Are you sure you're going to be all right with this, Kevin?'

'Do I…do I really have a choice?' my voice quivered.

She pursed her lips. 'Not really. But I don't see any other way. You'll be good and safe there.' She didn't dare look my way. I returned to counting the trees whipping by my window.

'When you go inside, find the Continental counter to check your bags. They'll direct you past security to the gate.'

'You…you mean you're not coming in with me?'

'I'd love to. It kills me to let you out of my sight. You know that. But I need to swing back home to check the oven before I check into the clinic.'

'Swing back home? It's over an hour away back to Salina. That makes no sense.'

'It won't take long; I'll drive fast. We'll burn the whole building down if I left it on.'

'But…I've never been on a plane before!' My heart pounded.

'Please don't do this to me,' she pleaded. 'You've been in an airport before, haven't you? I would just be walking you a little further to the gate. You can do that. You'll be fine. Trust me.' I had heard this pseudo-confident pep talk numerous times before. 'Flying is nothing. It's like…'

'Riding a bike?'

'Exactly!'

'And you remember I fell and broke my arm the first time you put me on a bike? You told me to trust you then.'

'It's completely different.'

'Because…I'll be…35,000 feet up in the air?' I felt light-headed.

'Exactly.'

'Interesting.'

'You'll be fine. Please. I really need to go and make sure I didn't burn the apartment building down.'

'I…I…' I gave up. The conversation exhausted me.

If I'd come anywhere near food that morning, I would have upchucked in my lap. Instead, I swallowed short gulps of air to keep the acid down.

She pulled up to the curb and shifted the car into Park. Her tone changed. 'Kevin, neither of us wants to do this, but we have to. I know this is so, so very hard on you. But I need to focus on getting myself better. You'll be with family. And I'm not going to be much fun.'

I gave her a long, lingering hug as I fought off the tears.

The few muscles on my body shook as I made my way to the ticket counter and the gate that would lead me to my maiden voyage to Cleveland.

I stepped onto the plane and assessed the situation. I found the emergency exits, pictured myself climbing over the four rows to launch myself to safety if necessary.

I pressed my head against the window during take-off and watched the grassy, rolling Kansas landscape unfold. The first few minutes were smooth, almost comfortable, until we began to crash. Or at least that's what I thought was happening when we hit our first patch of turbulence. I looked around wide-eyed to my fellow crash victims for comfort, but several were asleep and the others didn't seemed to care that we were about to die.

'Just a little turbulence,' the man in the aisle seat wearing a pin-striped suit reassured me.

We hit more bumps over the next few minutes, and I turned his way each time to be sure it was fine. If he's okay with it, then it must be safe, I tried to tell myself. But then again, why am I entrusting my life to this guy? He may be as ignorant about flying as I am. Or he might be drunk. Or he may have a miserable life and may be hoping to die.

I turned my attention to the stewardesses. I studied their features in search of any hint of panic or terror behind their plastic smiles. Are they going up the aisle because they've been summoned to the cockpit? Maybe the pilot had a heart attack. Maybe we're lost. Maybe we've lost an engine. Or a nuclear bomb has hit Cleveland, and we have nowhere to land.

A lifetime later we began our descent. As the plane banked into a turn, the wing's flaps opened outside my window. I gasped.

I turned to my friend on the aisle. 'It looks like the wing is falling apart. Should we tell the stewardess?' My finger was inches away from the Call button.

He chuckled. 'No, that's normal. That's how they slow the plane down.'

Did he mean that's how they crash a plane?

'It doesn't look like it's supposed to happen,' I mumbled.

I decided to sit there and die quietly instead of risk making a fool of myself. I closed my eyes.

I let out a small yelp when the wheels eventually hit the tarmac. I didn't know if we had crashed, landed, or both. Either way, I was just glad it was over.

My grandfather stood at the gate like a nervous limo driver. He was smaller than I remembered, with receding gray hair and a weathered face.

'Kevin, you've gotten so big.' Not really, but I appreciated the attempt. My skinny 12 year old body stood a mere 5 feet. My thick golden hair added perhaps another inch. My stature, hair and innocence were reminiscent of Hermey, the aspiring dentist from Rudolph, but without the unbridled optimism. Perhaps more like Charlie from Willie Wonka.

My grandmother hesitated a moment before enveloping me in a warm hug. Her bulging blouse smelled of stale moth balls. She was much shorter than the last time I saw her two years ago. She wiped bright red lipstick from my cheek as she released me. Her eyes sparkled behind her oversized tortoise-shelled frames.

My grandfather offered an awkward part-handshake, part-hug, part-stumble and took my carry-on bag. His polyester shirt smelled of stale cigarettes.

'It's so, so good to see you again, Kevin. How was your flight?' my grandmother asked.

I thought of the terror I had experienced, but just offered, 'It was fine.'

'Did they feed you?'

'Um, no.'

'You really should eat. You know it's very important for boys your age to get enough to eat. Don't you agree, Bill?'

He weakly nodded.

'I've read several articles recently that kids need to eat at least one serving of meat each day,' my grandmother continued as we walked. 'It's important that they get enough iron. We need to be sure you get enough iron while you're staying with us, Kevin. You also need to eat fruit. We need to be sure that you get enough Vitamin C. No one's getting scurvy on my watch. You know that explorers used to always get scurvy on those long expeditions to the North Pole and such, didn't you? But it turns out that it wasn't the common sailors who got the scurvy, it was the officers. The officers would eat the meat of the seals they killed and leave the innards for the other men. Well it turns out that the kidneys and livers and such, are chock full of Vitamin C. Did you know that? It's the innards.'

'Nope, never heard that.' I parried.

'I thought that was interesting. It served those officers right.' She paused. 'Scurvy... it might have been rickets; no, it was scurvy. Anyway we'll need to cook up some liver and onions this week.'

That didn't sound good at all.

We reached Baggage Carousel C and stood in a row like expectant fathers.

'So you just finished up fifth grade didn't you?' attempted my grandfather.

'Sixth. I'll be in seventh next year.'

'Seventh already? Huh. Where does the time go?' He let out a hacking cough.

My bags emerged onto the conveyor belt. My grandfather grabbed the bags and carried them to a faded, powder blue

Oldsmobile sedan in the parking garage. I felt particularly small with the entire back seat to myself. I analyzed the back of their heads, which barely poked up above the headrests. My grandmother's short hair was dyed auburn and unnaturally perma-fluffed. Not a good look. My grandfather's comb-over did a poor job of covering his shiny scalp. My hopes of emerging from puberty with a larger and improved appearance were dissipating ever so quickly.

I turned my attention to surveying the passing trees and buildings as we drove through the West Side suburbs.

'What do you think of Cleveland, Kevin?' queried my grandmother.

'Nice. More trees than I expected. Do you get many forest fires?'

'Uh, no. We don't get any of those here.' That made me feel better. 'I think you'll like it. It won't be quite as hot as Kansas, but the humidity will be higher so it will feel as hot. Not that I've ever been to Kansas.' She paused. My grandfather returned her glance.

'Remember the time, Bill,' she continued, 'that we drove back from Mexico on our honeymoon. We didn't drive through Kansas then, did we?'

'No, after we drove through Texas, we headed east before going up north.'

'You drove back from Mexico?' I interjected.

'It was your grandmother's idea.'

'It was fun. We flew down to Puerto Vallarta and rented a car and drove to Mexico City. Rather than just fly home, anyone can do that, we just drove it. It was great.'

'It was hell,' my grandfather countered. 'The roads were terrible. The food in the small towns was disgusting. We both got sick. What was so great about it?'

'It was an adventure. It was our honeymoon. It was fun.' She turned toward the back seat. 'Kevin, we made up the guest room. I hope you feel at home there. We hope you don't have to stay long; no, that came out wrong. We love having you here, but we hope your Mother gets better soon.'

'Me too.'

We pulled into their six-story apartment complex in the suburb of Rocky River. I searched around desperately for emergency stairs.

'Ever had a fire in this building?' I asked.

'No, not that I'm aware of.'

'How would we get out?' My breath shortened.

'The stairs are down the hall. I guess we would just use them.'

I strained my neck to find the EXIT sign at the end of the hall. I looked back the other way to find the other set of steps in case those were blocked. I didn't see them, but I was afraid to appear too weird if I pressed the point.

My grandfather unlocked their apartment door, and my grandparents walked right in.

I immediately took my shoes off at the doorway and held them by my side, waiting for a cue of what to do next.

10

'Your room's the one on the left.'

I stood still a few more seconds, slowly put my shoes upside down next to the door and walked across the shag carpet in my socks. The apartment had two bedrooms and only one bathroom. Mine was the guestroom, which looked like no guest had occupied it for years. The carpeting was yellow, the furniture was painted white and the walls were papered in lime-green flowers. A single overhead fixture emitted barely enough light for me to read.

'We already ate, but we saved you some pot roast. Do you want me to heat it up?'

'No thanks. I'm fine.' Eating was completely out of the question.

'Are you sure? It's your grandfather's favorite. We also have carrots and bread. It'll take no time at all.'

'No, I'm not hungry, and I'm pretty tired. I think I'll just go to my room and get my things squared away and go to bed early. I'm beat.'

'Well you should probably call your mother to let her know you got here safely.'

'No, she's not expecting a call tonight. I think I'll just go to bed,' I answered, and I escaped into my new room.

I methodically unpacked my suitcase and sat on the edge of my bed. The day had been exhausting. My body and brain were numb. But I had survived it. I feared that I would never be able to eat again, that my body would just wither away. My mind couldn't visualize a scenario in the future where I would eat normally again.

11

I didn't know how I would make it through another day, but I couldn't begin to get my arms around it until I had some time to sleep and reenergize my brain. I closed my eyes and tried not to hear the TV in the living room.

I woke up at least 20 times that night. Each time my grandmother's Hummel collection was staring back at me from a shelf on the wall. The choir boy's smile looked more like a sinister grimace, like he wanted to kill me.

Morning finally arrived and I struggled to sit up in bed. The thought of making it to the end of the day seemed impossible. Fifteen hours until I could finally return to the comfort of sleep, away from the fears of my life. Impossible.

My bladder was ready to burst, but my grandfather had taken up residence in the bathroom. I lay back on my bed until he finally emerged. I rushed into the bathroom and weighed myself after emptying my bladder. Ninety-six pounds. I eventually made my way into the kitchen. It was filled with the bitter smell of Maxwell House.

'Good morning, Kevin,' sang my grandmother. 'How did you sleep?' She had made a huge breakfast, complete with scrambled eggs, bacon, sausage, pancakes and banana bread, but my stomach had shut down since I started my journey back home in Salina.

I poked at the food on my plate. Bacon was my favorite food, the best food ever invented. At times like this when I was too nervous to eat anything else, a strip or two of bacon was the only thing that my stomach didn't reject. I suspect my stomach realized that it could let me wither away to nothingness, so it left me one concession and chose the fattest, highest-caloric item available.

I picked up The Plain Dealer on the chair next to me and fished through the classified ads to see what summer jobs were available. The thought of getting a job terrified me, but I needed to. I tried to fight through the fear.

Not much in the paper. A grocery store named Rego's had an opening for a stock boy. I circled that. A moving company was hiring, but you had to be at least 16 years old. Darn those pesky child labor laws. The Loews movie theatre had an opening in the concessions stand. I didn't see much else, but it was a start.

'Kevin, I ran into Mrs. Kenworth this morning,' said my grandmother as she placed more slices of bacon in the frying pan. 'She lives down the hall. She mentioned that her grandson, he's about your age, he's a caddie at the country club down the street. Westwood is the name of it. She says that they're always looking for good, young boys like yourself to carry golf bags. It may be fun.'

Carrying golf bags didn't sound like too much fun. 'Do you know how much they make?'

'No.' She paused. 'I didn't think it appropriate to ask.'

'I'll keep it in mind.'

'This caddying thing could be really good exercise. Boys like you need a lot of exercise, especially in these years when you're growing. This caddying thing could be just what you need to build up those muscles of yours. And you'd be outdoors...Of course carrying those bags seems like it could be awful hard on your back. It might give you scoliosis. We wouldn't want that, would we?'

'No.'

After I ate a piece of bacon, I stared blankly at the newspaper and willed my stomach to settle down so that I could move on with the day. After a few minutes, I got to my feet, but it was too much for my stomach. I hurried to the bathroom and threw up violently, but as quietly as I possibly could. My eyes were filled with tears as the convulsions stopped, and I felt a mixture of calm and disappointment in myself, my life. I listened to be sure my grandparents hadn't heard me. I went into my bedroom to collect myself.

I finally girded myself to face the day and headed for the door. My head was now throbbing. I grabbed three Kleenex on my way out -- one for the left pocket, one for the right pocket, and a backup in the right pocket just in case.

I went downstairs and straddled the old bike that my grandmother had gotten me for the summer. She had drawn me a map with the major roads and landmarks so that I wouldn't get lost. With each pump of the pedals, I pushed a little bit of the fear away. I reached Center Ridge Road and fought the traffic until I found Rego's. I locked the bike to a pole outside the store entrance, and prepared to present myself as a stock boy. I found the fortified manager's area near the back of the store. With each step, I was further and further away from safety in case a fire broke out. A swarthy man in a shirt and tie with an apron tied around his waist stood in the glass enclosed room.

'Excuse me, sir. Is this where I can apply for the stock boy position?'

'Oh, yeah,' boomed his baritone voice, 'that job has already been filled. It turns out that Sal's cousin, Connie? Well, her son needed a job and Sal didn't know that. So Tony's working here now.'

'So the job's no longer open?'

'No. Sorry, buddy.'

Filled? Already?

I rode my bike to the Westgate Mall, which had a multiplex movie theatre. The box office had not yet opened for the day, but a pale, gaunt, balding man stood behind the gate getting things ready for the first matinee.

'Excuse me. I was wondering whether the concession stand job was still available.'

'Well, of course,' he replied amidst the permeating odor of buttered popcorn. 'Give me a moment and I'll let you fill out the application.'

A few minutes later he opened the gate enough for me to slide under and handed me the application. 'You can sit over there,' pointing to the seat at the ticket booth.

The application took about 20 minutes to fill out. They sure did want to know a lot of information for a minimum wage position. It took me a few minutes to figure out how to properly respond to the questions about my military experience and my criminal history.

'I'm done. Do I give this back to you or should I drop it off somewhere?'

'Yes, give it to me, thank you.' He looked it over for a minute or two. 'Hmmm. Now, Mr. Campbell, what sort of concession or concession-related experience do you have?'

'None, really.'

'Now, what exactly attracts you to the concessional line of work?'

'I need a summer job.'

'Hmmm. And what do you think you would bring to this job as a concessionaire?'

I paused. 'Well, I have to ride my bike so I don't know how much I would be able to bring with me.'

'Why do you think you'd be good at the job?' he restated impatiently.

'I can be a pretty hard worker.'

He turned away from me. 'Okay, we'll call you if we need you.'

And with that, I had blown my first job interview.

This was harder than I thought, if I had really thought it through in the first place. I knew I needed a job, but I didn't really know what I was doing. Things had gotten pretty desperate for us since Mom lost her job. The fact that she reached out to her parents to look after me was a glaring sign of that. She wouldn't think of

16

stooping to take any money from them, so it was on my shoulders to bring in some cash for the family. I had never done anything like this before, and I wasn't very good at taking on new things.

Without knowing what else to do, I pointed my bike in the direction of the country club.

On either side of the imposing entrance to the tree-lined drive, two iron placards on granite structures announced Westwood Country Club – Members Only. Not completely convinced that non-members wouldn't be shot on sight, I tentatively pedaled my bike down the tree-canopied drive that paralleled golf holes on either side. The white colonial-styled clubhouse unfolded from under the branches, contrasting against the pristine green of the golf course. Along the circular driveway leading up to the clubhouse were parked Cadillacs, Lincolns and a couple Jaguars. I stopped to admire the scene. The grass seemed artificially green. The white buildings sparkled. It was perhaps the most beautiful place I had ever seen in my life.

I approached a man who was valeting cars.

'Could you please tell me where I can sign up to be a caddie?'

He took off running to retrieve a member's car from the parking lot without bothering to answer me, but he pointed in the direction of a small building on the other side of the clubhouse. Although painted white like the other buildings in the compound, the caddie house was a little more weathered.

As I entered the adjoining caddie yard, I was transported from stately grandeur of the rest of country club to Lord of the Flies.

About 50 boys between the ages of 12 and 18, all wearing the same blue T-shirts with a WCC logo, ran around like convicts in a prison yard without the guards. On the basketball court 15 or so boys were playing a version of basketball in which traveling and fouling appeared to be not only legal but encouraged. A boy was slammed against the chain link fence beside me as he flung the ball toward the hoop. On the other end of the court an older caddie driving a golf cart tried to run over two younger caddies. In another part of the graveled caddie yard, another group of boys played a makeshift game of stickball with a broomstick and a red-striped driving range ball. Three kids huddled around a small pile of scorecards and pencils that they had just lit on fire. Everyone was doing something. The quietest area was on a picnic table where an intense game of poker was underway. A pile of crumpled-up singles sat in the pot. The thumping guitar riff of The Knack's My Sharona blared just below the shouts and laughs of all the boys. It was a couple of midgets and a tutu-ed bear short of a circus.

I made my way into the caddie house, which was a bit quieter. Two large signs hung on either wall:

'Good caddies are not born. Boys become good caddies by being patient and ambitious.'

'No horseplay!'

I walked over to the small office in the corner where two high school age boys sat. I waited a full minute before getting up the nerve to peak my head in.

'Is this where I can sign up for caddying?' I said tentatively.

'Yeah, are you old enough?' said the blond-haired one behind a bemused smile.

'How old do you have to be?'

'Old enough to be able to take care of yourself,' said the brown-haired boy. 'Have you ever killed a man?'

The blond one stepped in, 'You have to be 12 and at least 5 foot 3.'

'Well, I'm twelve, but –'

'Strength is more important than height,' the other boy jumped back in. 'Let's see how many push-ups you can do.'

I stood there wondering whether they were serious.

'Come on! Get down and show us how many you can do.'

I slowly crawled to the dusty floor, keeping an eye on them for any sign of relief. I strained to push myself up with my skinny arms.

'One…Two…Three…Four…,' they counted out.

After the sixth one, my arms were burning and I collapsed to the floor.

'Not too impressive, my friend. Get up, and let's see how high you can jump.'

I pulled my humiliated self off the floor and jumped as high as I could. It was not high.

The boys were beside themselves in laughter.

The brown haired one grabbed me by the arm and started pulling me outside. 'We got to show this elf to Kovach.'

'Hey, Kovach! This shrimp wants to be a caddie. What do you think?'

Kovach was the boy who had tried to run over the two smaller caddies with a golf cart. Although you couldn't really call Kovach a boy. He stood 6' 4'' and his muscles stretched the limits of his caddie shirt fibers. He was probably only 18, but he had beard stubble so thick that you could almost hear it growing.

Kovach put his thick arm around me in the middle of the caddie yard and said, 'Hey, little buddy, what's your name?' Kovach's voice was surprisingly high-pitched, and he had a slight lisp.

'Kevin Campbell.'

'Kevin Campbell, huh? Where the hell'd you come from?'

'An hour or so outside of Wichita. I'm –'

'You're pretty short to be a caddie. Can you fight?'

'Um, I dunno.'

He scanned the caddie yard without listening for an answer. The caddie yard games halted and all eyes were on Kovach and me. 'Where's Mouse?' he yelled.

A freckled-face kid a little shorter than me was pushed from the crowd.

I wanted to run and vomit, but I was paralyzed.

'Mouse, this new Spook said that he could kick your ass.'

Mouse just sort of shrugged.

Kovach continued, 'I think we need to settle this with a traditional caddie slap-boxing match.'

Kovach assumed the dual role of ring announcer and boxing referee.

'In this corner,' he raised his voice to fill the whole caddie yard, 'from Fairview Park, Ohio. Current super flyweight world champion and Westwood Country Club super-Spook. Number 307 – Mouse McMurtry!!!'

A roar arose from the caddies, who all now had gathered to witness the spectacle.

'In this corner, from Wichita, Kansas. The challenger, in his boxing debut – The Wichita Kid!!!'

The crowd went crazy. We had no choice but to raise our hands into boxing position. I had never been in a fight before, much less a boxing match. Mouse looked like he knew what he was doing.

Mouse was first to strike with a slap to my left cheek. I was stunned since I barely saw him move. Next thing I knew, I felt another slap on my left cheek, followed by another one on my right. With my face stinging, I lamely reached out to slap Mouse, only to receive another 1-2 combo in the face. Mouse certainly was the crowd favorite. They roared with every slap he landed. The pummeling continued for another minute or so until Kovach stepped in and broke it up.

'Okay, okay, okay,' Kovach yelled against the boos. 'I think this one is over.'

He grabbed Mouse's wrist and lifted it into the air. 'By technical knockout, the winner and still reigning super flyweight champion – Mouse McMurtry!'

The crowd cheered.

I stumbled over to the fence and vomited up the few remaining pieces of bacon from breakfast.

'Oh, gross!' someone yelled. 'The little kid puked.'

Everyone took a couple of steps back.

I looked up and wiped my mouth. The crowd dispersed, and I heard the basketball game resume.

'There's a drinking fountain over there if you want to use it,' a boy about my size said. 'You should probably use it.'

I gargled some water to get the taste of bile out of my mouth, and then made my way to my bike.

Kovach intercepted me. 'You okay?'

'Yes,' I said, even though I was pretty sure I wasn't.

'The next time someone asks you if you can fight, the answer definitely is no.' He smiled. 'So you're looking to caddie?'

'I don't think so.'

'Come on, you can handle it.'

'I dunno.'

'Well show up tomorrow, and you can start your training. You're going to need to follow another caddie around for two rounds before you can caddie on your own. You won't get paid for that, but you have to learn what you're doing. Just go to the first tee tomorrow and find Mr. G, the caddie master. He's an old guy; you can't miss him. Tell him your name and he'll get you out on the course.' He handed me a booklet from his back pocket. 'This is the Caddie Manual. It'll help you with the basics.'

'Okay,' I mumbled.

My head was spinning; and it hurt too. What the heck just happened?

Chapter 2

I woke the next morning and briefly pondered my terrible options. There weren't many. I forced myself back to sleep.

When the clock read 9:30, I finally sat up. The caddie manual sat on the night stand. I turned to the Basics of Golf.

Common Golf Terms:

- Divot: A piece of turf dug from a golf fairway in making a shot
- Tee: A small mound or a peg on which a golf ball is placed before being struck at the beginning of play on a hole; also, the area from which a golf ball is struck at the beginning of play on a hole
- Par: An expert golfer's expected score for a particular hole of a golf course
- Birdie: A score of one stroke less than par on a hole
- Bogey: A score of one stroke more than par on a hole
- Handicap: An advantage given in the form of strokes that represents the number of strokes on average the golfer shoots above par for 18 holes

I flipped a few pages forward.

Expectations of a Caddie:

- Be prompt
- Be courteous and polite
- Never roughhouse or joke on the course
- Never chew gum
- Always wear a clean shirt and be sure your hair is combed
- Always address the golfer as Sir or Ma'am

I put it down and got out of bed. Every muscle in my abdomen was clenched. As I brushed my teeth in the bathroom, the brush hit the back of my mouth and made me gag. I desperately swallowed air to keep the contents of my stomach down. That worked for a minute or two until I could swallow no more. With the first small burp, the few remnants of what little I ate the night before heaved through my esophagus. God, I hated throwing up.

It left me weak, but at least it settled me down a little. I cleaned myself up and stepped onto the scale. Ninety-four pounds. I was terrified my weight would keep sliding down, but I also couldn't imagine being able to ever keep food down again. I looked at the mirror, and a skeleton stared back. I got dressed and tried to scoot out. I didn't want to bother with the charade of breakfast.

'I'm heading out,' I called into the kitchen. 'I'll be back sometime this afternoon.' I grabbed my three Kleenex and opened the door.

'But Kevin, I made you breakfast. At least have some fruit.' The door slammed behind me.

I rode my bike up the tree-lined drive, and locked it up on the crowded caddie yard bike rack. I wasn't quite sure where to go. I shuffled over to the first tee area to announce my arrival. I casually checked my zipper as I approached the break in the shoulder-high hedges. 15 caddies sat on green wood benches waiting to be assigned. They all looked at me. I checked my zipper again. I looked down at my golf shirt and back at the corps of boys in their blue caddie shirts. I stuck out like a clown at a funeral.

'Hey, it's the Wichita Kid,' said someone from a bench.

'Don't puke on me,' said another.

I put my head down and walked up to Mr. G, who directed operations on the first tee from an L-shaped desk area built into the corner of the pro shop porch. He was a small man, with a Kaiser Wilhelm mustache and glasses. He wore a golf shirt, plaid golf pants and white loafers.

'Are you 357? Where's your caddie shirt?' asked Mr. G as I approached.

'No, I...'

'357!'

Another boy sitting on the bench ran up to Mr. G.

'357, you have Mr. Adams.' Mr. G handed him a blue caddie card. 'Hurry up, son, he's on the tee.

''Mr. G, I'm Kevin ---'

'319!'

Another boy scurried up to the desk.

'319, you have Mr. Hannibal. Here you go. Now treat him well!'

Suddenly, he pivoted in my direction. 'What are you doing here, son? Did I call you up!?!'

'I'm Kevin Campbell. I'm a new caddie.'

'It's 10:00! Where have you been all day?!' He glared angrily at me, like I forgot to put the garbage out or dented his new car.

'What time am I --?'

'Roll call's at 6:30! Tee times start at 7:00. Look at these boys sitting there, they've been here for 4 hours. You can't make no money showing up here at 10:00. What's wrong with you?' He looked past me. '74!'

'I ---'

'What's your number? Where's your caddie shirt?'

'I don't have a number. I ---'

'Have you Spooked?'

'I don't ---'

'17! Well go sit on the benches, and I'll try to get you out soon. Campbell's the name, you say?'

'Yes.'

He wrote it down. Next time be here for roll call.'

I took a seat by myself on the only empty bench. My number? Spooked? 6:30 roll call? Was this guy insane? Were those actually white loafers on his feet?

I tried to think of other employment options, but what else could a 12 year-old kid do? Paperboys had to wake up even earlier than 6:30. I couldn't mow lawns because of my allergies. The Classified Ads had led me nowhere.

A boy from another bench sat down next to me. 'Hey there, Spook! I'm Dan Tulis.' He flashed me a wide grin.

I shook his outstretched hand and introduced myself. 'I'm Kevin Campbell.'

'Nice to meet ya, Spook.'

'Why are you calling me Spook?'

28

'Cause you're a Spook, Spook.'

'What's a Spook?'

'Do you have a caddie number yet?'

'No.'

'Then you're a Spook. You're a Spook during your first two rounds when you follow around another caddie. You're his shadow; his ghost; you know, his Spook. But really, all first year caddies are called Spooks. So, where you from, Spook? You talk kinda funny.' He had slightly squinty eyes to go along with a small mouth.

I told him where I was from and that I was spending the summer with my grandparents. 'How about you?' I asked Tulis.

'Oh, I live in Cleveland. In St. Pat's parish. That's where I went to school. I'm going to St. Ed's High School in the Fall.' He looked over at the other benches a few times as he spoke.

Tulis was only two years older than me, but he was a lot bigger.

'So what's the deal with Mr. G?' I asked. 'He seems a little…'

'Crazy? Senile? A Nazi? Yeah, he's all of those. He screws me all the time. This place sucks.'

'And who's the other guy?' I glanced over at the only other man on the first tee not wearing golf shoes. He had bushy blond hair that made his head look even larger than it was, sitting atop a spindly-thin body. He gesticulated wildly as he spoke to a member, with his arms tucked close to his body, as though his elbows were attached to his ribcage. His intimidating gaze and mirrored sunglasses were reminiscent of the prison guard in Cool Hand Luke. 'The one in the sunglasses?'

29

'That's T.Rex. He's the pro here. His real name is Bob Templeton. He basically runs the place.'

As Tulis and I continued our chat, another boy came over and sat down on the other side of me.

'Hey, Billy,' Tulis greeted him. 'This Spook thinks Mr. G is a crazy Nazi.'

'I didn't—' I attempted.

'Hi, Spook, I'm Billy Shaw.' He shook my hand. 'Really nice to meet you.' I began to relax a little.

After shaking my hand, Billy looked over to Tulis on the other side of me with his hand extended, 'Tulis, it's good to see you, ol' buddy!' Their outstretched hands met in front of me and immediately thumped me in the chest, sending me upside down backwards. Before I knew it, I was entangled in the bush behind the bench. A small branch burrowed into the base of my neck. I struggled to upright myself and to figure out what had just happened.

By the time I outwrestled the bush, my new 'friends' Tulis and Billy had escaped from the scene of the crime to the sanctuary and high fives of another bench.

I fought back tears as I examined a scrape on my elbow and checked my head to see if I was bleeding.

What kind of place is this? What had I done to deserve that? Is all of Cleveland this dangerous? I sat frozen. I wanted to flee but I knew everyone was still looking at me. I already couldn't wait for the summer to end.

'138!'

Dan Tulis slowly sauntered up to Mr. G.

'Hurry up, son! I haven't got all day! Take Mr. Stanton.'

Tulis slumped his shoulders and lazily searched for Mr. Stanton's bag among the 20 or so others lined up along the wooden rail fence that outlined the first tee. He looked over to Billy and began pushing his index finger into the hole formed by his index finger and thumb of the other hand. Billy turned to another caddie and said with a laugh, 'Looks like Tulis got Screwed!'

'Yeah, I had him a couple of weeks ago. He's not a bad guy, but he's definitely a Screw. He only gave me $6. I felt like handing it back to him and walking away.'

'At least it's not Five-Bills Wills. Now that guy is a royal Screw.'

'Look, they just brought out Booth's bag. I hope I get him.'

'Yeah, you're gonna get a Deal like Booth. You have a better chance of beating up Kovach than you do of getting Booth today. When are you going to understand that Mr. G only gives him to Senior Caddies and A caddies, not Spooks like you, Spook.'

'Quiet on the caddie benches!' yelled Mr. G. '310!'

Billy ran up to the desk and came back to the bench with his card.

'Who you got?'

'Smith.'

'Which one, David or Michael?'

'David.'

'You got Screwed.'

Soon after, Mr. G walked over in my direction.

'You,' pointing my way, 'you're out with 138.' I lost all feeling in my body.

'C'mon, son! You're on the tee.'

I lurched my way up to the tee. Tulis didn't acknowledge his prior assault on me; he just smirked and said, 'Hey, Spook. Don't mess up and make me look bad out here.' He briefly explained to Mr. Stanton that I would be Spooking this round for him. Mr. Stanton mumbled hello and grabbed a club from his bag. A boy a year or two older than me carried Mr. Brantley's bag. An older, bigger caddie carried two bags, or doubles, for Mr. McNabb and Mr. Johnson.

As each golfer teed off, the ball disappeared into the clear, blue sky like a rocket, never to be seen by me again.

'Nice ball.'

'That'll play.'

'Golf shot.'

'The hole opens up from over there.'

Everyone else seemed to have no problem following the shots. To my untrained eyes, they just disappeared into thin air.

The fairway down the middle of the long hole was so plush that I almost had trouble believing it was grass. It was more like fine carpeting, closer to Astroturf than to the crabgrass I was used to at home. The grass in the rough along each side of the fairway was longer but plush and a deeper green. I felt like I had stepped into a new world.

I tried to keep my distance from Tulis as we walked down the fairway. I wasn't exactly sure what he could do to me, but potential scenarios ranged from beating me up to pantsing me, with the outside chance of killing me in a remote area of the golf course and dumping my skinny, bloody corpse into a creek.

I quickly came to understand that caddying was much more involved than just carrying a bag. A caddie's job seemed to focus on ensuring that your golfer did not expend any extra energy beyond swinging a club and walking from shot to shot. It seemed that my job as a Spook was to ensure that Dan Tulis did not expend any extra energy beyond carrying the bag. Rather than teaching me how to caddie and explaining things to me, he just ordered me around like his minion.

Even from my inexperienced vantage point, I saw that Tulis wasn't a very good caddie. He pointed his face toward the sun to soak up rays instead of watching players hit. He walked slowly, lagging behind the group. He couldn't find golf balls in the rough. He made noise while the golfers were hitting. He constantly joked around with the other two caddies, but he was careful not to get caught by the golfers as he snapped his towel at the younger caddie or made an obscene gesture. He was a nuisance.

He threw me into the fire on the 5th hole. 'Okay, Spook, why don't you tend the pin on this hole.'

'Okay. What's that mean?'

'Wow, you really are stupid. Have you ever been on a golf course before?'

'Sure, I have,' I lied. I'd never actually been on a real golf course before, but my mom and I had played putt-putt a couple of times.

'Sure you have. The pin is the big stick with a flag on it that goes in each hole. Did you happen to notice those? When the golfers are putting and they're too far away to see the hole, you stand there holding the pin. Grab the flag so it doesn't fly around and distract them. When the ball comes near the hole, pull the pin out. When they're close enough that they can see the hole, you just pull out the pin and stand on the edge of the green. Again, hold the flag so that it doesn't fly around. Think you can handle that? It's pretty easy, even for an idiot like you.'

'Okay.'

'After they all putt out, stick the pin back into the hole carefully so you don't mess up the sides of the hole.'

When the members were ready to putt, I gingerly walked up to the pin and held it while Mr. McNabb lined up his putt. Little did I know that I had just violated several rules of golf and caddying.

'Son,' said Mr. Stanton from another direction, 'you're standing in my line.'

I looked down to see I was standing directly between Mr. Stanton's ball and the cup. This was my first lesson in golf -- layered on top of all of the common methods and procedures of caddying were the standard rules of golf. Violating these could cost your golfer valuable strokes. For example, a golfer or a golfer's caddie is not permitted to walk or stand in another golfer's imaginary line between the ball and its presumed path to the hole, lest the footprint alter the path of the impending putt. This seemed a bit silly to me since my sub-100 lb. body wearing sneakers did not put much of an imprint into the grass. Nevertheless, four balls on the green making four invisible vectors radiating from the hole made walking on the green like navigating through a minefield.

I moved to the other side of the cup to avoid Mr. Stanton's line, and stood at attention facing Mr. McNabb.

'Son, your shadow is over the hole,' Mr. McNabb notified me. I looked down on the green and sure enough my stick figure was casting a large shadow directly over the hole.

I shifted back toward the other side of the hole, being careful to avoid Mr. Stanton's line.

'Son, now you're standing in my line.' I turned around to see Mr. Brantley frowning at me. A dime marked the spot of where his ball lay. This was starting to seem unfair. My stomach tensed up.

I began to sweat. I found a small area where, if I stood awkwardly, I could avoid everyone's lines and still not cast my shadow over the hole. Tulis and the other caddie watched the spectacle from the safety of the next tee. They were nearly doubled over in laughter.

When all the golfers were close enough, they told me to pull the pin. I carried the yellow flag, which felt like it was twice my size, to the comfort of the edge of the green, careful not to drag it on the velveteen green. The blood in my head throbbed.

'Son, would you mind moving out of my line of sight?' Apparently these lines extended infinitely. Could this guy really be distracted by my standing on the edge of the green in line with the cup? This one seemed a bit excessive for me.

He waited for me to move to a position that was perpendicular to his delicate line. It annoyed me every time he called me 'Son.'

Tulis greeted me on the next tee. 'Nice job, Spook. What are you going to do for an encore? I think we're going to keep you away from the greens for a while. I want you to forecaddie on this hole and on the rest of them for that matter. Before these guys start teeing off, go run out about 150 yards along the edge of the trees and watch where they hit their balls. That's called forecaddying. Now hurry up and stay out of the way.'

I trotted off toward the row of pine trees. After about 20 seconds I slowed down to a shuffle. I glanced over my shoulder. Tulis waved me out further. I ran another 20 feet and stopped. He gave me another wave. I ran another 30 feet and stopped. Tulis looked back at the others and shook his head.

I was glad to be away from the rest of the group to collect my thoughts, but I felt conspicuously vulnerable standing all alone in the rough. I saw the golfers swing their clubs but I didn't see any of the balls until they landed. One almost hit me as it fell from the sky.

I successfully avoided tending the pin on the rest of the holes, but I still managed to break a couple more rules of golf. On hole 8, thinking I was doing Mr. Stanton a favor, I raked some old footprints in the sand trap before he hit his ball. How was I supposed to know that a caddie wasn't allowed to touch the sand until the golfer hit the ball out? On hole 12, we all were looking for a ball that Mr. Brantley had hit into the deep rough. I was so excited to be the one who found it that I picked it up and waved it in the air yelling, 'Here it is! I found it!' Okay, that move was pretty stupid. It was at that point that Tulis called me an embarrassment to the caddying profession.

All that previously transpired, however, paled in comparison to what Tulis coaxed me into doing on the 16th hole.

While the rest of the group was holing out on the 15th green, Tulis and I moved all the bags to the next hole. The 16th was an uphill par 4 with a blind shot to the green.

'Spook, when you forecaddie on this hole, it's a little different. Instead of standing in the rough like on the other holes, stand in the middle of the fairway.'

'Why…why do you do that?

'Well, it's a long hole so you can't see the pin from the tee.'

'Okay? You're serious?'

'Sure. And when they are about to hit their drives, jump up and down and wave your arms all over the place. They really appreciate that. Only really good caddies do that.'

Then he left to take a leak in the woods. He thought I was smart enough to know he was kidding.

He was wrong.

When the members reached the 16th tee, I was standing in the middle of the fairway as instructed.

'What in the heck is that Spook doing?' Mr. Stanton asked.

'Spook, get out of the way!' Mr. Brantley yelled.

I took a few steps to the left, but I was still firmly in the fairway. Mr. Stanton turned to the other caddies on the tee looking for an explanation. Tulis and the others just shrugged their shoulders. Not knowing what else to do, Mr. Stanton stepped up to hit.

On cue, I began jumping up and down waving my arms. The other members were flabbergasted. Tulis and his gang tried to act like they were as confused and surprised as the members. I continued waving my body around like a lunatic upon the pristine country club fairway.

'What the hell is wrong with that Spook?'

'That is the dumbest Spook I have ever seen.'

At this point they thought that I was beyond control, so they all tried to ignore me and hit their drives. Two of the drives went into the trees, not that I saw them. One barely made it past the Ladies' tees, and the final one came screaming at me, never getting above five feet off the ground, just barely missing me.

It was only when the foursome made their way down the fairway that I fully understood I had been duped and had screwed up yet again.

'Son, what in the hell were you...' Mr. Brantley just trailed off, not wanting to even begin to comprehend what my thought process was.

No one so much as made eye contact with me the rest of the round, including Tulis. I think he realized that he had pushed things too far, and he just wanted the round to be over as soon as possible.

As the golfers finished up on the 18th green, caddies lined up outside of the pro shop with the bags so that the members could clear their pockets of balls, gloves and tees and make the transition back to the real world.

'It was a pleasure caddying for you, Mr. Stanton,' Tulis robotically said.

Mr. Stanton paid Tulis $6 and retreated to the men's grille. Tulis unzipped the bag and fished around for golf balls.

'Did you lose something?' I asked.

'Get out of here, Spook. You've done enough damage. These rich members can afford it, and Stanton won't miss a few golf balls. I'm just taking my fair share from a Screw like him. I'm just balancing things out.'

Tulis continued to clean out Mr. Stanton's bag. I shuffled over to the caddie house and crumpled into a chair. I never wanted to see Tulis's or Stanton's face again. I tried to regain enough energy to ride my bike home. I had never walked that far in my life. My feet throbbed. With the course measuring more than 6,000 yards from tees to greens, the average round of caddying required walking about 6 miles, taking into account the distance between holes, walking to errant shots, etc.

Word spread like wildfire of my exploits on the course. Tulis had a field day recounting my idiocy as he peddled Mr. Stanton's golf balls for $.50 apiece.

'He did what?!?'

'Hey, where's the Spook who had the epileptic fit on 16?'

'The Wichita Kid? He must be the dumbest Spook in the world.'

I couldn't take any more abuse. I escaped the caddie house, grabbed my bike, and slowly pedaled home to my grandparents' apartment. They weren't home when I got there. I had never been more tired in my life, so I crawled into bed for a nap – not one of those where you collapse on the bed with your shoes on. This was much more serious. I stripped down to my underwear and climbed under the sheets. I needed to reset my brain too, to forget about the last few hours I had gone through.

I awoke two and a half hours later, just in time for dinner.

I was fully rested and I was starting to feel comfortable in the apartment. For the first time in days, I actually had the first slightest semblance of an appetite. I poured myself a small glass of milk.

'I'm so glad you're drinking that milk,' she said. 'It has the same thing in it that's in oyster shells. What's it called? Calcium. Milk is so good for you. It will build up those bones and muscle. Same thing oysters have.'

I held the glass up to the light and briefly inspected it. I drank some anyway.

'What's for dinner?' I asked.

'Roast beef,' she responded.

My appetite diminished. I hated fat and gristle. Even the thought of gristle could make me vomit.

'How was your first day at work?' asked my smiling grandmother as she spooned out hefty portions of roast beef, corn and au gratin potatoes onto my plate. I watched in dismay as the roast beef juice invaded the eastern region of the corn, the water from the corn attacked the potatoes and au gratin soiled the left flank of roast beef. Nearly as much as I hated gristle, I hated one type of food on my plate to touch another type of food.

'Fine...,' I responded as I surgically cut the fat off each piece of roast beef. I also ate my food in precise order. I ate as much as I was going to eat of each type of food and then moved on to the next. Once I was done with it, I never moved back for a few more bites. I started with the meat, my least favorite, and worked my way around the plate, finishing up with whatever I like most. Feeling increasingly uncomfortable in the spotlight of my grandmother's intent gaze, I finally started with a few bites of roast beef, followed by the corn and finally the potatoes. I kept my milk until the end, when I was done eating the food.

'I assume that all the other boys were nice to you.'

How could I explain to them that the boys were anything but nice to me? They had made fun of me, physically hurt me, humiliated me. I wasn't even sure I would ever go back.

'Yeah, they were okay.' I stared down at my carefully constructing three uneaten DMZs where the various food items had encroached beyond their designated borders. My stomach had constricted so much that I couldn't eat much, but it was nice to give my body some much-needed fuel.

'Did you run into Mrs. Kenworth's grandson?' asked my grandfather.

'No.'

'How come? Wasn't he there?'

'I don't know, there were about 75 caddies there. I only met a couple of them. And everyone goes by their number too. It seems like the younger caddies have really high numbers and the older ones have lower numbers. The caddie master is this really old guy, like older than you guys.'

'Wow, older than us? He must be old,' said my grandfather.

'No…you know what I mean.'

'I'm just kidding; go on.'

'And he calls everyone by their number – 77 do this, 328 do that.'

'Sounds pretty Orwellian,' said my grandfather with a smile.

I had no idea what he meant, but I smiled anyway.

'Yeah, it's a weird place.'

'So are you going back tomorrow?' asked my grandfather.

I thought again about Tulis. I hated to go back, but I didn't see any other choice. I felt trapped.

'I'll go back tomorrow and maybe start looking for something else after that.' I pushed my plate away from me.

'Is that all you're going to eat? You hardly made a dent in it.'

My stomach tightened. I thought I ate a lot, for me. 'Yeah, I'm not that hungry.'

'You don't eat much. We're going to need to fatten you up this summer. Put some meat on your bones.'

I hated that everyone thought it was their right to always comment on how much I ate, how skinny I was. Why couldn't people just leave me and my stomach alone?

'Be sure to drink the rest of your milk. It's good for you. It has oysters in it.'

I lifted the glass to my lips as I walked out of the dining room, but then emptied the milk into the kitchen sink.

Chapter 3

I dragged myself out of bed when my alarm went off at 6:00. My grandparents were still asleep. My grandfather was snoring. The skin on my arms and neck stung from sunburn when I put my tee-shirt on. I didn't want to return to the course, but I didn't know what else to do. My stomach felt surprisingly settled. I weighed in at 94 pounds. Holding steady. I sat on the bed for a few minutes, trying to think of an alternative way to make money, but the path of least resistance was to get dressed.

I entered the club just as the early morning rosy fingers of dawn appeared. There was a nip to the air, and the green fairways lining the club entrance were glistening with dew. I arrived just in time for the 6:30 roll call. All the caddies who were there lined up against the caddie yard fence while Mr. G read out the list of numbers in reverse order of caddies who worked the day before (last ones out the day before were the first ones out the next day.) As numbers were called, each caddie announced his presence, and Mr. G put his number on the list for the new day.

'...356...77...'

'Here!'

'34...'

'Here!'

'208...389...107...'

'Here!'

Caddies who were not there the day before were relegated to the bottom of the list, and usually had to sit around most of the day before going out onto the course.

Roll call was like one in a police precinct, at least based on my experience watching TV. Mr. G used the time after roll call to chastise the group for an increasing number of lost balls, pins untended and clubs not cleaned. As the list of infractions rolled out of Mr. G's mouth, he became increasingly animated.

'Boys, Westwood has the largest caddie program in all of Ohio, if not all the Midwest. But that all could end tomorrow. You keep this up, boys, and they'll replace you all with carts! You boys don't know how good you have it. The money you make! Why, when I was caddying here years ago, we got fifty cents a round, and if we were lucky, we got a stick of gum and a pat on the head as a tip. I was just talking to Mr. Stanton yesterday – he's on the club's board of directors -- and he said that in their last meeting a groundswell was underway to replace all of yous with a hundred new golf carts." To Mr. G, caddying was a threatened practice that was kept alive by the benevolent members of Westwood on behalf of the poor, unfortunate caddies. Our poor performance on the golf course apparently wasn't helping our cause in the matter.

After tearing into us for our transgressions on the course, Mr. G softened a bit and built us back up before finishing up roll call.

"You're good boys. I know you can do it. Now go prove me right."

'The Wichita Kid!' Kovach bellowed across the caddie yard as roll call broke up. 'You decided to come back for more.' He extended his huge hand.

I hesitated and then shook it as I mumbled yes.

'I heard you were doing some pretty good jumping jacks on the course yesterday. Why don't you do some for us right now?'

I checked his eyes to see if he really was going to make me do them.

'Come on, Wichita. Let's see your form.'

I did a couple.

'Come on, count them off.'

'One, two, three…'

'Come on, louder. No one can hear you.'

'ONE, TWO, THREE…' When I hit ten, I noticed that he had turned his attention to another Spook. I did another ten without counting, and then slinked away to the first tee.

I didn't have to wait long before Mr. G called my name and told me to get on the tee for my second round of Spooking.

'Well, if it ain't the Wichita Kid,' said Mouse, my slap boxing foe from the other day. He was assigned to the same group. 'Hey, sorry about the other day,' he said in a hushed tone. 'Kovach likes to treat the caddie yard like his own personal circus.'

'Yeah, no problem.'

'I did manhandle you pretty good though,' he said with a slight smile. 'My name's Pat, but everyone calls me Mouse.'

'I'm Kevin.'

47

'I'm caddying for Mr. Neagle and his Bionic Belly over there.'

Mr. Neagle looked like a vigorous World War II vet with skinny arms, skinny legs and a protruding gut that defied the laws of anatomy and physics. At some point in his life he must have made the fateful decision to stop buying larger pants to corral his ever-expanding paunch and to belt his pants low on his hips underneath his belly. 38 inches…40 …42 …44 …oh, screw it, 34 inches.

'We've got Rickles with us and Alice Cooper.'

Rickles was a red-head carrying two bags. Tom Cooper was a chunky kid with glasses.

'Why, it's the Wichita Kid,' said Rickles in a grating voice. He was tall and skinny and had a bumper crop of zits sprouting from his forehead.

'Go run out and forecaddie, Wichita,' Mouse instructed.

I took two steps and turned back around, 'Where's that on this hole, again?'

He raised his eyebrows. 'Out about 150 yards on the left.'

Back on the tee, Mr. Neagle and the other members silently greeted each other. Someone made a joke and the rest of the group cracked up. Only the faint remnants of laughter reached me as I arrived at my designated post. I was alone with the birds and a couple of cicadas.

After the group teed off I hummed the new Gloria Gaynor song while I made my way to Neagle's ball.

Rickles appeared through the trees. 'Nice song, Spook. Are you appearing here all week? And, no, I don't think you will survive.'

Mr. Neagle showed up with Mouse. As he struck the ball, he unearthed a toupee-sized piece of grass and dirt that landed 10 feet in front of us. I began to walk to his next shot.

'Hey, Wichita, you want to pick up that divot before you walk by it?' said Mouse.

'The what?'

He sighed. 'Hey, man, that piece of grass lying there. It's called a divot. You need to replace it, or there would be holes all over this course.'

'I thought there were holes all over the course. 18 of them.'

He squinted at me to see if I was being a smart ass. I wasn't.

He laid his bag down. He picked up the tuft of grass at my feet.

'This is a divot.' He walked back to where Neagle hit his shot. 'You lay it back down exactly like it was,' he fit it back into the ground like a puzzle piece. 'Then you step on it.' He twisted it with the ball of his feet. 'You've got to really push it down or else it won't grow back, or it will stick to a member's cleats. This is pretty basic stuff. Are you sure you Spooked before?'

We met up again at Mr. Neagle's next shot.

'How far we got?' he asked me.

I looked around and pointed to the small pine tree. 'There's the 150 yard marker.' I proudly declared.

'That's nice, how far are we from that?'

'I don't know, I haven't walked there yet. 20 yards? Maybe 30?' I did know that I had taken 392 steps since I left the tee, but I didn't think anyone was interested in that.

49

He laid down the bag. He took a series of giant steps until he reached the imaginary line extending across the fairway from the 150 marker.

'It's 12.' He picked up the bag as Mr. Neagle approached.

'How far we got, Pat?'

'162. The pin's up, though, so figure 155 or so.'

'6 or 7 iron?'

'I'd hit the 7.'

Mr. Neagle yanked out the 7 iron and hit it onto the front, right side of the green. Mouse handed him his putter before retrieving the divot.

'Mouse, that is one awful Spook you got there,' said Rickles as we forecaddied on the second hole.

'He'll be fine. Wichita, who were you out with the first time out?'

'Tulis. Dan Tulis.'

'It figures. Tool is an idiot. You got a lot to learn.'

Mouse talked me through the basics of caddying over the next few holes – how to rake traps, how to tend pins, when to speak, when to shut up.

We had brought our bags 150 yards ahead as the members teed off with their drivers on hole 6. 'The most important thing about caddying is keeping your eye on the ball and being able to find it in flight after the golfer hits it. Losing balls is just about the worst thing a caddie can do.'

'You can say that again,' chimed in Rickles.

'Why? Are balls that expensive?' I asked

'Not really, especially for these people. But the golfer has to take a one-stroke penalty if he loses the ball. They care about that much more – although with some of the cheap guys out here, I think they care about the cost too. You need to line the ball up with something else, a landmark, like a tree, usually a tree, and then walk in a straight line to the spot.'

Neagle hit his drive. It flew over our heads into the middle of a large oak tree.

'Jack Martin!' said Mouse. The ball struck a branch and bounced out into the rough. 'Works every time.'

Mouse turned to me. 'See it?'

'I think so.'

'It's in the rough, so line it up with that skinny brown tree. Draw an imaginary line between you and the tree. The ball is about 10 yards short of the tree. So just walk toward the tree and stop 10 yards short. The ball should be right there.'

'Why'd you say Jack Martin?'

'Superstition. Jack Martin was the club champ years ago. On the last hole of the championship one year, he hit his drive right into the middle of a tree. It bounced high in the air into the middle of the fairway. If it had stayed in the woods, he almost certainly would have lost, but the tree gave him a perfect lie. His next shot landed cleanly on the green and rolled right into the cup to win the championship.'

I walked toward the brown tree, but I looked around for a minute and when I looked back, there were five skinny brown trees that all looked the same. I started looking around frantically.

'What happened?' asked Mouse. 'Didn't you line it up with the tree?'

'I did. I just couldn't remember which tree I lined it up with.'

'You're an idiot.' Mouse chuckled. He pointed to the ground. 'The ball's right there. Keep working at it. You'll catch on.'

Mouse set the bag down about 20 feet away. Right next to the ball.

'Son, you got that missile I launched over this way?' called Mr. Neagle as he approached.

'Right here, Mr. Neagle.'

'Boy, it sure did clear some terrain.' He pulled a club from the bag and said, 'Let me try this weapon.' A faded tattoo briefly exposed itself from beneath the sleeve of his golf shirt as he addressed the ball. He hit the ball into the sand trap short of the green. 'Dammit,' he said. 'Bunker.'

On the next hole, we were on the tee when Neagle hit his drive near the trees on the left.

'Jack Martin!' said Mouse and Mr. Neagle as the ball hit a tree and bounced to the right.

A few holes later, while we were waiting for the group ahead of us to finish putting, Mouse explained the numbering system. 'It's really pretty simple. There are about 250 caddies, even though only about 100 caddie regularly. New caddies like you are B caddies.

Those numbers start at 300 and go up from there as guys come on board. I think we're at around number 400 right now. Have you seen the caddie cards Mr. G hands when he assigns you a golfer at the beginning of the round?'

I nodded.

'At the end of the round the member rates you – Excellent, Good, Fair and Poor. Once you get 20 Excellents you become an A caddie and you get a number in the 200s. So first year caddies have the 200s and the 300s and above. Second years are in the 100s, third years are 50-99, fourth years are 25-49, and so one until you get to Number 1 like Kovach.'

'What happens after that?'

'Well you can't caddie after you hit college. You have to get a real job then. They make sure that no one turns caddying at Westwood into a career choice. And that way everyone kinda moves up every year, and there's a new Number 1 each year.'

After the round we ran into Kovach as we brought Neagle's bag back to the bag room.

'The Wichita Kid! And Mouse!' He shook each of our hands. 'You two were out together? Any fisticuffs out there?'

'No, we were fine,' responded Mouse.

'Mouse, how'd my little man do?'

'He's got a lot to learn, but he'll do okay.'

'Wichita, how come you stopped doing jumping jacks? I turned around and you were gone this morning.'

'I...um'

'I'm just kidding you. And don't worry about yesterday. Tool is a jerk. He screwed you over. We'll take care of him. Have you finished your second round of Spooking?'

'Yep, all done.'

'Then head on over to the caddie house and get your number.'

Mouse walked over with me but Mr. G wasn't in his office, so we sat on one of the picnic tables in the caddie yard.

'So how do you like caddying so far?' Mouse asked me.

'It's okay. I liked today a lot better than yesterday. How long you been caddying?' I asked.

'This is my first year. I started in April on weekends as soon as it started to warm up. All my brothers caddie, or at least used to, so it was kind of a given that I would become a caddie.'

'How many brothers you got?'

'Five. Two of them are in college so they're too old to caddie now, but they both were the #1 caddie when they were seniors in high school. The two others are caddies now. Todd is number 2, behind Kovach. He just graduated from St. Ignatius. Paul is going to be a junior next year. He's number 34. Peter is 55. It was pretty much just assumed that I would become a caddie when I turned 12.'

'Holy crap, that's a big family.'

He shrugged. 'I don't know. It's not that unusual in St. Angela's, the parish I live in. There are a lot of families in my neighborhood with six or seven or even eight kids.'

'So what's up with all this about Screws and Deals? What's Neagle? Is he a Screw?' I asked.

'He's a medium Screw. B Caddies are paid a flat rate of $4 plus a tip, usually a couple bucks. A Caddies make $6 plus tip. An experienced caddie who carried doubles usually makes about $18-20. Neagle's nothing terrible, but definitely not a Deal. He paid me $6 today. A Screw like will pay a B Caddie like us about $5. A Deal will be like $7. And it's all about the tips. It has nothing to do with whether the golfer is nice or a good player. I'd take the nastiest duffer out here if they paid me right.'

'Aren't good golfers easier to caddie for?'

'Not always. Guys with lower handicaps usually want a lot more attention. You're constantly washing their ball, reading their putts, kissing their butt. They're also more apt to become a real jerk if you lose their ball. Like Mr. Booth – he's the biggest Deal out here by far. He'll give you $15 for a round, but you'll earn it. His bag is huge, like 40 pounds, and you have to go to the practice green before he plays and round up his balls after he practices his chipping. You have to wash his ball before every putt and tee shot. He's a pain. And don't even think about messing up. He'll tear you a new one. But I'd caddie for him any day, because he pays.'

'How many times have you had him?'

'None. Spooks like us don't have to worry about that. We just take our Screws until we earn enough good ratings to become an A Caddie. And even then, it's usually older kids who get Deals like him.'

We got up to see if Mr. G was back.

'So, why do they call you Mouse?'

'When I was really young, maybe 5 or 6. My dad caught a mouse in a mousetrap. My mom was freaking out; she was so scared of it. And my brothers were arguing about who would pick it up and throw it out. I just walked over, picked it up by its tail and tossed it into the garbage. It was no big deal; it was just a mouse. I guess since I'm kinda small, the name kinda stuck.'

We found Mr. G sitting in his office. It was a small room with a chair, a small metal desk and old paint chipping off the ceiling. On the walls were small racks with little slots that held index cards numbered from 1 to 406. Each card contained the personal information for the caddie who held each number.

'Mr. G, I've finished my two rounds of Spooking. What do I need to do next?'

'Huh?' He looked up from sorting through the snack bar take for the day. 'Well, let's see here, son.' He looked up at the wall and pulled down the next blank index card. 'Looks like the next one is 407. Here, fill out your name, address, and phone number on this card.'

And just like that, I had my number, which would identify my rank and persona for the next couple of months.

407...407. The more I said it, the more I liked it. It had a mysterious, secret agent feel to it. Or maybe I was just coming to grips with being a number instead of a name.

'Here are two caddie shirts. You owe me $10 for these two,' instructed Mr. G, 'If you need any additional shirts, it'll cost you $10 each.'

I fished through my wallet for a $10 bill, which was a lot of money to me. So far this caddying gig had cost me $10 and a good part of my dignity. At this pace, I was going to be in debt and in the loony bin. Without even asking me, he had picked out Small sizes, and even those left me some room to grow into them. They were light blue cotton of marginal quality, with dark blue piping around the end of the sleeves and around the neck. They would be my uniform for the rest of the summer.

Chapter 4

'Who's up for a game of jungle ball?' 113 yelled across the caddie yard the next morning after roll call.

Within seconds a dozen kids assembled on the basketball court.

Since roll call had wrapped up, I wandered the caddie yard starkly alone. I wore the same blue shirt, but I wasn't one of them. I had never made friends very easily. I had never been to summer camp and we had never moved to a new city, so I was never faced with having to make friends, or even acquaintances, to survive. I was used to being by myself; I even liked it. Mom worked every day and never came home until 6:00 or so. I could read or watch TV or make up stupid games for myself. But being alone in a crowd was lonely. I hated that.

I had spent the first hour, which seemed to last a lifetime, sitting alone in a cold Naugahyde chair in the caddie house, counting the number of times the basketball bounced between each shot. The cacophony of the caddie yard was occasionally interrupted by Mr. G's peppy voice over the loudspeaker, calling caddies over to the bench on the first tee.

'Number 4, coooome-a-runnin'!'

'217, coooome-a-runnin'!'

'34, coooome-a-runnin'!'

Mr. G no doubt had been working on that well-rehearsed cadence for decades.

I walked back outside. I had no intention of volunteering to play jungle ball, but one of the boys organizing the next game looked at a few of us standing on the fringes, 'You in for jungle ball?'

It was easier to join in than not, and I was dragged into the melee.

'How do you play?' I asked a boy at the edge of the group.

'Basically there are no rules. You just try to get the ball and score a basket while everyone tries to kill you. If you make it, you get to shoot up to three foul shots. If you miss a foul shot, everyone tries to get the rebound and score. Pretty simple.'

The first several minutes of the game I couldn't figure out how to get the ball without getting killed, so I desperately avoided it. A rebound finally came my way. As soon as it hit my hands I hurled it back toward the hoop over the encroaching horde. Airball. The second time I touched the ball, I dribbled twice. Bad mistake. When I turned to shoot the ball, two charging bulls attacked me. One swatted the ball away. The other swatted me away. I hit the pavement and smashed my elbow hard against the ground. The game continued around me.

I crawled my way off the court to assess the damage. My elbow was killing me and I had an ugly scrape that stung badly. I fought off tears as I went into the bathroom to wash it off. With the muffled screams of jungle ball outside the bathroom walls, I looked at the lonely figure staring back at me in the mirror.

I found a seat again in the caddie house. After a while, an old lady flung open the door and shuffled in, leaning heavily on a walker.

'Pick up that pop can!' she barked at me.

'Hi, Mrs. G,' sang Alice Cooper.

She stopped and glared, and then shuffled with her walker into Mr. G's office.

Time crawled. As much as I was afraid to go out onto the course my first time as a caddie, I couldn't wait for Mr. G to call my number over the loudspeaker to save me from this purgatory.

I tested out my stomach and ate half a hot dog and 2 Fla-Vor-Ices.

I had been battling my nervous stomach for as long as I could remember. I vomited every day of school when I was in the First Grade. I was afraid to leave my Mom each day and to venture off into the real world away from the comfort and security of home. Sometimes I vomited at home; usually at school. Sometimes in the boys' room toilet; usually on the classroom floor or hallway. My best friend in first grade probably was Jim, the school custodian. He came by our classroom almost daily and whispered to me in the back of class, 'Where today, Kevin?' He had an earthen, unshowered smell to him and his voice croaked from too many cigarettes. He sprinkled a few handfuls of Zep crystals over the vomit to dry up the mess. Thirty minutes or so later he shuffled back in with his dark blue jumpsuit, and swept up the remains. He never made more of a scene than he had to.

Mrs. Upton, my first grade teacher, wasn't as understanding as Jim.

The splashing sound of puke hitting linoleum was always quickly met with her reprimands.

'Kevin Campbell, not again! Look out, kids, make sure you don't step in it. Did anyone get hit? Mary Ann, go tell the janitor we've had another incident. Kevin, go stand in the back of the room until someone comes in to clean this up.'

This led to a vicious cycle of my becoming so nervous of vomiting, that I would indeed vomit. My vomiting tapered off a little in the second semester when I tried giving it up for Lent. It declined more in the second grade after I escaped the wrath of Mrs. Upton, and I began to hide my problem by not eating and by being more discreet when I threw up. Sometimes my stomach shut down for a week at a time, and I went days eating only a cracker. It was pretty exhausting. It was fine that my mom knew about it, but we already were unlike the other families in Salina. I didn't want to be any more different.

During that time, I had trouble explaining what my stomach felt like when I became nervous. I told Mom that it felt like a hamster running around on a circular treadmill in my belly, first slowly and then going progressively faster. Ever since, we blamed my stomach problems on that hamster. We even named it -- Herschel. I imagined him as a benevolent chap, who perhaps wore a bowtie, and who didn't mean to cause me any harm. I generally didn't like talking to Mom about my nervous stomach, even though she always assured me that everything was all right. Animating it made talking about it a little easier. Mom was very supportive, letting me eat what I wanted, hugging me whenever I got nervous, but I still felt like it was a weakness, and I was ashamed of it.

'407, coooome-a-runnin'!" Finally, the call came.

My first assignment was as a runner for a cart. Westwood was so committed to its caddie program that even those who rode in a cart were required to take along a caddie. The runner's job was to run ahead to forecaddie on every hole to find balls, rake traps, and tend pins. Not much to it.

'Hi, Mr. Guelcher, my name is Kevin. I'll be caddying for you and your guest today.'

He took a final drag off his cigarette, tossed it to the ground and put it out with his white Footjoys. 'Yes. Hi ya, son.' He turned to his guest. 'Looks like they're putting a runner with us today, Warren.' His spikes clicked the cart path rhythmically as he marched to the tee.

Warren turned my way and acknowledged my presence. His stocky figure only reached 5 feet. With his Roman nose and down-turned mouth, he looked like a short totem pole figure, or a co-worker of Fred's at the Bedrock Quarry.

The other two golfers, Mr. Morgan and Mr. Lanning, walked and had number 65 carrying their two bags. He was a typical skinny 14 year old with feet that were disproportionately larger than the rest of his body. He had a brother and everyone called them the Elvis twins because they always wore souvenir caps from Graceland.

As I ran out 150 yards along the tree line to forecaddie, my heart was racing in recognition of this momentous occasion. I was beginning my first career and, if all went as planned, I would be earning income for the first time. The only thought that ran through my head was, 'Don't screw this up.' I had to prove to myself and to everyone else that my Spooking hijinks were an aberration.

As the golfers approached the tee, I snapped to attention, leaning slightly forward, right hand saluting to block the sun from my eyes. The pressure forecaddying put on a new caddie was intense. Golfers assumed that, because the forecaddie was closer to where the ball was going to land, he should find every ball. In reality, he was 150 yards away from the tee, so it was often impossible to pick up the ball coming off the driver in the first place. Especially on a cloudy day like that one, picking up a 2-inch wide white projectile against a white sky could be challenging, if not dangerous.

Mr. Guelcher was the first to tee off. I strained my eyes as he put his 24-handicap swing on the ball. I heard the delayed thwack of the club hitting the ball, but saw absolutely nothing come off of the club head. I frantically looked up and down the fairway for the ball to appear. About 4 seconds later, the ball magically fell out of the sky, landing about ten yards beyond me. I jumped a little, but at least I knew where it was. The next two members teed off successfully. I didn't see either of their shots until they landed safely in the fairway.

Mr. Guelcher's guest teed off, and I turned to the fairway to see where it would land. The only problem was that it never appeared.

After waiting several seconds, I turned back to the tee, where everyone was looking at me.

'WHERE'D IT LAND?' yelled Mr. Guelcher.

I put my palms up and shrugged my shoulders, 'I DON'T KNOW,' I yelled back.

Mr. Guelcher stormed off the tee and got into his cart. My hamster, Herschel, started to race in my belly. Mr. Guelcher was going to yell at me. I was going to lose more balls, and he would yell at me some more. He would tell Mr. G to fire me. I'd be humiliated. I'd have to look for another job again. I wouldn't be able to find another job. My Mom and I would run out of money, and --. I looked around for the nearest tree and threw up. I wiped my mouth and tears from my eyes when Mr. Guelcher pulled up in the cart.

'Caddie, where'd it go?' asked Mr. Guelcher.

'I don't know,' I replied sheepishly.

He glared at me behind his green prescription sunglasses. He sniffed. 'What smells like puke?' He turned the cart into the grove of trees.

We looked for the ball for 5 minutes but didn't find it. The foursome let Mr. Guelcher's guest take a free drop. I was dripping wet in guilt. I had failed.

After everyone hit their next shots, I stood next to the cart midway down the par 5 first hole, waiting for the group ahead. Mr. Guelcher already had smoked two cigarettes and he lit up his third.

He hocked up a big loogie and spit it onto the freshly-cut fairway inches from my feet, 'Boy, were my sinuses running last night, Warren.'

He followed that up with a loud fart that reverberated against the vinyl golf cart seat. ''Scuse me,' he said under his breath, as though he had just sneezed.

The second hole ran parallel in the opposite direction to the first hole, so caddies didn't bother to make the trip up to the #2 tee. Upon approaching the #1 green they just dropped their bags in the rough between the two holes. Caddies gave their members their drivers after they finished the first hole, and caught up with the golfers after they teed off on the next hole. This gave caddies an opportunity to decompress early in the round without the members around.

'If I had a swing like Guelcher's guest, I'd just walk directly off the course now and never return,' the Elvis twin said to me with a smile. 'You're the Wichita Kid, right?'

'I guess so. My name's Kevin.'

'No offense, Wichita, but you looked like a real, bona fide Spook back there.'

'Gee, thanks.'

'You've got to learn the Caddie Fake. No one sees every ball that's hit off the tee when you're forecaddying, especially when you're looking into the sun or it's a really overcast day, but you have to act like you've got it all the way. So after they swing their club, look up in the sky and slowly move your head like you're following the flight of the ball going past you. Ninety percent of the time you're going to see the ball land, and it will look to the members like you had it all along.'

'What about the other 10% of the time?'

'Well, you're pretty much screwed. Assuming it doesn't hit you, you just have to kind of mess around, tying your shoe, adjusting the bag strap, whatever you can do so that you can follow the member to his ball. Never let the members know that you have no idea where the ball is.'

I ran ahead to forecaddie again on the 4th hole before the foursome teed off. Number 4 is a par-3, about 175 yards over a gully. Forecaddies were positioned off to the side in front of the green at the crest of the hill, which dipped down about 20 feet into the gully. As I looked back to the tee, which was slightly uphill, I was looking directly into the sun. Mr. Guelcher was the first to tee off. He took the club back, followed through the ball, and I again saw nothing. This time I tried the Fake. I looked up into the sky and slowly rotated my body toward the green, following the arc of the imaginary ball. Suddenly, a chorus arose from the tee.

'FORE!'

I abandoned the Fake and covered my head with my arms. A millisecond later a stinging pain ripped through the side of my knee. I felt like I had been shot, and I must have looked like it too. I lost my balance and fell backward downhill and went somersaulting down into the gully.

I lay face down in the thick, wet weeds. I did a mental check of all of my body parts to be sure that I had not broken anything. I slowly stood up, and although my knee was throbbing I was able to walk with only a slight limp. By the time I climbed my way out of the gully, the golfers were making their way up toward the green.

I was embarrassed, but I expected just a smidgen of sympathy from Mr. Guelcher for almost ending my life. Instead, he threw Rule of Golf 19-2-b at me.

If a competitor's ball is accidentally deflected or stopped by himself, his partner or either of their caddies or equipment, the competitor shall incur a penalty of two strokes.

His face behind the green sunglasses was red with anger as he drove up in the cart.

'Caddie, where's my ball? You cost me a two stroke penalty. You okay?'

'I think so. Sorry.'

We found his ball buried in the weeds at the bottom of the gully. He made 3 futile attempts to swat his ball out of the gully, but then he picked it up and gave himself an 8 on the hole.

I started to question my future as a caddie. Maybe I wasn't cut out for the job. Maybe I just wasn't talented enough to follow a white ball as it flew through the air. Maybe the arcane rules were beyond my immature and feeble mind.

Herschel started running on his treadmill in my gut, and I began to sweat as the pressure mounted to salvage this round, and perhaps my job. I decided that I needed to work harder the rest of the round to overcome my mistakes so far. I vowed to 'go the extra mile' to serve my golfers' every needs. I became a whirling dervish, hurling myself across the fairways and greens.

The result was a caricature of my Spook self. Rather than simply stepping in a golfer's putting line on my way to tend the pin, I ran across the putting surface stepping in three golfers' lines. Earnestly trying to find Mr. Guelcher's errant shot, I broke into a full sprint during his guest's backswing. I raked a trap before the golfers had a chance to hit their balls out. I was a caddying nightmare.

On the 8th hole, I tended the pin for Mr. Guelcher, right hand on the flag, left hand behind my back, back straight as a 2x4. A tornado couldn't have moved my body.

'Excuse me, son,' I heard Mr. Morgan say to my right. He had white hair combed straight back, and bright yellow shirt. 'Could you please move your feet a little? You're standing in my line. It's not your fault, my ball mark is pretty tough to see.'

'Sorry,' I grimaced in shame. I carefully shuffled my feet 12 inches and turned back toward Mr. Guelcher. He just shook his head and sighed.

When the group putted out and we made our way to the next tee, Mr. Morgan put his hand on my shoulder and said quietly, 'Relax, son. You'll catch on. Besides, this isn't exactly splitting the atom. The world's not exactly going to fall apart if you mess up out here.'

'Thanks,' I mumbled.

At the pit of despair, my life changed dramatically after the 9th hole. Next to the 10th tee stood a halfway house. The members entered the front and sat down at one of four tables for 10 minutes or so to have a bite to eat. The caddies were served from a window in the back. As I hung back to let the Elvis twin go first, I caught a glimpse through the window of the most beautiful green eyes I had ever seen. My stomach went on immediate notice. My hands went numb by the time the Elvis twin got his Coke and hot dog and I stepped up to the window.

'What can I get for you?' she asked with a pleasant, but confident, smile. Just below where her long brown hair stopped, her nametag proclaimed "Maureen."

'I don't want anything,' my voice squeaked.

'Nothing?'

'Um, I'll have a Coke.'

'That's it?' she sang.

'I'll have a Coke.'

'Is that two or one?'

'A Coke.'

She danced back to the fountain and poured me my drink.

She came back and handed me the drink. I reached out, but I had no feeling in my hands. 'That'll be 50—" The drink dropped from my hands and onto my shoes. I screamed like a bomb had just exploded.

'Oh, I'm so sorry,' Maureen said. 'Did you get wet? Let me get you another one.' She raced back to the fountain. I looked down at my fizzing shoes.

'Nice job, Wichita,' offered the Elvis twin. 'You're smooth with the ladies.'

Maureen came back with a new drink and a wet rag. 'Are you okay, a…a, what's your name, by the way?'

'Kevin.' I wiped my legs with the rag. 'I'm okay. Sorry.'

'Well, I'm sorry, Kevin. That's never happened before. I'll see you later.' She disappeared back into the halfway house.

Perhaps inspired by Maureen's eyes, I pledged to work even harder on the back nine. After Mr. Guelcher and his guest hit their shots, I took their clubs and returned them to their bags. This was outside of my official cart caddie duties, but I was trying to offer the highest level of customer service.

'Son, I can do that myself.'

'Son, that's not where my pitching wedge goes.'

'That's not my bag, caddie!'

But I would not be deterred.

As we finished up, I was proud of myself for completing my first round. 'It was a pleasure caddying for you, Mr. Guelcher,' I said as I handed him my card.

He grunted and walked into the pro shop to record his score. He came back out a few minutes later and handed me $5 without saying a word or even looking me in the face.

Mr. Guelcher's guest looked my way, sighed and shook his big Bedrock head as he walked to the clubhouse.

Mr. Morgan gave me a quick wink as he walked by and said, 'Hang in there, kid.'

I was just glad that it was over. Not even counting the cost of lunch and Cokes, I was still $5 in the red so far because of the caddie shirts.

That night I tossed and turned the entire time. I couldn't take my mind off of Maureen. Girls were an absolute mystery to me; a terrifying mystery. Most of the girls in my class back home had shot past me in height, which intimidated me. Kissing a girl was almost as remote a possibility as marrying one. Most of them weren't interested in me anyway. I had never come close to kissing a girl. In 6th grade, I developed a crush on Dawn Crabtree. She had brown pigtails and huge brown eyes, and most importantly she was still shorter than me. I stared at her endlessly in class. For a solid two month period, I ate very little at breakfast and lunch because I was afraid of being caught off-guard in an impromptu conversation during the day with Dawn. I didn't want to blow my rare chance of impressing her by blowing chow all over her. My infatuation ended when I found out that she liked Billy Taylor, a much bigger kid in my class. They started going together. My disappointment was outweighed by the pleasure of being able to eat again.

I figured that Maureen was two years older than me. As I lay in bed, I imagined that I would rescue her from a band of terrorist guerrillas that attack Westwood. They take the entire club hostage

72

and set up the halfway house as their headquarters. I happen to be hiding outside under the caddie window. When one of them comes around the corner on patrol, I trip him and take his gun. I take out each of the guerillas with single shots, including the one holding Maureen by the neck. I am her hero. As I refined the details of my rescue, I drifted to sleep. In my dream I was chased by a giant pair of green sunglasses; soon a pack of them was chasing me, faceless but with white golf caps resting atop. Before long, it was an army hunting me up and down the hills of Westwood. A menacing laugh echoed in my head, interspersed with the reverberation of Mr. Guelcher clearing his sinuses.

My next two times out I again ran for carts. One would think that, since I was just barely bigger than the average golf bag, I would consider this to be a good deal; but being a runner sucked. First, the member usually didn't want the runner there. He had just paid for a cart and now he had to pay for a snot-nosed kid to run around with it? Second, a runner rarely was with the golfer, so developing rapport with him was difficult. They quickly forgot my name and only acknowledged my presence when I screwed something up. Third, true caddies are born to carry bags. Only first year caddies were runners. Being a runner was like stamping a large 'S' on my forehead for 'Spook.'

I didn't like being out on the course caddying so far. But at least it beat the loneliness of the endless hours in the caddie yard, and at least I was bringing home some money. To make matters worse, Maureen wasn't at the halfway house either round. My near-puking each time we hit the 9th hole was all for naught.

I hoped that carrying a bag would make me like the job a little more. Real caddies carried bags. They didn't run after carts. And it would show Maureen that I was strong enough to be a real caddy. I worked up the nerve to ask Mr. G during a relatively quiet moment on the first tee if he would please let me carry a bag.

'Can you handle it?' he shot back, examining me from head to toe.

'Yep!' I immediately answered, realizing that I hadn't even considered that I couldn't.

'Okay, what's your number?'

'407'

He looked down at the list and made a small pencil mark next to my number. 'Okay, son. Now don't let me down.'

I went back to the bench and eagerly awaited my turn to prove myself.

About a half hour later, Mr. G called out, '407!'

I snapped to attention and ran to the desk.

'407, you're out next.' He handed me my caddie card with Mr. Ronkowski's name on it.

I checked the plastic tags attached to each bag on the bag rack until I found Mr. Ronkowski's name. The bag was gigantic. I took a deep breath before I hoisted the brown leather bag onto my right shoulder. The cow hide hung just barely off the ground. Even after adjusting the strap, the bag still hung low, and there was nothing I could do to adjust the weight.

Mr. Ronkowski approached. He was proportionately as huge as his bag. At about 6'5", 275 pounds and a full beard, he looked like a lumberjack who was dressed up as a golfer for Halloween. His face held a Boss Tweed scowl. I flashed back to Mr. Guelcher, glaring back at me through those green sunglasses, and feared for my life.

I politely introduced myself.

'Hi, Kevin,' he replied. 'You gonna be able to carry this big bag?' While extremely deep, his voice was pleasant.

'Yessir.'

Mr. Ronkowski greeted Mr. Booth, and they went to the practice green to putt. I left the bag on the rack and walked to the water fountain to wet one end of my caddie towel. I had seen other caddies do this so that they could keep the clubs and balls clean. Now that I was a real caddie, I had to act like one.

I got back to the bag just as Mr. Ronkowski returned from the putting green.

'We're up next, Kevin. I'll see you on the tee.' He pulled out his driver.

I picked up the bag, put it on my shoulder and began making my way to the tee. After two steps, the bag suddenly crashed to the ground. The shiny clubs slammed onto the black asphalt path. The clang temporarily silenced the tee area, and all eyes were on me.

'That better not have been my bag!' yelled Mr. Booth. 'Caddie, was that my bag?'

'No, Mr. Booth,' his caddie assured him.

I was stunned, holding an empty strap. The caddie bench was full of boys failing to suppress their laughter.

Mr. G race-walked over in his white loafers. 'What's going on here, 407? You ask me to give you a bag, and then you drop the bag? What's wrong with you, son?'

'Are you okay, son?' asked Mr. Ronkowski.

'Yes, I'm okay. I'm so sorry. I don't know what happened.' I reattached the strap by clipping it back onto the metal loop.

'Well, it's a little scratched, but I guess it's okay,' said Mr. Ronkowski as I put the clubs back in.

Still confused, I walked up to the tee and stood next to number 127 who stood next to Mr. Booth's enormous bag and a doubles caddie who I'd noticed everyone called Stinky. I don't know why they called him that; he didn't seem to be any more unkempt than the rest of us. 127 was a skinny kid with pale skin and wild, bushy red hair.

'They fixed your bag, Spook,' 127 mumbled out of the side of his mouth.

'What?'

'They fixed your bag,' he said in a hushed tone.

'What does that mean?'

'I'll explain next hole. Don't worry, we'll get them back.'

After the foursome teed off, I led the pack on my way to Mr. Ronkowski's ball. I wanted to prove to everyone that his bag was no problem for me. I placed the bag down next to his ball and leaned the bag out so that he could select his club.

'Um, Kevin, you're on the wrong side,' he said. Caddies were supposed to stand on the right side of the ball (for a right-handed golfer). This position ensured that the caddie would not be hit by either the club or the ball. So much for my perfect round.

While we forecaddied on the next hole, 127 introduced himself as Howie Weston. 'Tool got you back there,' explained Howie. 'When you left the bag at the rack to go wet your towel, I saw Tool unhook your bag strap from the metal loop and reattach it to the plastic loop that holds the plastic membership tag.' Howie showed me how the strap unhooks. Sure enough, the bag tag must have broken because it was nowhere to be found. It must have been lying on the ground back at the tee. 'We do it all the time to each other. You got to keep alert, Wichita. I've trained myself to always check the strap before I pick up the bag if I've ever left it alone even for a second. Tool's one of the biggest jerks out here. I hate that kid. Luckily for us, he's in the foursome behind us. We'll get him back.'

Howie held the pin at the edge of the 2nd green as the members were holing out when he caught my attention. He subtly rolled the bottom metal end of the pin in the dewy grass. He then dipped the pin into the sand trap and rolled it around until the end was covered with sand. After the members holed out, he walked over to the cup and jammed the pin back into the hole.

'Just watch Tool try to tend that pin,' he mumbled to me with a grin.

The forecaddying spot on the 3rd hole was right near the 2nd green. While our foursome walked from the tee to hit their second shots, we were able to watch from the fairway as Tool tended the pin near us. He stood in the proper caddie position to tend the pin – right hand on the bunched-up flag, left hand behind his back, feet together. As the first golfer putted and the ball neared the hole, Tool reached his left hand around to grab the pin out with both hands like he had done hundreds of times before. But this time it didn't move. He tugged again and couldn't budge the pin out of the cup, and the ball kept moving toward the hole. After the third unsuccessful tug, with the ball only three feet away from the hole and on target, Tool began to panic. He put all of his might into the fourth tug just as the ball reached the hole. This time the pin came out of the hole, but the plastic cup came with it too. The ball richocheted off the cup and came to rest about three feet from the hole.

Howie's suppressed giggles came out like a squealing piglet. Tool shot a glare our way. I looked away. Howie innocently shrugged, then turned to me and started tearing up laughing, 'That has never worked so well. Usually it just makes it hard to pull the pin out. I've never seen someone pull out the entire cup before. We've got to do that a few more times.'

Howie sanded the pin on the 3rd and 5th holes. He left the 4th clean just to keep Tool guessing.

'Between caddying for Booth and sanding pins, I'm working my butt off here today,' Howie said as we forecaddied on the 6th hole.

Booth teed off and his ball headed for the trees.

'Jack Martin!' yelled Howie as the ball hit the tree, but it dropped deeper into the woods. 'My God, Booth is playing like an absolute pig today. I even kicked his ball out from behind a tree last hole, and he still messed it up. Now it's time for the Caddie Towel Trick.'

'What's that?'

'Watch and learn, my young friend.'

Howie made his way over to Booth's ball as the golfers left the tee. He casually dropped his towel on top of the ball, like the towel had just fallen out of his hand. When he picked the towel back up, the ball came with it. He walked about 20 yards further and 10 yards closer to the fairway -- just enough for the golfers not to question it -- and dropped the towel again, leaving the ball on the ground when he picked it up.

'Boy, I hit that one better than I thought,' said Booth as he approached Howie.

'Yes, and it's a pretty nice lie too.'

Booth lined up his next shot and knocked the ball onto the green.

I found myself walking in stride with Mr. Ronkowski.

'So where do you go to school, son?'

'I go to school back home in Kansas. I'm just visiting for the summer.'

'Oh.' We continued in silence.

I wasn't much in the mood for talking anyway. His bag was taking a mean toll on my shoulder. By the end of nine holes, I was in such agony that I hadn't even thought about Maureen as we approached the halfway house. I massaged my shoulder to try to work the pain out of it.

'Hey, man, you gonna make it?' asked Howie.

'I'll be okay.' As much as my shoulder hurt, I didn't want to go back to running for carts, and I didn't want to admit to myself or to anyone else that maybe I was too small to caddie. 'Maybe there's something wrong with that strap.'

'Don't worry. You've just got Spook Shoulder. Everyone gets it their first few times out. In fact, I still get it the first time or two that I caddie each summer.' He looked around quickly. 'You didn't hear it here, but even Kovach gets it each year.'

'Kovach gets Spook Shoulder?'

'Yep, even Kovach. It'll get better.'

I wasn't sure that Spook Shoulder was its proper medical term, but I did know the body just wasn't designed to carry bags full of golf clubs. Maybe Spook Shoulder was the body's way of telling us that it was rejecting the idea. I was just afraid my arm would fall off before the Spook Shoulder got any better.

When we arrived at the halfway house, Stinky ordered his food, and I stepped up to the window. And there she was again.

'Hi, Kevin,' her face lit up.

'Can I have a Coke?'

'You want it in a cup or should I pour it directly on your shoes?'

'A cup will be fine.' I met her smile.

'Thanks,' was all I could add when she came back with my drink.

'Come on, move it,' ordered Howie, 'I'm thirsty too.' I sat down at the bench.

Howie joined me a minute later. 'She's pretty cute,' I nodded toward the window.

'Um, yeah, I guess. You do know she's Mouse's sister, don't you?'

My stomach sank. 'She is?'

'Yeah, all the McMurtrys work here, even the girls.'

I got back up and stole a glance at Maureen. I tried to find a resemblance to Mouse, but other than the Irish looks, they didn't really look much alike. Or so I convinced myself.

Mr. Ronkowski was the first out of the halfway house. He finished off his beer in a wax paper cup.

'Watch this, boys.'

He teed up his ball and then put the cup over the ball. He swung through the cup, and the ball ripped through and shot out into the middle of the fairway.

'Doesn't go quite as far, but something about the shape of the cup makes it go dead straight.'

'I don't think that's legal,' called Mr. Booth from the halfway house.

For the entire back nine, my Spook Shoulder flared up each time I put the bag on. I rested it at every opportunity and subtly massaged it each time I put the bag down for Mr. Ronkowski to take a shot. As I struggled through the final holes, I like to think that the irony was not lost on Mr. Ronkowski that this 90-pound weakling was carrying a bag for such a large man. He could easily have picked up and carried me and the bag without much effort. A couple of times he looked at me and said, 'You okay?' I assured him each time that I was, even though I wasn't. But my pride wouldn't let me admit my pain.

At the end of the round, I told Mr. Ronkowski, 'It was a pleasure caddying for you, sir.' I didn't mention what disdain I held for his golf bag.

The hulking man looked me in the eye and said with a warm voice, 'You did a good job, Kevin.' He handed me a memo-sized signed document with a carbon-copy beneath it. It was a country club chit for $7. I smiled.

I brought the chit over to the caddie house, where Mrs. G cashed it for me in Mr. G's office. Despite my fear that my shoulder would need to be amputated, I finally felt like a real caddie.

Back at the apartment, I washed out an old Maxwell House can to use as my piggy bank. I found a pad of paper and began a log of each person I caddied for and how much money I made. So far I had made $24. I had to make a lot more. I had planned to take the next day or two off, both as a reward to myself and as a way to let my aching shoulder recuperate, but I was going to have to caddie more loops than my current pace in order to make any significant money.

There was a knock at my door.

'Come in.'

It was my grandmother wearing a pink bathrobe. She took a tentative step into the room. 'How are you doing, Kevin?'

'I'm fine. Everything is great.'

'You've hardly been home at all the last week. Are you sure you're not working too hard?' She had a soft, old-fashioned voice.

'Yes, I'll be fine.'

'Looks like you've got some money saved up there.' She looked at the Maxwell House can. 'Things have been tough, haven't they, Kevin?'

'It really hasn't been that bad…well, at least until lately.' I knew that was a lie, and I never took the time to consider how big a lie it really was.

She tilted her head and wrinkled her forehead. 'Well, don't work yourself too hard. Your Grandpa and I want to spend some time with you this summer.' She paused. 'Have you talked to your Mom today?'

'No, have you?'

'Kevin, we never talk to your Mom.'

'Never?'

She shook her head.

'Has it always been like that or only since she got sick recently?'

'We love your mother so much, but to be honest there's always been a certain wall between us.' Her eyes drifted to a set of framed grade school pictures of my mother with slight variations of the same dutch boy haircut. 'When she decided to move away right after college, we started hearing from her less and less. We didn't even meet you until you were over a year old. The last couple of years there's been virtually no communication. You can imagine our surprise when she called a few weeks ago to ask us to take you for the summer.'

'Yes, I've been meaning to thank you for that—'

'Oh gosh, Kevin, we would do anything for you. You're our grandson for gosh sakes. My first thought was how this whole situation had impacted you. Grandpa and I didn't know what to expect when you came off that airplane, and just look at you. You're a wonderfully healthy, well-adjusted boy.'

Well, not totally, I thought.

She stood in silence for another 30 seconds, then let out a deep sigh. 'We just want you to be happy.' She looked at her watch and looked back at me urgently. 'You need to get some sleep. Your brain grows when you sleep. Actually, your whole body does, but especially your brain. You better get to sleep.'

'Good night, Grandma.'

'Goodnight, Kevin. Sweet dreams...' She turned off the light switch.

As the darkness filtered through the room, I let her words sink in; well, some of them. Happy? I was just trying to survive. Each day was a struggle for me. I wasn't ever completely relaxed. I certainly had never been completely happy; I hadn't even been shooting for it.

Mom took me to a doctor a couple years back to see if my stomach problems were due to any physical condition instead of nerves. I had gone through a week or so when I couldn't keep any food down. I hoped that they actually would find something wrong, so that maybe we could treat my problems, but deep down I knew there was nothing wrong with me physically. Dr. Isaac poked and prodded my belly and set me up for a screening. The next Saturday we went down to a hospital in Wichita.

'Don't worry, Sweet Bugs.' she said in the waiting room. 'Remember that Curious George had to go through the same procedure when he ate the crossword puzzle piece.'

I had to drink a chalky barium drink while a technician took images of my stomach. It actually was pretty cool to see the liquid traveling down my esophagus on the screen.

We returned to the doctor's office the next week, and Dr. Isaac proclaimed that my stomach was fine. Easy for him to say. With no additional help to be lent from the medical community, I was left to fend for myself.

I rolled over in my bed and turned my thoughts to golf. I pictured a golfer hitting balls, not any golfer specifically, more like a composite of all of the swings I had seen over the last couple weeks. Golf swings are like finger prints – no two persons' are the same. Each golf swing adapts to the person's unique characteristics, their height, the length of their arms, their weight, their mental makeup. So as I lay in bed, I created a generic golf swing in my head. I tweaked things here, adjusted things there to try to come up with the perfect swing. After a hundred swings or so, I drifted to sleep.

Chapter 5

Tool's squinty eyes were laser beams the next day throughout roll call. I looked around for Howie to take some of the heat for sanding the pins the day before, but he was nowhere to be seen.

Mr. G had taken down all the numbers and was finishing up his final thoughts for the morning.

'218, are you here today?' Mr G called out. 'There you are. You don't have dungarees on today, do you?'

'No sir.'

'Boys. I had to send 218 home yesterday because he had dungarees on with rivets. Do you know what rivets do to a golf bag? Scratches up the sides. Now I hate to send any of you boys home, but you got to follow the rules.'

'114. Mrs. Hamlin told me that you did a nice job for her, that you're a really good boy. Good job son.'

'Brooowwwn-nose' taunts flooded the caddie yard. Mr. G ignored them.

'And I've gotten a couple of complaints from the members that it's been getting noisy in the caddie yard when they've been playing the 9th hole. So tone down the horseplay, boys.'

Mr. G closed up his black book and headed to the first tee. I tried to lose myself in the ebbing sea of blue shirts, but Tool intercepted me.

'Hey, Spook, you think you're pretty funny sanding all those pins yesterday?' He stared down at me and poked his finger into my chest. He wanted to fight, and fighting just wasn't part of my makeup. Actually it was less the fighting and more the bleeding and pain that I was pretty sure I wouldn't be fond of.

'I don't know –'

'Don't try to deny it. I know you did it, and I'm gonna get you back, Spook.'

Just then, Kovach came over. 'Is there a problem, Tool?' Tool was about 6 inches taller than me, but Kovach was at least 6 inches taller than Tool.

'No, Kovach. No problem.' Tool slowly walked away, his eyes locked on mine the whole time.

I kept my distance from Tool and kept in general proximity to Kovach, without annoying him, for the rest of the morning. I bided my time until Mr. G finally summoned me to the sanctuary of the first tee.

I sat on the caddie bench awaiting my turn when the green-bespectacled Mr. Guelcher appeared around the corner of the pro shop. My limbs went cold. I couldn't be assigned to him again. I could almost smell the suffocating smoke from his cigarettes. My heart skipped a beat, perhaps a minor heart attack, as he hesitated a step when he saw me sitting on the bench. I went into all out panic mode as he walked over to Mr. G and the two of them stood chatting as they kept looking my way. Mr. G looked concerned. He nodded and shook his head as Guelcher spoke. Guelcher shot me a couple more looks as he walked to his bag on the rack.

Mr. G called out, '407! Get up here!'

I ran up to the desk with blood pounding in my temples.

'Son, did you caddie for Mr. Guelcher and his guest last week in a cart?'

'Yessir.'

'Well, apparently a couple days ago, Mr. Guelcher received a phone call from his guest from his home in Florida. He informed Mr. Guelcher that he had half of Mr. Guelcher's clubs in his bag in Florida, and he correctly assumed that half of his own clubs were in Mr. Guelcher's bag in Cleveland.'

He looked at me as if waiting for a response. I had none.

'Son, that's exactly why many of the members here are looking to replace all of the caddies with carts.'

I paused, a bit confused, 'But weren't they riding in a cart?'

'Are you getting smart with me?' His eyes bulged.

'No, I was just—'

'The members don't have to let caddies run with carts, and if caddies continue to make boners like you did, they're going to change the policy and many of you caddies will be out of work. Now go sit your keyster back down on the bench.'

I walked back to the bench feeling guilty for nearly bringing down the caddie program and still feeling a bit confused. I had never heard the word boner used in its original meaning.

It was clear to me that I needed to avoid Mr. Guelcher for the rest of the summer. I didn't know what he could do to me, apart from making four hours a living hell for me, but I didn't want to find out. I added another name to my list of enemies.

I sat back down on the bench alone. I wanted to shrivel up and disappear.

A while later Mouse joined me on the bench just as Mr. G yelled my number, '407!'

I shot to attention.

'Try not to mess this one up,' Mr. G said as he handed me the card.

'Who'd you get?' asked Mouse as I sat back down.

'Mr. Morgan. I think he was in the group my first time out, when I caddied for Guelcher and his guest. He seemed like a really nice guy. What do you know about him?' I began to panic that Guelcher would be playing with him again.

'Never had him, but he's been in the group a couple of times before. I heard he used to be pretty good. He doesn't hit the ball very far, but he's deadly around the greens. I think he's like a 7 handicap or something.'

'Is that good?'

'Yeah, pretty good. Basically a handicap is how many strokes you average over par. Par is 72, meaning if you play the course the way it's supposed to be played – landing the ball on the green in 2 shots on a par 4 or 3 on a par 5, that's what they call regulation, and two-putting each green – you'll have a 72, but just about no one is that good. Most people are like an 18 handicap, meaning they usually shoot around 90, or 18 over par.'

'So Mr. Morgan usually shoots, like, 79?'

'You're like a genius, Kev. Yes.'

'I don't remember him being that good when he was in Guelcher's group. Then again, I was very busy at the time being super-Spook.'

'He doesn't hit it very far, but he hits it straight. And he has a great short game.'

I got even more nervous. I hadn't caddied for someone nearly that good before. 'If he's so good, why is Mr. G giving him a B caddie like me? Is he a screw or something?'

'Not too bad, he's just one of those guys that flies under the radar. For some reason he always plays with these old guys who pretty much suck. Like Guelcher. He's kinda old, so no one thinks of him as being very good. And he always plays with Screws so no doubles caddies want him. He'll be easy to caddie for. He hits it short and straight, and he's never in trouble so you won't lose any balls. He should be fine.'

'Do you think Guelcher will be in his group?' I asked a little too desperately.

'How should I know? Why do you care?'

'I dunno.'

Mr. Morgan approached his bag with a confident stride. He wore a pink golf shirt that could only be worn by someone thoroughly comfortable with his masculinity.

'Hey, Sport,' Mr. Morgan greeted me at his bag. 'Am I lucky enough to have you as my caddie today?'

'Yes, Mr. Morgan, my name is Kevin.'

'Glad to have you along today, Kevin.' He squinted a little. 'Weren't you in my group a couple weeks ago?'

'Yes, I think so.'

'I thought I remembered you. Well, let's have some fun today.'

His swing was as smooth as a waterfall, wristy like old film clips of Bobby Jones. He would have looked comfortable in a pair of knickers. He predictably hit his drive 220 yards down the middle of the fairway. As we walked off the tee he handed me his driver and asked the standard first question, 'So, where do you go to school, Kevin?'

'Well, I'm not from Cleveland. I go to school back in Kansas. I'm visiting my grandparents who live just down the street.'

'Oh really? What are their names?'

'Bill and Margaret Coyle.'

He thought for a second. 'Hmm, I don't believe I know them. So tell me, where do you go to school?'

I looked over at him.

I began hesitantly, 'Well, I just finished the sixth grade at the public school where I live. It's called Cottonwood Elementary School. I'm supposed to be going to the junior high in August.'

'How many children were in your grade?'

'Only about 90, but the junior high is much bigger.'

He hit his next shot low and straight, about 180 yards, with a 3-iron. He left himself about 75 yards to the green. He landed the next shot onto the middle of the green and two-putted for par. He followed that up with a short but straight drive on the second hole.

We stood together on the second fairway as the rest of the foursome searched the woods on the other side for Mr. McGowan's ball.

'So how do you like Cleveland?'

'It's okay, so far. I really don't know anybody though. Just my grandparents.'

'I remember when I joined the army when I was 18. I had never been out of my hometown and away from the security of my friends and family. It scared the crap out of me. I had a pit in my stomach the entire first month. Even when I joined this country club 20 years ago, I didn't know a soul, and it took a while to feel at home.'

I liked that he didn't tell me that everything was going to be okay. He just assured me that it was normal to be afraid. No one his age ever talked to me that way.

'And how do you like caddying so far?'

'I guess I like it okay,' I lied. 'I'm still pretty new at it.'

'You know, I caddied when I was your age,' he said with a twinkle in his eye.

'Did you caddie here?'

'No.' It was his turn to hit. The ball landed short of the green and rolled up just onto the green. I handed him his putter.

'No, I grew up on the East Side. I caddied at a club named Canterbury over there. I lived in Cleveland Heights, used to ride my bicycle over to the club. I moved over to the West Side right out of college and have lived here ever since. You probably haven't noticed this yet, but Cleveland's like two separate cities; two cities with a common downtown. Have you been downtown?'

'No, not yet.'

'Well the Cuyahoga River runs through the Flats just next to downtown, and it cuts the city into two really different sides. I think of it as the point in the country that separates the East and the Midwest. The East Side is older and wealthier than the West Side. Shaker Heights, in the heart of the suburbs over there, is one of the wealthiest zip codes in the US. There are a lot more WASPs and Jews over there, whereas the West Side is much more ethnic, more Irish Catholic.' He swung his putter at a blade of grass. 'I fit in a lot better on the West Side. We weren't poor, but my dad worked for the Water Department for 30 years. The West Side is less into status. It's less cosmopolitan, but people tend to be a bit more down to earth, more Midwestern.'

We turned to watch Mr. McGowan finally make it onto the green.

'They actually have a club over there named The Country Club. Can you believe that? Westwood's the oldest club on the West Side and it's not nearly as stuffy as any of those over there. Most of the members here are accountants, doctors, small business owners or lawyers, like me. We're not the CEO's, we don't have the old money. But, I don't know, I like it here.'

He hit his next shot short of the green, chipped up close and sunk his par putt. He played the next four holes in a similar, unassuming way -- knocked it up close in regulation, chipped it near the pin and hit the putt. It was a thing of beauty.

On the 6th hole, Mr. Morgan had reached the par 4 in regulation and had about a 20-foot putt for birdie. He turned to me and said in a fatherly sort of way, 'Kevin, never leave a birdie putt short. This is the one situation on the golf course where I throw conservatism out the window. Two-putting for par is like kissing your sister. Anyone can par a hole; birdie chances are rare. Don't waste them by hitting your putt like a girl. If you don't hit it far enough, you never give it a chance to drop in the hole. Remember, never leave a birdie putt short.'

He made a run at the birdie, but missed it an inch to the right.

'Nice putt, Walter,' called Mr. McGowan. 'That's good. Pick it up.'

'You know I don't take gimmes, especially when we're playing for money.'

'It's a $2 bet,' replied Mr. McGowan.

Mr. Morgan lined up his putt, and tapped in for par. He shot Mr. McGowan a smile as he retrieved his ball from the hole.

McGowan hit his putt three feet short of the hole. 'That's a gimme, Howard,' called out Mr. Morgan. 'Remember, Kevin, 90% of putts that don't reach the hole don't go in.' He handed me his putter and walked away.

'Interesting.' I pondered that one for a few seconds.

Mr. McGowan gratefully picked his ball off the green and moved on to the 7th tee.

The path to the 7th tee intersected the path going to the 16th tee with a drinking fountain at the junction point. Caddies on the front 9 were just hitting their groove, building some rapport with their golfers. Caddies on the back 9 were on the home stretch; they could smell the cash awaiting them a mere 900 yards away. Mr. Morgan and I walked side by side when we came across Howie making his way from the 15th green.

'Hey, Steve,' he said to me straight-faced as he walked by.

Mr. Morgan looked at me quizzically.

Howie spun back around to address me again, 'Steve, your parole officer came by again. He left his number at the caddie house. I'll catch up with you later.' He turned and continued walking to the 16th tee.

Mr. Morgan cracked a smile. 'Friend of yours?' he commented.

'I guess so.'

'So, do you like school, Kevin?' he asked as I handed him his putter a few holes later.

'It's okay, I guess.'

'What do you want to be when you grow up?'

'A doctor,' I replied without hesitation.

'A doctor,' he repeated. 'Very good. You better study really hard. My father was a doctor. What a wonderful profession. You get to meet all sorts of people and help them, and you get paid well while you do it. Well, keep studying hard.' His smile followed him all the way to the green.

I really did want to be a doctor, but I didn't have the heart to tell him that the only reason I wanted to be one was that I was always scared of being drafted into the army and put onto the front lines and killed. Most doctors sat back at the bases or in the Pentagon and gave soldiers physicals or shots. Sure, I had seen M.A.S.H., that TV show about doctors in the Korean War, and I knew that some doctors had to be a little close to the gunfire, but even then, none were ever shot. Medical school was my ticket out of combat, so I didn't even care that I hated my 6th grade science class.

Mr. Morgan ended up parring every hole except the last, which he bogeyed, to card a 73 for the round.

'Not a bad day, huh, Dr. Kevin?' he said with a big grin at the end of the round.

When I told him it was a pleasure caddying for him, I really meant it.

'Maybe we'll do it again.'

I was pretty spent as I walked back to the caddie house.

'You gonna go out again?' asked Mouse.

'Again?'

'Yeah, you gotta go out twice a day if you expect to make any money.'

'Yeah, okay,' my mouth uttered even though the rest of my body screamed No Way. 'Do you think we'll be able to?'

'Let's go over to the first tee and see how many kids still need to go out their first time. Some just give up and go home by now.

We can put our name on the bottom of the list. Hopefully there will be enough people golfing this afternoon.'

Parked in front of the circle at the club's entrance was a silver sports car like I had never seen before. 'What on earth is that?' I said to Mouse.

'That's a DeLorean. It's stainless steel; you clean it with a Brillo pad. Look at the doors. They open from the top. It's awesome.'

'Whose is it?'

'Mr. DeLorean. It's his uncle or something that owns the company. This is one of the first ones ever made. They make them over in Europe. They're going to start selling them here in the next couple of years. Everyone's going to want one. They're going to be huge.'

I pressed my face against the window to look at the interior.

'Hey!' Yelled one of the car parkers. 'Get away from that car, caddies.'

Mouse and I scurried over to the tee.

Howie was seated on one of the benches. The first tee was fairly empty. 'How ya doing?' said Mouse. They shook hands.

'If I was any better,' replied Howie, 'I'd be on vacation.'

Howie reached out his hand to me. 'And how are you, Steve?'

'That was a good one, Howie. Luckily, Mr. Morgan didn't buy it for a second.'

It felt great to sit on the bench. My feet were killing me. My new Keds sneakers hadn't quite broken in properly. I untied them and took off my shoes and socks. I had developed blisters on several of my toes.

'Man, that looks nasty,' commented Howie.

'Any way to stop this from happening? My feet are killing me.'

'Not really,' replied Howie as he took off his shoes and socks. Both he and Mouse wore Chuck Taylor high-tops, as did about half of the other caddies. They were cheap and they dried out more quickly than other shoes when the grass was wet from the morning dew or the rain. 'It takes a few weeks to turn the blisters into calluses, but I'm always getting new ones.' He pulled his shoes and socks off. 'I usually just pop them and let the puss drain out.' He lanced the skin of the largest blister by pinching it between two finger nails. 'Oooo, that feels much better. They hurt a lot less after that.'

I almost fainted.

He lanced another blister and then shoved his butt-white foot toward Mouse's face. 'Here, Mouse, can you take care of the next one for me? Maybe cut it open with your teeth.'

'Ahhh! Get that Franken-foot away from me,' screamed Mouse as he barely escaped the monster.

Howie drained three or four more blisters before putting his socks and shoes back on.

'Sloan was in my foursome this morning,' Howie said to Mouse.

'Did he Sloan you or any of the other caddies?'

'No, but if he did, I'd kick his ass.'

'I think you'd enjoy it,' teased Mouse.

'Yeah, right.'

'Who's Sloan?' I interjected.

'He's this creepy member,' explained Howie, 'who likes to sneak up behind his caddie, slide his putter between the caddie's legs, and then yank it back so that the putter head racks the caddie in the balls.'

'Why the heck does he do that?' I asked.

'Who knows?' said Mouse. 'He thinks it's funny or something.'

'Or he's some kind of pervert,' added Howie.

'Has he ever done it to one of you?' I asked.

'No!' they both quickly answered.

'I heard he did it a couple of weeks ago to 328,' said Mouse.

'Yeah, I heard about that, but I asked 328 that afternoon, and he said he didn't get Sloaned. Didn't your brother say it happened to someone in his group one time?'

'My brother Todd claims it happened, but he didn't see it.'

'Well, whether he does it or not, Sloan is a creepy guy.'

'He's really weird looking, and he's got this deep monotone voice, and he hardly ever talks. When he does, it's more of a grunt than actual words. He's just a weird guy.'

'I'll be sure to keep clear of him,' I said as I made a mental note.

An hour or so later, Mr. G assigned Howie and me to a two-some, the Gallaghers. I introduced myself to Mrs. Gallagher.

Howie introduced himself to Mr. Gallagher, 'Hi, my name's Napoleon, and I'll be your caddie today.'

'Nice to meet you, Napoleon.'

Howie grinned as the Gallaghers took the tee.

'You gotta keep things fun out here,' he told me while we forecaddied on #2. 'With so many caddies, most members usually don't remember caddies' names. Besides, the Gallaghers hardly ever play.'

Halfway through the front nine, I wasn't sure that my body was going to make it. In addition to my aching shoulder, my feet were killing me. I collapsed on the caddie bench at the halfway house.

'Man, you've got to take care of those blisters,' said Howie. 'Yank those shoes off and pop 'em.'

'But...'

"Pop em!"

"Isn't that just asking for them to get infected?' Not to mention the pain that I feared.

'Never thought about it. I don't think there's much chance of that happening.'

'My mom always taught me to be very careful about open cuts. I'm pretty sure it could become infected. It could be very serious.'

'Well, your mom doesn't have to walk nine more holes, but it's up to you.'

I considered it for a moment, but all scenarios resulted in having at least one of my feet amputated.

I limped my way through the back 9. With my blisters coupled with Spook Shoulder, I paced the fairways with a Quasimodo gait.

Mrs. Gallagher's golf bag was my Esmeralda. I finished the round, but at least my feet were attached. Barely.

I made $14 during the day, bringing my total for the summer up to $38. My whole body hurt, but I realized that caddying two rounds a day was the only way that I would make any real money.

Back home, my Grandma left a plate of chicken and vegetables in the refrigerator. I ate it cold; didn't even wait to heat it up. I ate it all. I was too tired to even think of throwing it back up. I collapsed into bed.

Chapter 6

'Boys, being a caddie is much more than lugging a bag around the course for four hours.'

Mr. G had finished roll call on a quiet Wednesday morning and was now pacing back and forth in the caddie yard like General Patton. 'They can train a monkey to lug a bag, but they can't train one to caddie.'

'What about Tulis?' Howie offered.

All the caddies cracked up. Mr. G didn't crack a smile. 'Now many of you are good caddies, but I want all of you to be great caddies. A great caddie takes into account the wind and whether the pin is in the front or back of the green so that you can adjust the distance you mark off. A great caddie knows his member's abilities well enough after the first hole to recommend the right club for each situation on the course. He can diagnose a swing fault on the spot and, if asked, suggest a slight correction based on the golfer's natural swing. An exceptional caddie, serves as a golfer's cheerleader, his best friend on the course, his psychologist. He compliments the golfer when he hits a good shot and keeps his mouth shut when he hits a bad one. When a golfer unravels during an important match, a great caddie can pull him together by taking his mind off of the situation. Those things come with time. Learn from the Senior Caddies when you go out on the course with them.

'Now I'm not saying all this so that I look good or so that you can feel good about yourselves. You work hard and it leads to more of this.' He rubbed his fingers together. 'The golfers will pay you more cash. It's also easier for you out there if you can get your golfer to play better. I'm looking out for all of you. I want you all to succeed. Any questions?'

'No, Mr. G....'

'Any questions?!?'

'NO, MR. G!'

He packed up his lists and walked over to the first tee.

'Stay where you are!' Mouse's brother Todd yelled to the assembled caddies. 'We're going to do Caddie Clean-up and then some Caddie Calisthenics!'

Todd McMurtry, Rickles and Kovach kept everyone lined up against the fence. Typically, Wednesday was the slowest day of the week. Saturdays and Sundays were the busiest. Mondays the course was closed. Tuesdays were saved by Ladies' Day in the morning. Thursdays were the second slowest, and Fridays usually picked up around lunch, when men would get an early start to their weekends. With Mr. G sequestered at the first tee and the surrounding bushes protecting the caddie yard from the view of members, Kovach was able to impose his iron fist upon the younger, smaller caddies. About 75 of us were lined up. I had positioned myself to be as far away from Tool as possible.

'All Spooks take one step forward so we know who you are,' yelled Rickles.

About 25 kids stepped forward.

'Alice, grab those two Spooks next to you, get the brooms inside and sweep out the caddie house. I want it spotless!' Kovach ordered Tom Cooper.

'You four,' yelled Todd. 'I want you to pick up every single scrap of paper in the caddie yard. If I see one piece of garbage on the ground afterwards, it's Caddie White Benches for all of you.'

Kovach walked over to Howie. He towered over Howie's skinny, red-headed body.

'127!'

'Yessir,' he responded with eyes wide open.

'Someone sanded a bunch of pins on Tuesday, and I have a good feeling it was you.'

'I swear, Kovach, I had nothing to do with that,' he squeaked.

Kovach turned to the crowd, 'Does anyone else want to fess up to sanding the pins on Tuesday?'

A smattering of 'No's' tumbled from the frightened masses. He turned back to Howie. 'I had trouble pulling the pin out on the 2nd hole, the whole goddamn cup came out. I looked like an idiot to Mrs. Chambers. You may have cost me a buck or two.'

A glimmer of a smile passed across Howie's mouth.

'You think that's funny?' asked Kovach.

Howie's smile erased. 'I swear I didn't do it.'

'Well, let's teach you a lesson anyhow.' Kovach grabbed Howie by the underwear and gave him the Mother of All Wedgies.

"No, please! Don't do that! Come on, man. I'm sorry, I won't do it again.'

Kovach lifted Howie off the ground above his head. He hooked the back of Howie's underwear on the top rung of the fence about 6 feet off the ground.

'Awww. Come on, Kovach. Let me down. Come on.' Howie flailed his arms and legs futilely. He looked like a turtle that had been picked up by its shell.

Todd and Rickles picked up some pebbles from the caddie yard and tossed them in Howie's direction.

'Cut that out, guys. You're going to hurt me.' One pinged off his head.

'You!' demanded Kovach as he headed toward another kid. 'What's your number?'

'356.'

'Why the hell didn't you step forward when we called all Spooks?'

'Um, I don't know,' 356 mumbled.

'Todd,' called out Kovach, 'looks like the Caddie White Bench for Mr. 356.'

He strong-armed 356 to the caddie house wall to begin his Caddie Re-Education program.

'Lean against the wall,' Kovach instructed, 'like you're sitting in a chair. I want your legs bent at a 45 degree angle. Don't rest your hands on your knees like that. Sit there with your palms up. You need to build up those skinny legs so that you can walk up and down the hills out on the course.'

'Oh my god. That kills. How long do I need to do this?' protested 356.

'Until Caddie Cleanup is over.' He turned back to the crowd. '127! How you doing up there?'

Howie had given up the struggle and hung from the fence with his arms folded. He looked almost bored. 'Kovach, can I come down now?'

'If you can get yourself down, you're free to go. Otherwise you'll need to stay up there until Caddie Cleanup is over.'

Todd continued to dole out tasks.

'You three, empty all the garbage cans – every one – into the dumpster.' I was happy to have skirted that one.

Todd made his way toward my direction. 'You,' he yelled to the kid next to me, "Grab one of the brooms and sweep the basketball court.'

Kovach returned to the ranks.

'You!' demanded Kovach. 'Is something funny? What's your number?'

'124!' He was no longer laughing.

'Looks like caddie broom stick for this one.'

Kovach pulled 124 into the middle of the caddie yard while another Senior Caddie retrieved a broomstick from the caddie house. 124 had to hold the broomstick down as though it were attached to his forehead and had to spin his body around its axis until he became so dizzy that he couldn't stand up.

'Kovach! Everything is taken care of except for the bathrooms,' announced Todd.

Kovach first walked over to 356 to check on him. He slapped 356's burning thighs. 'That feel good? We're doing you a favor here. You'll be running up those hills your next time out.'

He then surveyed the row of caddies to determine who would be selected for the worst task. Usually it was reserved for the Spook who gave them the most lip during Caddie Cleanup, but that day he walked over to Tool.

'Tool!'

'What?'

'What do you mean 'what'? Get out here.'

'But I'm not a Spook.'

'Close enough. Get out here.'

He took two small steps forward. Tool was 4 years younger and 100 lbs. lighter than Kovach.

'You're on toilet duty today.'

'What?!? No way. Come on, I'm not even a Spook.'

'Don't argue. You've got the toilets. You can pick whoever you want to help you.'

Tool stopped protesting and surveyed the line of Spooks. When his eyes reached me, he sneered. 'I'll take the Wichita Kid.'

My body went numb.

I soon found myself alone with Tool in the smelly bathroom. We had a bucket and some cleaning materials.

Tool pointed the wrong end of a plunger in my face. 'So you think messing with me on the course is funny, and then you can hide behind your big friends like Kovach?'

'No,' I mumbled.

'What's that?' he shoved the plunger handle against my throat. 'Listen, you little turd, I've had enough of you. Kovach isn't here now to protect you.' He looked over at the door to be sure no one was coming. 'You're going to clean this whole bathroom and clean it good.' He dragged me over to a toilet stall. The floor was wet with piss and water from leaky pipes. He pushed me to my knees and grabbed me by the hair. 'Now clean it. Lick it clean.'

I whimpered and struggled to get up, but I couldn't break free from him. The toilet was disgusting, like it hadn't been cleaned in weeks. My stomach started to turn and I gagged.

'What's wrong, Wichita? Clean it up.'

Just then my stomach erupted. I vomited all over the toilet.

'Ugghh! Gross!' Tool let go and stumbled out of the stall. 'What the hell is wrong with you? That's disgusting.'

It's the only time I could remember that throwing up actually helped me. Tool didn't want to come anywhere close to me. I got up and latched the stall door and assessed the situation. I used some toilet paper to triage the vomit. I hadn't gotten much on me. Most of it was on the toilet bowl.

'Leave me alone, Tool, or I'll throw up on you.'

'Stay in there. I don't want you near me.'

'I'll clean the stalls if you just leave me alone,' I offered.

'Fine with me, freak.'

He slid the bucket under the stall door and I methodically cleaned up my vomit. What wasn't on the toilet fairly easily flushed down the drain in the middle of the floor. When I was done, I moved to the next stall. Tool cautiously stayed near the door.

I cleaned the rest of the bathroom, gagging only a few times on the stench. I also cleaned myself up and rinsed out my mouth.

Tool and I emerged from the relative darkness.

'I'm done, Kovach,' Tool declared. He gave me a shove and rejoined the other caddies against the fence. I was shaken but felt like I had won a strange victory.

Kovach went over to Howie and retrieved him from the fence. He patted Howie on the head, 'Good job, Spook. I think you've had enough for one day.'

'Okay,' yelled Kovach. 'I noticed that some of you Spooks are looking a little out of shape so we're going to line up for Caddie Calisthenics. It's very important that you guys be in top physical shape. When you're caddying for Mr. Booth and you're pulling out your best brown-nosing, you can't fall apart physically. We're here to help you with that.'

We started off with jumping-jacks.

'One...Two...Three...Four...'

'Come on, guys. Let's work hard,' Todd yelled from the sidelines. 'Mr. Wills expects the most for his five bills. We need to ensure that every penny is worth it to him.'

'FORE!' screamed Kovach as he picked up a basketball and fired it into our ranks as hard as he could. Spooks a-scurried. 315, a skinny kid with glasses, dropped to the ground after being hit squarely on the head.

'I didn't tell you that you could stop!' Kovach screamed at us. 'Five...Six...Seven...Eight...'

Kovach checked on 315 to make sure he was okay. The kid was a bit dazed as he readjusted the glasses on his face. 'Now I did that for your own good,' explained Kovach. 'You always have to be on your toes on the golf course. A player could hit a bad shot, and it could hit you in the head. I may have just saved your life. I'm here to help.'

We moved on to cherry pickers. We had to hold our arms out parallel to the ground while we rapidly snapped our fingers until our shoulders burned with pain.

'Keep those arms up, boys,' yelled Todd. 'You need to build up those shoulders if you ever expect to carry doubles. Kovach has never lifted a weight in his life, he's gotten that big just doing cherry pickers.'

'FORE!' screamed Kovach as he fired the basketball again. We were all looking for it this time, and the ball glanced off of 320's thigh. 'See? Thanks to me, you're already better prepared.'

Next we did deep knee bends so that our legs were better conditioned to walk up and down the hills on the course.

'Come on, make it burn. The ladies members like to see you guys in your shorts. Do it for them.'

Finally, we moved on to Saturday Night Specials. We set up in a push-up position and were instructed to move our hips in a circular motion. I couldn't figure out the golf-related rationale for that one.

'Okay, guys,' yelled Todd. 'We're done here. Can you all thank Mr. Kovach for all his help this morning? He's always committed to making you better caddies.'

We muttered our thanks to Kovach, and the crowd dispersed.

'Hey, Spook. How are your blisters treating you?' Mouse sought me out as the caddie cals wrapped up.

'I could barely walk when I woke up this morning.'

'Good. They should only hurt for a couple of months. You'll be fine. You want to join us over here for some Caddie Golf?'

'Sure...I've never played before'

'That's okay. I'll teach you. You got a penny?'

I fished around in my pocket.

'That's okay, I got an extra one.' He tossed one to me. 'It's basically the same as regular golf, but you use a penny instead of a ball. The picnic table over there is the green, and the knothole there in the middle of it is the hole. You pitch the penny onto the table and you slide it across the table to putt. You play 18 holes with par 3s, 4s and 5s.' I looked around for more picnic tables. 'Just one table,' he said. 'We just make up different holes each time. It may seem pretty unexciting, but it's addictive. I guess, just like golf. He lofted his penny into the air, and it landed softly on the picnic table. 'It's easy.'

I tried to do the same and the penny went over my head and landed behind me.

'Nice shot. Try again,' encouraged Mouse.

I picked up the penny off the gravelly dirt. I moved a few steps closer and tossed the penny underhand. It hit the table and immediately rolled off.

'You need to hold it between your thumb and fingertip and spin it. It kind of rolls off your index finger when you release it.'

I tossed it toward the table again. It landed under it.

'That's the sandtrap,' he explained. He put the penny on the fingertips and slapped the bottom of the picnic bench, sending the penny through the narrow vertical space between the bench and the table. It landed on the table. 'That's how you do that.' Mouse appeared to be the Jack Nicklaus of Caddie Golf.

'What's up, gentlemen?' announced Howie.

'How's the underwear feeling, Howie?' asked Mouse. 'Did it hurt being up on the fence?'

'No, it actually felt pretty good.' He pulled on his stretched underwear. 'I'm thinking of hanging out there some more this afternoon. You teaching Super Spook here how to play Caddie Golf?'

'Yeah, he needs some work,' replied Mouse.

'How are those feet treating you today, Wichita? You should have listened to me yesterday and popped those blisters. You looked like my grandmother carrying that bag on the last hole. And she died three years ago.'

'They still hurt,' I replied. At least I still have them though, I thought.

'Are we going to play?' asked Howie.

'Yeah, here comes Tim,' said Mouse.

'How are things hanging?' Tim asked Howie.

'Very funny. Tim, this is the Wichita Kid.'

'What's up,' Tim shook my hand. 'What's your real name?'

'Kevin.'

'I'll stick with Wichita. What's your number?'

'407.'

'Christ, you're brand new. I'm 344.'

'Wichita is the one that kicked Mouse's ass a couple weeks ago,' Howie continued. 'Mouse was afraid he'd do it again, so I guess he befriended him.' Mouse didn't take the bait, but he granted Howie a slight smile. 'Wichita, Tim goes to school with me at St. Christopher's. We're both going to be in the 8th grade.'

'You guys ready to play?' asked Mouse.

Everyone nodded.

'How about Kevin and me? First hole is a par 4. Hit the fence pole over there and then to the hole.'

Tim tossed his penny at the fence pole. 'So Howie, did you actually sand those pins or did Kovach nab the wrong guy?'

Howie threw his penny. 'Of course it was me. Who else enjoys a good pin sanding better than me?'

Howie hit a long putt to win the hole. 'You guys are one-down after one. My hole – par 5. Go around the tree. Hit the bike tire, then to the green.'

'I just try to stay on Kovach's good side. That guy is psycho.'

'He's not a bad guy. And he's actually pretty smart. He's going to Purdue next year.'

'Yeah, but that's to play football. Nice shot.'

'But he got something like a 1200 on his SATs. He's no dummy. Hit the tree! Yes.'

'He acts like he's about as smart as an ape.'

'I think he's pretty funny.' Mouse landed his penny next to the hole.

'You won't be saying that when he gives you a wedgie. Believe me.'

'So are you dating your underwear now?'

My penny hit short of the table and landed under.

'Man, you really are terrible at this,' Tim said to me.

It was the first time anyone directed the conversation to me. But I was happy.

A few hours later, Howie and I sat on the caddie bench next to the first tee. I attentively observed Mr. G manage the operations. He was in his late 70s and stood a mere 5 foot 6, but looked like he had the strength and energy to kick every single caddie's butt.

'What's the deal with Mr. G?' I asked Howie. 'What's the G stand for anyway?'

'His real name is Arnie Gramlich,' Howie explained.

'That explains why he runs this place like a Nazi.'

'He's okay. He's tough, but he's fair. People make fun of him behind his back, but everyone respects him to his face at least. He's been around here forever. He'll tell you about the old days if you're hanging around here late in the afternoon. He started caddying here during World War I when he was around our age. Even when he had a family and he worked in the warehouse of May's or Higbee's or one of the department stores, he kept caddying on the weekends. The rules must have been different then. He then became the full time caddie master during the 50's and has been running the place ever since. He's really the reason the program is what it is today.'

'I wonder what he does during the winter?'

Howie shrugged. 'I hear he keeps busy around the club. He and Mrs. G go down to Florida for a couple weeks. But that may have tapered off with Mrs. G being fairly sick the last few years. Members love him, and they make sure he's taken care of.'

'Why does he always wear those white loafers?'

'Style, Wichita. He's got style.'

'127,' yelled Mr. G. While Mr. G had an uncanny ability to keep track of hundreds of caddies by number, he had an equally uncanny inability to know any caddie's name.

As Howie made his way to the desk, Mr. Gallagher came around the corner. His face lit up when he saw Howie.

'Hi, Napoleon!'

'Um, hello, Mr. Gallagher.'

'Mr. G, Napoleon is an excellent caddie. I'm just hitting the range today, but next time I play, I'd love to have Napoleon again.'

'That's good to hear.'

Mr. Gallagher continued toward the range.

'Let's see here, Napoleon. You take Mr. Penfield.'

Howie kept his head down as he grabbed the card from Mr. G and shuffled back to the bench.

'Who'd you get, Napoleon?' I chuckled.

'That guy never plays. What's he doing here again today?'

While we continued laughing, a kid a couple years older than me, dressed in jeans and a golf shirt, came out of the pro shop, hopped into a cart and drove away.

'What's that kid doing driving a golf cart?' I asked.

'He's a Pro Shop Boy. I hate those guys. While we're busting our ass out here, they work in the air conditioned bag room. All they do is pull out the bags when a golfer is ready to play. At the end of the round, they clean the clubs and put them back in their cubbie holes. The only other thing they do is manage the balls on the driving range. They get to drive the tractor, the one with the cage on it so they don't get hit, they get to drive it all over the range, picking up all the golf balls. It's pretty cool, but those guys are wusses.'

'And they get to drive carts? I'd love to do that.'

'Yeah, if one of us even stepped foot in a cart, they'd fire us. But those guys get to drive them all over the place. They walk around like they're all better than us caddies. No one likes them. We should have Kovach kick their butts someday.'

'How do you get to be one?'

He looked at me sideways. 'I think a couple of them used to be caddies. I don't know about the others. They must know T.Rex somehow. You don't want to be one of them. They're lame.'

I looked back at the pro shop door and over at T.Rex, coolly overseeing the first tee from behind his aviator sunglasses. Air conditioning? Driving golf cart? Not having to lug a bag 6 miles for a $6 pay-off? Maybe, somehow, the pro shop would be my escape hatch out of caddying.

'407!'

I shot to attention.

'Take one of Mr. Kerry's guests.'

I was in the group behind Howie. I walked over to the bag rack where Mr. Kerry fawned over three other men, talking and laughing nervously.

'You guys have enough tees?'

'It's some great weather we've got, huh?'

'Looks like were on the tee next.'

I looked for a guest bag that wasn't yet claimed by a caddie until I paired up with a sorry looking, black vinyl bag with no head covers. It belonged to Kerry's guest, Mr. Simmons, a gangly, nerdy guy with wire-rimmed glasses and a white belt that matched his white golf shoes. He seemed neither to know where to stand nor what to do with me after I introduced myself.

'Okay, Bob,' Mr. Kerry said to Mr. Simmons, 'why don't you lead us off.'

What I saw next would have scared small children.

Mr. Simmons took the club back with all of the grace of an ostrich in distress. I was afraid he dislocated one or more of his arm, hip and knee joints as he paused briefly at the top of his backswing and followed through the ball.

Fffffssssshhhhhhhh.

The club head barely made contact as the ball popped up into the air a couple of feet and landed inches from where it began.

Mr. Simmons tried to laugh easily, as though this was not an uncommon result. 'I think I'll try that again.' Kerry looked around the first tee and laughed very uneasily.

This time, same ugly swing, but the ball at least made it about 100 yards, landing amidst the trees that circle the second green.

'That was better,' offered Mr. Simmons.

Kerry's host-worthy grin became increasingly artificial.

Mr. Simmons sliced his way through the first hole, which meant playing the adjacent second hole in reverse.

'Do I get to subtract any of these shots when I play the next hole?' he asked as his fourth consecutive shot landed on the second fairway.

When Mr. Simmons teed off the second hole, finally playing it in the correct direction, Howie approached from the foursome behind us. 'Start doing the caddie rain dance, Wichita. That guy is an embarrassment.'

I looked up into the sky. There were some cumulus clouds, but nothing threatening enough to bail me out. I had become somewhat of a meteorological expert since my great fear of tornados kicked in two years ago. I had never really been too afraid of the weather before, despite the fact that we lived in Tornado Alley. No tornados had touched down anywhere near Salina when I was really young. But one evening in May two years before, an unholy storm swept across the Kansas plains. A bunch of tornados touched down in the state, which wasn't unusual, but one hit New Cambria, the town closest to us. It destroyed a farmhouse, killing an entire family, including a boy my age. It was like a switch was flipped on in my brain. Tornados could kill me. I immediately became a vigilant monitor of bad weather. My heart skipped a beat and Herschel churned every time I heard the 'Beep. Beep. Beep.' on TV alerting viewers of a severe weather warning. Since we lived in an apartment complex, I ran down to the basement laundry room every time I heard the first clap of thunder, sometimes in my pajamas. I scanned every threatening weather system that made its way across the skies, looking for unusual activity. I spent a great deal of my time in class looking out the window, on constant alert for suspiciously dark clouds. Outside on the playground I kept vigil for perceived changes in barometric pressure.

Mr. Simmons' golfing prowess did not increase with the number of strokes that he took. I discovered parts of the golf course that day that I previously did not know existed. I felt like Lewis or Clark on the fifth hole when I uncovered a creek deep in the woods that I had never seen before. I lost a bunch of balls through the first nine holes, but I figured that most of them weren't my fault.

I saw Howie again at the turn. 'You look like you need help. I'll do the caddie rain dance for you.' He attempted a Navajo ritual step, but looked more like a bad impersonation of James Brown. 'Did that guy break 100 on the front?'

'Maybe just barely,' I replied.

'This is fun,' Howie continued, 'you have two unknowns working for you here. First, if it rains, you usually get paid for a full round even if you get stopped on 11 or 12. Secondly, you have the chance for the guest Slip on top whatever the member pays you. That could be anywhere from $1 to $10 if the guy is either rich or an idiot. The Slip could magically turn a Screw round into a Deal. On the other hand, if the guest steps in and pays, you could get royally screwed because he doesn't know how much to tip. Guests are a complete wildcard, Wichita. A couple of weeks ago, I had a guest of Mr. Fletcher's. The guest gave me $8 and headed for the clubhouse. I lingered around the pro shop until Mr. Fletcher came out and then he gave me a chit for $8. I hustled back to the caddie yard as fast as I could before they figured out that they paid me twice. Other times though, guests haven't given me nothing. This is great.'

'I'm glad it's so much fun for you. I'm just dreading chasing this guy around the course for another nine.'

'When your Spook Shoulder's in pain, pray for rain. Isn't that how the saying goes?'

I stared blankly.

'I think I just made that up,' he said.

As the foursome teed off the 10th to start the back nine, a cold wind stirred up as a cloud temporarily blocked the sun. Perhaps Howie's homage to the Godfather of Soul actually had some power to it. Westwood was just a mile or so south of Lake Erie, which brought along its share of nasty weather. Systems kicked up off the lake and often caused dramatic changes in the skies. I had to keep on my toes to detect any sudden changes.

By the 13th hole, clouds had taken over every bit of formerly blue sky, and the temperature had dropped about 10 degrees. My attention was almost solely directed toward analyzing each band of darker clouds that entered the horizon. I lost two balls that hole.

Although it seemed obvious to me, no one else seemed nervous that our lives were in jeopardy. Howie's caddie rain dance kicked in too late. The rain began to fall as we approached the 15th green, the furthest point on the course from the clubhouse. They were huge raindrops that had a metallic smell to them. The wind whipped up and we abandoned the balls on the green and headed for the shelter where the path between the 15th and 16th intersected with the 6th and 7th. The irons in my bag clanged in unison as I sprinted through the aquatic assault. A lightning bolt flashed instantaneously with a crack of thunder.

'Drop the bags!' yelled a guest.

I abandoned my bag in the rough and continued my sprint to shelter.

'Go get the bag, you wuss. The thing'll get soaked out there,' said the doubles caddie after I took a few steps.

I planted my foot, which slipped on the grass, and I fell on my butt. I got up, ran back, picked up the bag and scurried the remaining way to the shelter. I was soaked.

We were in the furthest possible place on the course from the clubhouse. Seven of us huddled in the wall-less shelter as the rain became a steady sheet. I was sweating underneath the coating of rain, even though I was cold. There was nothing to do except stare at the rain and hope it stopped.

After a half-hour, the rain still showed no sign of letting up.

'Let's call it a day, folks. Grab your umbrellas. Boys, grab the bags. Let's head in,' announced Mr. Kerry.

Mr. Simmons was nice enough to extend me part of his umbrella, but we kept bumping into each other so I opted to make most of the long trek alone with a towel hung over my head. I really couldn't get any wetter.

Sure enough, the rain suddenly stopped as soon as we made it to the clubhouse. I told Mr. Simmons what a pleasure it was witnessing his 150 strokes on the first 15 holes.

'Thanks, Kevin,' he replied, standing there awkwardly. 'It was a pleasure for me too.'

I took his bag over to the guest rack and dried his clubs in exaggerated motion and occasionally checked to be sure he was recognizing my hard work.

Still nothing.

'Mr. Simmons, would you like me to take the clubs to your car?'

'No, that's okay,' he said while looking down at his watch.

'Anything else I can do for you?'

My lingering paid off. He sensed his duty. He pulled out his wallet and fished around.

'I don't seem to have any Ones,' he said mostly to himself. 'Here you go, Kevin.' He handed me a $5 bill just as Mr. Kerry emerged from the pro shop to pay me.

'I just made $12 for my last round,' I announced to Mouse back at the Caddie House.

'Nice. How'd you do that?' He was soaking wet himself.

I told him about the guest's Slip. 'What hole did you get stuck on?' I asked.

'I wasn't out. I was in a Caddie Golf match with the Carrito twins, and we were all tied up when the rain hit. We had to finish out. Hey, I'm grabbing something to drink in the caddie house. You want anything?'

'No, but I'll go with you.'

I was feeling pretty good about myself. Not only had I survived the storm, but I had started to see some fruits from my labor. I was up to $50 for the summer, and I no longer was looking like a special ed reject on the course. Things were looking up. Just maybe, I thought, I could be a good caddie.

Inside the caddie house, Kovach sat in Mr. G's office, sorting through a huge stack of caddie cards that the members filled out after each round. Caddies were rated either Excellent, Good, Fair or Poor.

'Mouse, get in here.' Kovach called from the office. 'Haven't you been made an A caddie yet?'

'No, not yet. I think I'm pretty close though.'

'Let's see...' Kovach thumbed through the binder that Mr. G used to keep track of each caddie. 'According to this, you've got 15 Excellents. Only 5 more to go. Good job. I'm sure you'll pick up a couple more, too, after I sort through these cards.

'How about you, Wichita? How are things going with you? What's your number? 407?'

'Yeah.' I eagerly awaited my results.

He turned to my summary page. 'Let's see...1 Excellent, 2 Goods, 2 Fairs, and a Poor. Not so good, Wichita.' He looked up at me sympathetically.

I was shocked. Six times out and only one Excellent? At this rate I would never become an A caddie. I knew I was bad at the beginning, but I didn't know I was this bad.

'It'll get better,' said Mouse. 'Let's go play some Caddie Golf. The rain looks like it's stopping.'

I was deflated. The rain indeed had stopped, and the dark clouds were clearing. But the gloom still hung above me.

'No, I think I'll head home. I haven't been around there much.'

'Where is home anyway? You're staying with your grandparents, right?' asked Mouse.

'Yeah. They live in the Magnolia apartments, about a half mile on Detroit Road.'

'Where are your parents?'

'My mom is traveling all summer for work.' I lied. 'My dad, well, I never knew him. They were never married.' I didn't lie. 'I better head home.'

I hopped on my bike and pedaled down the club drive.

When I got back to the apartment, the phone was ringing. I picked it up. I wasn't very good with phones.

'Hello?'

'Sweet Bugs! Where have you been?' She sounded tired.

I hadn't spoken to my mom since I'd arrived in Cleveland. My hands went cold. I tried to settle my stomach down.

'How are you, Mom?'

'I'm doing okay. The doctor says I'm making a lot of progress.'

'That's good. Do you think you'll be done by the end of summer?'

'I hope to, but don't pressure me, Kevin. I don't need pressure.'

'Sorry, Mom.' There was an awkward silence. My stomach started churning.

'How's Cleveland, sweetie. Are your grandparents treating you okay?'

'Yeah. They're treating me really nice. Although I don't see them much. I started caddying at the country club nearby.'

'Caddying? Like golf?'

'Yes.'

'Is that safe? With all those hard golf balls flying around? And…'

126

'It's fine. Yes, it's safe, Mom. It's just a lot of work. And a lot of sitting around. The bags are really heavy, and you have to walk for miles.'

'That sounds awful,' she said quietly. 'I'm sorry to put you in that situation.'

'It's okay. I'll be fine.' Another few minutes of silence. 'Well, I just got home. Can we talk in a few days?'

'Yes, that'll be fine. Remember that I love you, Sweet Bugs.'

'I do. I love you too.'

I went into the bathroom and threw up.

Chapter 7

The following Monday, when the course was closed, I invited Mouse to go swimming at the apartment pool. My Grandma made me bacon and eggs before he came. I scarfed them down and had a second plate of eggs. After breakfast I stepped onto the scale. 100 pounds! What the heck was going on? I had never cracked the century mark in my life.

'I'm so glad that you boys are going to use the swimming pool today. You can build up those muscles doing the crawl stroke. Swimmers have big shoulders. That would be good for caddying. And the sunshine would be good for you too. You look a little pale.'

Mouse buzzed up from the entrance, and as I walked down to meet him down at the pool, I tried to think of why I suggested swimming in the first place. I was never much for water. I didn't even like to get my body wet. I dreaded the shower every morning and tried to bathe as little as socially possible, which was becoming more difficult as my nascent puberty was making my hair greasier.

The pool area was about half filled. I scanned the empty lounge chairs for two together. The closest had just been vacated by a big, hairy man, so those two were obviously out. The next closest looked like they had a couple bird droppings on them. The furthest were next to a woman in a wide-brimmed straw hat.

'Well, hello!' she exploded as I began to put my things down. She looked to be in her late 70's. She was unnaturally tan. 'We haven't seen you two around here. Then again we haven't been around here in the last three weeks due to a urinary tract infection that I had, and then Harry had to get his prostate removed.'

I looked over at her husband, and judging from the vacant stare on old Harry's face, I could only assume that a prostate was one of the lobes of the brain.

'Interesting.'

'So, do you boys live here or are you visiting someone? We've lived here for 30 years and we love it.'

'He's my friend; just visiting,' I motioned toward Mouse. 'I'm staying here with my grandparents, the Coyles.'

'Oh yes, George and Ida! They're wonderful people.'

'Thanks, but actually their names are Bill and Margaret. They live in 521.'

'Exactly! And where are you visiting from?'

'Salina, Kansas, about an hour outside of Wichita.'

'Oh, Michigan. We just love it there. Harry was stationed there during the war, actually in Wisconsin, but we just love that area. The cold, the snow, the wind. It's just beautiful. We were newlyweds when we lived there. We had met once before the war and Harry sent me just the nicest letters from North Africa, and when he came back home, the first thing we did was get married. I was 18 and he was 26 and we've been married since.'

'Interesting; but I'm actually from near Wichita. Kansas.'

'Right. We used to drive up from the army barracks on the Canadian border to the lake up there…Lake…Lake…what's its name?'

'Michigan?'

'Right. But we've been in Cleveland ever since the late 1940's. I can't really remember which year we moved into our house – 1949? 1951? Something like that, definitely an odd number. We had a nice two-story house in Lakewood. It was about seven blocks from the lake. We raised all of our children in that house. You know, you look like my grandson Luke. He's 13 years old, or is he 14? I can't remember. He lives in Albany. Luke plays basketball, but his favorite sport is baseball. He's very intelligent too. He reads at an 11th grade level. He wants to be a doctor. A cardiologist, I think. Do you play sports?'

'No, not really, I –'

I looked over at Mouse, who was working hard not to laugh.

'Oh, you should. They have wonderful programs here. They have baseball, football, basketball. Of course, you're not from here so you wouldn't benefit from those, even if you did play. I'm sure that they have sports programs back in – where did you say you were from again?'

'Uh, Michigan.'

'Oh, yes. I hear it's a nice place.'

'Okay, we'll be right back. We're going to swim now.'

Mouse took a few running steps and jumped right in. I sat on the side and let my feet acclimate to the temperature.

'Come on, Kevin, you've got to get wet some time.' I weakly deflected Mouse's splash with my hand.

'I'll be in; give me a few minutes. I just need to warm up a little.' I sat on the edge with my feet dangling into the cold water.

'You look like you still have your shirt on.'

I looked down at my arms. From mid-bicep down, I had a pretty good tan. But the rest of my arms and torso were as white as chalk. The tan line from my shirt couldn't have been more precise if I had used tape. 'Your caddie tan isn't much better.'

'At least I'm smart enough to get in the water so that no one sees it.' He looked around the pool area. 'Hey, there are some pretty hot girls here.'

'Shut up,' I laughed. 'It is pretty awful. I'm kind of afraid that everyone is going to die at the same time and I'm going be the only one left to call for ambulances.'

'I'd just sneak away if that happened. Disappear. At least the lifeguard is pretty cute. Not really hot like my Sambuca woman, but she's okay. Have you seen the Sambuca woman on the 13th hole?'

'No, I don't think so.'

'You'd know her if you'd seen her. Her house is right at the 150 marker. She lounges by her pool underneath an umbrella that has Sambuca written all around it. She's a goddess. Tall, tan, thin, great body. I think I love her.'

He dunked his head under water. He splashed me again when he resurfaced. 'Are you ever going to come in?'

'Soon. My feet and ankles are just getting used to the water. I'll jump in in a few minutes.

I had never met anyone else who'd flunked a Beginners' swimming class. I did it three times. I had a rare, self-diagnosed physical condition that prevented my body from floating. I literally sank like a rock. The previous summer, in my final attempt to graduate from swimming first grade, I was an 11-year-old invalid in a class of 9-year-old guppies. By then I had learned enough of the basics to keep me from drowning (I put the crawl into 'crawl stroke'), but the back float was my Waterloo. When I got my third and final flunkie card in the mail, I committed myself to a terrestrial lifestyle. There was just something about water and me that didn't get along. I didn't understand why people liked water. Water killed humans. Man was meant to spend life on land. That's why we had lungs, not gills.

'Speaking of girls, I haven't seen Maureen around lately.'

'Why?' He said in a sing song voice. 'Does someone like my big sister?'

'No. I mean yeah, I like her. She's really nice. I dunno.'

'She had a few days off last week, but she's working tomorrow. She's been spending a lot of time in the bag room. I think she has the hots for one of the bag room boys.'

'Really?' I hoped my disappointment didn't show. 'Those guys have it great.'

'They're wusses,' said Mouse. 'They couldn't carry a bag 18 holes if they tried.'

'Is that bad?'

133

He splashed me again. 'So don't they have pools in Wichita, or something?' I appreciated him changing the subject.

'You mean Salina.'

'Whatever. So what's it like in this crappy town in Kansas, anyway? You never seem to talk about it.'

'It's okay; not that much different than around here. There are a lot more farms, a lot less trees, and a lot less people.'

'How big is it? How many people?'

'About 40,000.'

'What do you guys do for fun?'

Fun? That wasn't something that I associated with Salina. 'Same as anywhere, I guess.'

'How'd you guys end up there?'

'My mom grew up here, but she left right out of college; happy to get out of Cleveland, for some reason. She got a job with a bank in St. Louis called 3rd Federal. She lived in St. Louis for a couple of years, but right after I was born, a job opened up to help run a bank in Salina, and Mom jumped at it.'

'And where's your dad?'

I paused for a second. 'Don't know. Never had any idea.'

Mouse was silent for a moment or two, and then he dunked himself under again.

Suddenly I felt a hand grab my ankle under the water. Mouse pulled me in off the edge.

The water was freezing cold. I was in agony. But slowly, very slowly, it warmed up.

Chapter 8

The next day was a scorcher. At 8 am it already was in the 80s. Mouse and I met up with Tim Kenworth, and Number 77, who everyone called Buddha, for a game of Caddie Golf. I put it together that Tim was the grandson of my Grandma's neighbor.

Buddha indeed was fat, but he actually was Filipino. Mouse had explained to me that apart from the small number of Filipinos, who could more easily fit into the Catholic culture, the West Side was almost completely devoid of Asians. I don't think I saw another Asian all summer, and I'm sure one didn't set foot on Westwood property while I was there. Not that Salina was any better. We only had one Asian family that I was aware of. They had twin boys a couple years older than me who everyone called Ping and Pong.

We were on our third hole of Caddie Golf when Howie showed up. He had a thin line of blue ink from the bottom of his ear to the center of his throat and another on his arm.

'What the hell happened to you?' asked Mouse. 'Did you lose a fight with a ballpoint pen or something?'

'Oh, crap,' Howie responded. He licked his arm and tried to rub the ink off with his hand. 'My brother and I were playing Mugger in New York last night.'

'What the heck is Mugger in New York?'

'My brother and I play it all the time. One guy acts like an unsuspecting tourist walking down a New York street. The other guy is the Mugger with a knife; but we use a ballpoint pen instead of a knife.'

'Good choice.'

'The tourist walks by,' continued Howie, 'and the Mugger is like, "Hey you, come here," and the other guy is like "What, what do you want?" and the Mugger is like "Come here, I just want to talk to you," and the tourist is like "Hey, I don't want any trouble," and so on until it escalates into a knife fight. Whoever stabs the other guy with the knife wins. And then we switch places.'

'You need more hobbies,' said Tim.

'Looks like you lost,' said Mouse.

'Actually, not. You should see my brother. He's covered with ink,' replied Howie.

'Isn't your brother like 5 years older than you?' asked Tim.

'Six, actually, but I'm scrappier.'

'That's the saddest thing I've ever heard. Let's get back to the game,' said Mouse. 'Kevin and I are up by two. My hole. Par 4, off the tree to the hole.' He tossed his penny and it hit the tree right in the center.

'Hey,' interjected Howie. 'Did you guys see how big the Ohio Lottery has gotten? It's up to $50 million. I can't imagine what I'd do with that money. The first thing I'd do, though, is pony up to buy a membership to this place, and then make you guys caddie for me and order you around.'

'You would definitely be a Screw,' said Mouse.

'Absolutely,' agreed Howie. 'Especially to you guys. Oh, and I would request Tool and not tip him at all. It would be great.'

'Keep dreaming,' said Tim. 'Like they would let riff raff like you join this place.'

'They'd have to,' responded Howie, 'I'd be rich. What would you guys do if you won the lottery?'

Tim and I both thought about it for a few moments, and I jumped in first.

'I'd first throw a big party for everyone back home where I would be the guest of honor. Then I'd buy my Mom and me a house. Finally, I'd put the money away in a bank account and live on the interest.'

'You may be the most boring person on the face of the earth,' jabbed Tim. 'I like the idea of a party; I'll go with that. And I'd buy a house too, but it would be a huge one right on the lake. I'd buy a fleet of seven sports cars, one for each day of the week. I'd buy the best of everything – stereo, golf clubs, bike, everything. I'd spend it all. Life is too short.'

'And you, Buddha?'

Buddha was silent for several moments. Finally, 'I'd buy a lot of food...And a big house.'

'Yes, food and shelter. Very practical, very wise. What do you think, Mouse?'

He thought for a second. He picked up his penny and put it into his pocket. He finally smiled and said, 'Well, first I would buy my own house so that I'd have my own space, with none of my brothers. Nearby them, but definitely my own place. But I'd need my Mom there to cook for me – well, I'd figure that out. Then I'd take whatever's left over and make a movie of my life.'

'A what?'

'I'd make a movie. It would be a Hollywood blockbuster. I'd take all of the money and spend it on the movie. I'd be immortalized forever.'

'Yeah, as a loon!'

'It would be great,' Mouse continued. 'Think about it, what a better way to spend the money than to make a movie that would debut in every theatre in the nation, with, like, Burt Reynolds starring as me.'

'I hadn't noticed your 'stache before, Mouse,' I needled.

'Yeah, wouldn't that midget Billy Barty be more appropriate?' said Howie.

Mouse continued wide-eyed. 'Better yet, I'll star in the film and hire the best-looking actresses to play my love interests. There'd be tons of love scenes. This definitely won't be rated PG. And I'd get the ugliest actors in the business, like Marty Feldman, to play my brothers. Wilford Brimley would definitely have to play Mr. G. Tim, get his agent on the phone and see if he's available. I'd be nice to you guys. Kevin, I'd get Oliver from Brady Brunch, to play you.'

'Interesting,' I replied.

'Tim, I'd get Gilligan to go back in time and play you.'

'Very funny.'

'Howie, this would be a big step up for the actor who plays Ronald McDonald. He'll have a big role playing you.'

'Screw you.' He unholstered a book of matches and flicked one at Mouse. I jumped away and stared at it until I was sure it burned out.

We quit our game of Caddie Golf and spent the next two hours filling out our cast lists for the movies for each of our lives until Mr. G called Mouse over to the first tee.

'Act like you didn't hear it, Mouse,' suggested Howie.

'No, I've got to head over,' said Mouse.

'In that case,' said Howie, 'I think I need to drop the kids off at the lake in a bad way.' He headed to the bathroom.

'I need food,' said Buddha. He headed inside to the snack bar.

Tim and I sat together for a few minutes in a strained silence.

'You want to play some Caddie Golf?' I offered.

'No, I think I'm going to see what the Carritos and those guys are doing. I'll catch up with you later.'

Tim went over to another picnic table where the Carrito twins and three other boys sat. He greeted the group with a big smile and handshakes. Why did everyone shake hands here, I wondered. Kids in Salina sure didn't. My number wasn't going to be up for a bit so I practiced my chipping on the table we had been using.

Pablo and Kenny Carrito's parents had immigrated from Panama when the boys were toddlers. They were the only caddies who could claim at all to be 'of color,' and they stuck out even more noticeably against the whiteness of the club's membership. While they were twins, they were anything but identical. Pablo was tall and thin with glasses. Kenny was short and chunky with braces.

Twenty minutes or so later, Tim called out to me as his friends arose from the other table. 'Hey, Kevin. Would you mind moving? We want to use that table for a game of Caddie Golf, and that's the better table.'

'Sure, no problem.'

I put my penny into my pocket and walked to the caddie house to grab some lunch.

For the first time in days I found myself alone. Mouse and the guys were the first group I had ever hung out with. At home, my only real friend was my Mom. She didn't let me leave the apartment when she was working, and when she wasn't, I was her constant companion. It seemed like we spent most of our time running errands and cleaning. Over the years, I had spurts of hanging out with kids at school, but I mostly kept to myself. My stomach interfered with one of my early friendships in the 3rd grade. I sat next to Joey Pahlson, a short kid, whose family had just moved to Salina from the next town over. The Ringling Brothers Circus was in Wichita, and he invited me to go with his parents and his brother one Saturday morning. About 20 minutes into the drive, my nervousness got the better of me and I threw up all over the back seat of the car. I blamed it on carsickness, but I caused everyone to miss the circus. I doubt they ever got the grape juice stains out. Joey and I drifted apart after that.

I sat alone in the Caddie House and ate my hot dogs, Funions and Fla-vor-ice.

By the time I was called over to the first tee at 1:00, the mercury was tickling the mid-90s. Mr. G walked down the line of benches and handed out salt tablets to any caddie who would take them.

'Got to keep hydrated out there, boys. Drink plenty of water, but not too much or you'll double over with cramps. Or you'll get the runs, and no one wants that.'

He looked down at his list. 'Number 1!'

Kovach sauntered up.

'Are those new shoes, Mr. G?'

'You're a funny man, Number 1.' He handed him his caddie card. 'Get your keyster out of here before I kick it.'

Just then I saw my old friend Mr. Guelcher appear around the corner of the pro shop. I was sure that my name and his were fated to intersect on Mr. G's list. I scurried up to Mr. G in an effort to interfere with my foreseen destiny.

'Mr. G, please don't give me Mr. Guelcher,' I said a bit too desperately. The vision of his green sunglasses streaked across my memory. 'I'll take anyone except Mr. Guelcher. Please, I'll take anyone.'

'Okay, 407,' he said without looking at me, 'take Mr. Sloan.' I deflated.

I shuffled back to the bench. Howie grabbed the card out of my hand, and almost fell over laughing.

'Well, you avoided Guelcher. Good job, Kev,' laughed Howie. That guys Sloan is a pervert,' advised Howie. 'Keep your eyes on him.'

141

Sloan indeed was an odd guy. He had coke-bottle glasses, a greasy combover, and an unfashionable goatee. His exaggerated pear-shaped body waddled as he walked. He looked like no other member.

He didn't say a word to me until the 5th hole.

'What'd you say your name was?'

I would have been less shocked if a passing squirrel had spoken to me. I cleared my throat. 'Kevin.'

'How old are you?'

'12.'

'You have a young face. That's good. When you're older and all your friends are screwing old hags, you can still be screwing young chicks.'

'Huh.'

That was all. I started thinking that he might be insane.

On the 8th hole, I was holding the pin on the side of the green, waiting for the foursome to putt out when I felt something hit the back of my knee, and it unbuckled. After I regained my balance, I turned around to see Mr. Sloan quietly chuckling.

On the 9th tee, we had to wait a while for the group ahead of us to putt out.

'I heard a joke the other day,' chimed in Mr. Lawton. He was short and stocky, with thick wavy brown hair and large, somewhat bucked teeth, which made him look like a beaver or a wolverine, depending on your impression of him.

'A group of kids are in class, and the teacher is giving vocabulary words and asking the kids to use them in sentences. So she throws out the word "navigate." And a few kids raise their hands, including Dirty Ernie, who always said dirty words. So she picks Mary.

"The boat navigated the river."

"Very good, Mary. Next word is delegate."

And no one raises their hand except Dirty Ernie, who's going crazy in the back.

"Anyone know this?"

Luckily for the teacher, Johnny raises his hand. "The president delegated power."

"Oh, very good, Johnny. The next word is..." she looked down...she paused "...is urinate."

Dirty Ernie's hand shot up. What could she do, she thought? His is the only hand up! He'll surely say something dirty with this word. But she had no other choice.

"Okay, Ernie. Urinate."

"Teach, Yer-n-8. If you had bigger knockers, you'd be a 10."

Everyone laughed hard for a good half minute. Lawton teed up his ball.

Two holes later, walking down the fairway, I felt and heard something hit the bottom of my golf bag. A few steps later I heard it again. I looked back, and Mr. Sloan was walking right behind me, trying not to let on that he was hitting the bag with the club.

I began to panic a little. Was this the precursor to getting Sloaned? What would I do if he did it? I definitely would report him to Mr. G, but would I retaliate in any way immediately? I'm not sure I had the guts to stand up to a member directly.

On the 13th hole Sloan hit his second shot into the row of birch trees that separated the hole from the single story houses on Hilliard Road.

'Jack Martin,' he mumbled. It rattled around the branches and landed next to the yard of the legendary Sambuca Woman who Mouse told me about.

Sure enough, there she was, lounging under an umbrella emblazoned with the popular Italian liqueur – white bikini, long flowing brown hair, Jackie O sunglasses, mid-afternoon cocktail in hand. She was as attractive as Mouse had described and much more exotic. I wanted the world to move at slow motion as I spent the next minute or two on my yacht, docked on the Riviera with my Mediterranean paramour. I was whisked away from Westwood, away from Cleveland. Did she just catch me looking at her? Was that a smile she just flashed me? A woman like this possessed a sexual exoticness that was utterly mysterious to me. She was so much more mature and complex than the girls my age, so much more erotic than any female member. It was like she was from a different race, was a different life form, one that didn't exist in Salina, and one that appeared to be rare in Cleveland as well. It wasn't that she was rich -- her house was rather modest -- but she probably didn't eat the same things regular people ate.

'Boy, I'd like to screw her.' Sloan's mumbled voice whipped-sawed me back thousands of miles to reality. It was like a wet towel landed on my head.

When we reached the green, I tended the pin. After placing it back in the cup, I walked by Mr. Sloan. The rest of the foursome was up on the next tee getting ready to tee off. I hesitated for a step remembering to take his putter from him. Just then, I felt the putter in my crotch. I jumped and let out a short scream in the middle of Mr. Lawton's backswing. He took a chunk of dirt, and the ball dribbled off the tee.

'What is wrong with that kid?' he said to no one in particular, but loud enough for me to hear.

It wasn't the classic 'Sloan' that I had heard of, but he did shove his putter into my balls. I turned around and Sloan just looked at me and snickered. I wanted to punch him, to explain to everyone what he did, but I knew I couldn't. I just wanted to the round to be over. I had had it with caddying. I was going to march into Mr. G's office and tell him what happened and quit my job. For once I was going to stand up for myself.

After the round, Sloan came out of the pro shop and muttered, 'Looks like I left my wallet back in the locker room. Leave the bags here and follow me down, and I'll take care of you.'

I looked at Kovach for a sign of reassurance. He just shrugged. Anywhere inside the clubhouse was strictly off limits to caddies, and this was especially weird with Sloan.

I had no other choice but to follow him down the path that led through the men's grill. I stopped short when we reached the locker room door. 'I'll just wait here.'

'Suit yourself. I'll be out in a minute.'

The dimly-lit men's grill was a sea of middle-aged white male conformity. About half of the low-slung cocktail chairs were filled, mostly by golfers, with a few members in their business suits. Alcohol flowed, cigars were lit, gin rummy was played. My eyes fixed on a short figure at the end of the bar with his back to me. It was Mr. G with beer in hand, yucking it up with a member and the bartender. The only females within grenade range were the teenage waitresses.

I drifted toward the exit near the trophy case. On the wall were the etched names of each club champion since the club's inception. The newer names were somewhat recognizable, but as my eyes drifted back in time frame by frame, the names were less familiar. Some guy named Fred Hoefelder won 10 of the first 12 championships. In the column next to the champions' names were the runners-up. I scanned that as well and halted in the early 60's.

Runner-Up:

Walter Morgan1961
Walter Morgan1962
Walter Morgan1963
Walter Morgan1964

Walter Morgan1967

'Here you go, caddie. Here's your money.' Sloan handed me $7, a buck more than I usually got.

I turned and left without a word.

The sun stung my eyes when I got back outside.

I sat down on a picnic table trying to figure out what to do about what Sloan did to me. My anger had subsided a lot. I didn't want anyone to know that he did it to me, but I didn't want him to get away with it.

After a while, I gathered up the courage to talk to Mr. G about it, hoping that he would know the best way to handle the situation. Hopefully, Mr. G could get him kicked out of the club, or at least reprimanded. I could at least save future caddies from becoming one of Sloan's victims.

Mr. G was back from the grille, sitting alone in his office. He looked up. 'Yes, 407? Can I help you with something?'

I paused for a few seconds. 'No. I don't need anything.'

I left the office feeling ashamed of myself.

I needed to find a different job.

Chapter 9

'So how are you doing today, Kevin?' asked a smiling, cologned Mr. Morgan as we walked down the first fairway.

'I'm okay...I caddied for Mr. Sloan yesterday,' I felt pounds of tension released from my body as I spoke the words.

'Ol' Donnie. He's a strange character.'

'Yeah, he's a pretty weird guy.'

He lowered his voice. 'I've heard some odd stories about that guy. His wife, who by the way is not an unattractive woman, she comes from a lot of money. Donnie bounced around from job to job until he finally just gave up putting in the effort and just started hanging out at the club most of the time. He has a crowd of guys he pals around with, but I don't really know anyone in the club who is good friends with him. He's a pretty odd guy to talk to.'

'Yeah, I kind of agree.' It helped to get some validation from Mr. Morgan.

'So tell me about where you're from,' he asked on the fifth hole. 'Where is it? In Kansas?'

'Yes. Salina. About 100 miles outside of Wichita.'

'What do people do for a living in Salina?'

'A lot of farming, obviously, but there's also a pretty large beef processing plant, Hampton Farms, where a lot of guys work. It's been pretty tough recently. Some people work down the road in Fulmer. There's an oil refinery or something there, but that's been struggling for a while. My mom says that at some point they're going to run out of people to lay off.'

By the time I stopped talking we had reached his ball.

He grabbed a 6-iron and put the ball in the middle of the green.

'That's happening a lot with rural plants,' he said, as I handed him his putter. 'Jobs are disappearing as new technology brings about automation. We're seeing the same things happening here in Ohio. From what I understand, even the low-level jobs in places like Kansas are being snapped up by Mexican immigrants who don't mind the awful conditions as much. It's getting tough to make a living.'

'Nice shot, Steve,' he yelled across the fairway to Mr. Anderson.

'So it's tough to find a job here too?' I wanted to continue the conversation.

'It is for any blue collar jobs. Cleveland's industrial economy, which for a long time was based on steel, has just been decimated the last few years. But no one here at the club, for instance, is affected much. Doctors, lawyers, that type of thing is fine.'

'What about banking?'

'Yes, there are a lot of banks here. Society, National City; they seem to be doing fine.'

My spirits rose a little. Since my Mom worked at the bank, we were pretty insulated from the industrial troubles that hit Salina. But she had her own troubles.

For the first time, I thought that Cleveland may be the solution to our problems.

'Kevin, you must be a good luck charm,' Mr. Morgan said at the end of the round. 'I shot 73 again.' He handed me my money. 'I hope we can do it again real soon.'

'Thanks.' I said. 'I'd like that.'

That night my grandparents took me out to dinner for my Grandma's birthday.

'Kevin, we're going to The Mark, on Lorain Road. That's in North Olmsted,' my Grandma informed me from the front seat. 'It's my absolutely favorite restaurant; isn't it, Bill?' My Grandfather nodded numbly. 'We went there with the Jacobsons when we first bought our house over on Parkview Terrace. They have the most wonderful salad bar, although the carrots were a little wilty last time we were there. And the celery was wilty too, now that I think of it. It's a wonderful place.'

We pulled into the parking lot, and the bottom of the sign said that they served Steak – Chicken – Seafood. Pretty much covered the gambit. I wondered why they didn't just throw in mutton and veal to round things out.

The restaurant was fairly dark, and we were seated at a square table with old, maroon high-back chairs.

'Now, feel free to order whatever you want,' my Grandma declared to me as the maître d' handed us our menus. 'I like The Mark Steak, it has a special seasoning, and Bill's going to have the stuffed shrimp. And they have a fabulous salad bar. Very fresh.' My Grandpa closed his menu.

151

I honed in on the seafood section in an attempt to keep my dinner as gristle-free as possible.

'Is it okay if I have the Alaskan King Crab Legs?' I requested. I had only tasted them once before, when my Mom ordered them for her past birthday dinner. They were about the best thing I had ever had in my mouth. And no fat or gristle.

'Anything you want,' said my Grandma.

My Grandpa re-opened his menu. They were the most expensive thing on the menu. 'How about the shrimp?' he suggested. 'It's kind of the same.'

'Oh, let him get the crab legs,' retorted my Grandma. 'Do you really want that, Sweetie?'

I nodded my head.

My Grandpa closed his menu, and we ordered.

My stomach immediately began to churn. The pressure was on to eat the crab legs now that I had ordered the most expensive thing on the menu.

'Let's head to the salad bar,' said my Grandma.

'I think I'll stay here,' I replied. 'I don't want to ruin my appetite.'

After they left the table, I saw a huge flame shoot up from the grill behind the serving station next to our table. I felt the outer reaches of the heat on my face. I looked to the front of the restaurant to plan my escape route in case the fire managed to get out of the control of its confines of the grill and spread to the rest of the kitchen and through the entire restaurant. I found a side exit as well, which would serve as my backup escape route.

'What are you looking at, Kevin?' asked my Grandpa upon his return. He put down his salad, which was covered with ranch dressing.

'The fire. Just seems like it's a little out of control.'

'That's just the grill. What are you afraid of?'

'Nothing.'

'What are you talking about?' asked my Grandma as she carried her salad back to our table. 'These carrots are wonderful. What's Kevin afraid of?'

'Nothing,' I stated again.

'He was looking at the fire like it was going to come out and bite him,' said my Grandpa.

'No, I wasn't. I wasn't.' They were unconvinced. 'It's just that there was a family in Salina, the Carsons, one of the boys is my age, Andy. He was in my class two years ago. They had a fire in their house last summer. Their dad was out of town on a business trip. The fire started when their TV shorted out, and it spread through the house. His mother and his little sister, Amy, were killed. Andy and his two brothers made it out.'

'Oh my gosh, that's terrible. No wonder you're afraid of fire.'

'I'm not, really.' Out of the corner of my eye, another ball of fire arose from the grill. 'Well, maybe a little, but it's no big deal.'

'Is that why I keep finding the TV unplugged when I try to turn it on?' asked my Grandpa.

'Yep, sorry about that.'

'Don't worry about it.'

The waitress arrived at our table with a tray filled with food. My stomach shut down. I couldn't eat. The pressure was too great. The plate full of crab legs was piled high. I'd never be able to finish it all.

'That looks good, Kevin,' commented my Grandma.

I couldn't even acknowledge her. I feared that with the slightest movement of my body I would vomit all over the table. I sat stone still.

'Come on, sport,' said my Grandpa, 'dig in. You ordered them, you gotta eat them.'

I stared straight ahead. I swallowed saliva and air to keep everything down.

'What's wrong, Kevin?' asked my Grandma. 'Are you okay?'

I nodded my head slightly up and down.

'Then go ahead and eat.'

I kept looking straight ahead. Didn't move. Tried with all my will to settle myself down. Just relax, just take one bite and you'll be okay, I told myself.

'What the heck's wrong with him?' asked my Grandpa.

'Kevin, are you okay?' I heard from the other side.

Again, I just nodded slightly and slowly.

'I can't believe this,' said my Grandpa. 'He orders the most expensive thing on the menu, and then doesn't eat it? Are you sick, son?'

'Just leave him alone.'

'Is everything okay here?' asked the waitress. 'Are you okay?' She touched my shoulder.

'He's fine,' my Grandma answered for me. 'Do you have any Alka Seltzer in the back? Maybe you can bring us some?'

'I'll check,' the waitress replied and disappeared.

'It's okay, Kevin,' said my Grandma. 'Just eat what you want and when you want.'

They continued to eat in strained silence.

The waitress returned with a bubbling glass of Alka Seltzer. I left it sitting there on the table.

'I'm going to need that when the bill comes,' commented my Grandpa.

As they continued to eat in silence, I kept thinking that I had killed my Grandma's birthday dinner. But as the minutes ticked away, I slowly began to relax. I focused on my Grandma's words that I didn't have to eat anything and everything would still be fine. My muscles uncoiled a bit to where I could at least move. After a few minutes, I reached for a crab leg and slowly broke the shell. I pulled out the red and white meat and dipped a small piece into the butter. My body warmed up as the delicious crab went down my throat. It actually felt good in my stomach. I can do this, I thought. If I can just make a reasonable dent in the mountain of crab legs, I thought, I can salvage the evening.

The dinner began to return to normal.

'Bill, did you see that gas prices rose another ten cents last week?'

'Yes, it's those damn Arabs over there in the desert that are strangling us.'

'I don't know about that, I just thought it was interesting that a gallon of gas costs more than a gallon of milk now. They should invent a car that runs on milk instead of gas? We have all the milk we need in this country, and we wouldn't have to rely on any of those Arabs anymore.'

'Brilliant,' he chuckled.

She just shrugged.

I managed to get down about half of the crabs. And more importantly, kept them down. I didn't touch my baked potato, but I thought I managed to circumvent disaster.

'I don't think we'll be ordering any of those crabs again,' said my Grandpa as he perused the bill.

That sunk my spirits again. I beat myself up on the drive back to the apartment. What kind of nut job can't even eat a normal dinner at a restaurant? What's wrong with me, I asked to no one?

I called my Mom to check in with her when we got home.

We were quite a pair. It was at about age 7 or 8 that I realized my family life was a bit different. Sure, there were other families that didn't have a dad, but at least they lived in a house. My mom and I always lived in an apartment, and we moved from apartment to apartment every six months or so. There weren't many apartment buildings in Salina, so we worked our way into a somewhat regular rotation. After we spent some time in a particular unit, my mom deemed it to be too contaminated with germs, and we moved on to a 'fresh' one.

It didn't really bother me that much; I didn't know any better. I just learned not to collect too much stuff. The shortest we stayed was two weeks, this one time after a neighbor visited one day with her smelly poodle. Mom spent most of the day shampooing the carpets and mopping ammonia on the linoleum, but it wasn't clean enough for her.

'Kevin, I feel really bad that we have to move again,' she told me, 'but we have to. It's for your own protection, Sweetie. I think the place is clean enough, but I just can't be sure. We'll keep the next place ship-shape.'

Mom's fear of germs had halted my first break in show business.

'Come on, Mom. The play starts in an hour and I still have to get into my costume at school.' We were putting on Peter Pan, and I was playing one of Captain Hook's stooges. I hadn't been able to eat a bite all day. I only had one line, but I was terrified that I would forget it.

'I'll be right there. I just have to put my dress on.'

She scurried into my room. 'Can you zip me up?' She looked beautiful in her new blue dress. It was kind of an old lady style but somehow it made her look years younger.

'Mom, did you notice this spot here?'

She turned her back to the mirror. 'Oh, crap! I just bought this.'

157

She stared at the dime-sized spot, analyzing it for a full minute. 'It's not that noticeable, is it?' She tried to shrug it off, but she analyzed the spot again. Her face turned from disappointment to concern. 'Kevin, what do you think it is? It looks like blood.'

'I don't know, Mom. It just looks like a spot. Could be anything.'

'Kevin, could it be blood? Do you think it's blood? What does it look like to you?'

'I don't think—'

'Oh my God, what if it's blood? Someone could have tried the dress on before me and bled on it. Tell me it's not blood.'

'It's not blood, Mom. It looks brown.'

'Blood looks brown after it dries.'

'It really doesn't look like it. Come on, the play starts in less than an hour.'

'It might be blood; I've got to take this off right now. It'll only take a minute.' She disappeared into her room. I stared at my watch. I heard the shower run.

About 15 minutes later a more relaxed Mom came out of her room wearing an old dress and carrying a plastic bag. 'We'll have to return this tomorrow. Now where are the keys? We have a play to get you to.' She stopped, spun around and looked at my hands. 'Kevin, you touched the dress. Did you wash your hands?'

'No, I didn't touch the spot.'

'But the spot could have spread germs to the rest of the dress. Go wash your hands. Actually, you probably have touched your clothes, your face, your hair since then. Do me a huge favor and jump into the shower real quick.'

'Mom, the play starts in about a half-hour and I have to get into my costume—'

'Pleeease.'

I figured that giving in was easier and actually perhaps quicker than trying to reason with her.

I ran into my room, showered and emerged in less than five minutes.

'Where are the clothes you had on?'

'They're in my room.'

'Can you put them in the hamper and then we'll leave.'

I gathered them up. 'Can we go now?'

'Did you wash your hands after you touched the dirty clothes?'

I washed them in the kitchen sink.

'I'm sorry, Kevin. You're such a good boy. Thank you. I love you so much.' She kissed me on the head as we walked out the door.

My teacher confronted me when I finally showed up. 'Where have you been, Mr. Campbell? The play started 5 minutes ago.'

'We had some trouble leaving the house.'

'Well, we're too busy to get you in costume. Jeff is going to have to deliver your line. You better hope he doesn't forget it.'

I watched the entire play backstage, sitting out of the way on an old wooden crate, a little relieved I didn't have to deliver my line.

'The doctors say that I'm progressing really well,' she said over the phone. 'Hopefully it won't be long before we can be together again.'

'That's great, Mom. I can't wait to see you again. What types of things are they doing?'

'They're just trying to get me to accept that the world around us has lots of germs and that germs don't kill people, well actually they do, but not as easily as I seem to think. So they're trying to expose me to stuff that normally would scare the heck out of me. Yesterday I touched a garbage can – put my hand right in it – and then went twenty minutes without washing my hands. It was one of the hardest things I've ever done. I was so grossed out by it. But I did it. You would have been so proud of me.'

'That's great, Mom. That's really great.' For the first time, I entertained the thought that she would never get fully better. 'Hey, it's Grandma's birthday today. Do you want to wish her a happy birthday?'

'Um, not really.'

'Grandma,' I yelled. 'Mom wants to talk to you.'

I stood there as my Grandma and Mom had a brief, cordial conversation. My Grandma's eyes were moist as she handed back the phone to me to say goodnight.

I got ready for bed and weighed myself. I was up to 102.

I looked over at my shoes next to the bedroom door. Back home my mom put my shoes in the washer each night. It became a ritual for us. I always took my shoes off outside the front door.

When I woke up each morning, they would magically appear clean in my bedroom on a piece of newspaper. Actually I liked the feeling of the hot canvas of my Keds on my feet after she took them out of the dryer. It never bothered me -- she was the one who did all the work – except the few times she forgot to run the dryer and I had to go to school in cold, damp shoes. She bought me a new pair every couple of weeks because the Keds didn't hold up too well to this regimen. Now, after so many rounds on the golf course, my shoes looked beat up and dirty. Wonderfully dirty.

Chapter 10

'Okay, getting it on with Mrs. Karnes on the first tee in front of everyone, Mrs. Harrison where no one could see you, or death?' asked Howie Weston during a game of playing caddie golf Mouse and I were playing with him.

'I'm going to have to go with death,' I replied with a nervous laugh.

We both looked at Mouse for his decision.

'How many people are on the first tee?' Mouse inquired.

'No less than 20,' shot back Howie.

'Are there lights on or off with Mrs. Harrison? I mean, how well can I see her?'

'Lights are on.'

'Is the death a short, instant one, or is it long and painful?'

'Long and painful. Come on, we need an answer!'

'I hate to say it, but I'm going to go with Mrs. Harrison.'

'Oh, noooo!' erupted Howie. 'She's a cow!'

'At least she's not Mrs. G."

All our heads shot into the direction of Mr. G's office. We were all silent for a moment until we were sure she hadn't heard us.

'Why aren't there any better looking members out here?' asked Howie.

'It's because so many of the members are Catholic,' Mouse opined. 'No one is divorced, so there aren't any trophy wives.'

'And Catholics are ugly?'

'No,' Mouse backpedaled. 'It's just that all the members are old. You can't be young and have enough money to join Westwood. All the members are at least 40.'

That seemed to satisfy us. Regardless, it was generally accepted that women were second class citizens at the club. Women were allowed to play on Tuesday mornings, and after 2:00 other days only if accompanied by their husbands. Some men would become irate if Mr. G let a couple onto the course at 1:30, even if no one else was on the course. The prevailing viewpoint was that letting women play whenever they wanted would make it more difficult for the male (i.e., real) golfers to get a tee time, and that women were poor golfers who would clog up the pace of play.

Nearly all caddies liked to caddie for men. They were better players, and they tended to pay more. I liked caddying for women. They were nicer. I also thought it was easier caddying for women. They never hit the ball far enough to lose it. And after their drive, you just let them work their way down the fairway with their 3-wood until they got close enough to hit an iron to the green. Simple. Every other caddie could barely stomach the Caddie Death March every Tuesday morning, but I liked it. I guess I always felt more comfortable interacting with women.

Later that afternoon Dr. and Mrs. Sullivan came around the clubhouse corner. They were new members and very few caddies knew them, so they hadn't yet been placed into their appropriate Screw or Deal caste. There were only two of us caddies left around, and I was happy I got assigned to Mrs. Sullivan instead of to Dr. Sullivan.

While Dr. Sullivan was extremely quiet and barely acknowledged his caddie's existence, Mrs. Sullivan greeted me with a big smile. She also didn't carry herself like other members. She had a refreshing salt-of-the-earth quality about her. Her second shot on the first hole sliced into the trees in the right rough. She handed back the club and laughed, 'Boy, Kevin, that shot really stunk, didn't it?'

We talked the entire round. Mrs. Sullivan seemed truly interested in my life in Kansas, what my mother was like, what I liked to do for fun. She told me that she had four sons, so maybe she just felt natural talking with boys like me. She also was gracious. When I couldn't find a ball that she hit into the trees, she told me that it was okay, it wasn't my fault. Why couldn't the other members understand that everything wasn't the caddie's fault?

She wasn't a knock-out, but with brown hair, sky blue eyes and a great smile, she had a Sally Field-like cuteness. She had the type of looks that were going to hold up well as she aged. As far as I was concerned, they didn't make 'em like that in Kansas. On top of that, Dr. Sullivan tipped me very well.

I actually enjoyed my round of caddying. I wanted to caddie for Mrs. Sullivan every round. If things didn't work out with Maureen, I wanted to marry Mrs. Sullivan.

I had a wonderful dinner of beef stew that night with my grandparents. I started to gain back some of the pounds that I had lost earlier in the summer. I ate all of the potatoes in my bowl, then all of the carrots and left most of the gristly beef in the bowl.

'It's really nice to have you home, Kevin.'

'Thanks, this stew is really great.'

'Be sure to eat your meat. You need the iron and the protein. When Bill was working, he was home every single night for dinner, never missed it. So I wasn't used to it when you haven't been home for dinnertime because of your job.'

'What did you do before you retired?' I asked my Grandpa.

'He worked at the steel factory –'

'I can answer him, Margaret. I worked for US Steel. I spent 30 years with them. I was an accountant. I spent most of my time managing the books for their factories here.'

'He was the assistant controller for the Ohio unit for the last few years.'

'That's neat. We have a bunch of factories in Salina.'

I had never bothered to try to picture him outside of his role as my crotchety grandfather.

'I put in 30 years of my life with them,' he continued. 'And then when times hit the skids, they laid me off. Five years short of my full retirement. Can you believe that? After all the time I put in for them.'

'That stinks,' I chimed in.

'Sure does.' He took a huge bite of stew.

* * *

166

I met up with Howie and Tim in the caddie yard the next day.

'So either of you guys ever caddied for Mrs. Sullivan?' I tried to act casual.

'No, never heard of her.'

'Me either. She a deal?'

'No, nothing great. I just caddied for her yesterday afternoon.'

They seemed to buy that explanation.

'I caddied for T.Rex last night,' Tim said as his penny landed softly on the picnic table.

'You know, T.Rex actually isn't a bad guy, but he really sucks as a golfer,' continued Tim. 'I don't get it, the guy's a pro; how can he be that bad?'

'Lay off the guy,' chimed in Howie, 'how well do you think you would hit the ball with 10-inch arms?'

'It confuses me. Supposedly he's a great teacher,' Tim continued, 'but judging from some of the swings I've seen from some of these members out here, it doesn't look like it. I was caddying for the Williamses last week. T.Rex has Mr. Williams standing at a 45-degree angle and chopping down on the ball like he's chopping wood. He actually says that each time he hits – 'Like chopping wood'! Mrs. Williams, with her huge chest can't follow through correctly, so T.Rex taught her to follow-through holding the club directly over her head. So she ends up swinging normally and then kinda jumping up in the air facing the hole with the club straight up in the air. It's embarrassing. I understand that you have to work with people's natural swings, but at some point he has to stop them from looking like idiots.'

'So did you brown-nose T.Rex to become a pro shop boy?' asked Howie.

'I did my best, but he wasn't biting. I've been working that angle for weeks.' Tim was one of the few caddies who freely admitted that he wanted to work in the pro shop.

I had made absolutely no progress in my hopes of trading in my life as a golf sherpa for the cushy life of the air-conditioned bag room. Caddying for Sloan was the straw that broke my back. I just didn't like caddying. Unless it was for Mrs. Sullivan, and I couldn't do that every day.

'Wichita, you'd make a good pro shop boy,' teased Howie.

'Nah, pro shop boys are wusses,' I weakly retorted. I, of course, would have given my left golf ball to get the call from T. Rex.

'Well, excuse me, boys, but I need to take a grumpy.' He headed for the bathroom.

'You know, crapping's cool and all,' said Tim, 'but you really ought to see a doctor.'

Howie shrugged. 'It's the most natural thing a man can do,' he said and headed for the bathroom.

I walked over to the first tee. With no sign of Mrs. Sullivan anywhere, Mr. G assigned me to Mrs. Thomas. She had white hair, tanned leathery skin, and was in pretty good shape for a woman I guessed to be about 65. Like most women at the club, she couldn't hit the ball very far, but she was pretty consistent.

Joining the group was Mrs. Thomas's friend Mrs. Barker. Mrs. Barker was obsessed with lavender. Everything on her was lavender -- her clothes, her eye shadow, her golf shoes, her nails, her golf bag – even her woods were custom-painted lavender. What I'm sure started with an innocent attraction had turned into a fetish. Everything she owned was lavender. I could only imagine what her home looked like.

She approached the tee with all of the exaggerated excitement that she could muster. 'Come on, Dorothy, let's show this golf course what it's got coming to it,' she exclaimed to Mrs. Thomas.

She took the club back around her plump body and held the swing high at its apex for a full second before descending slowly through the ball. When she handed the lavender driver back to her caddie, she was a bit out of breath.

Mrs. Thomas was very nice without being fake. She also had an enduring intensity for the game. When she hit a bad shot, she frowned, clenched her fist and exclaimed, 'Sugar!' or 'Rats!' Had she grown up in a less innocent time, she would have had quite a mouth on her.

At the turn she gave me a couple of ginger snap cookies that they kept in a jar on each table of the halfway house. I wolfed them down; not that I particularly liked ginger snaps, but because I hadn't eaten breakfast and would have gladly eaten a golf shoe if someone had offered it to me.

'So are you all set for the back nine, Kevin?'

'Ymzz.' Shards of ginger snaps flew from my mouth. She kept looking at me. I chewed feverishly. I failed to generate sufficient saliva to swallow. Finally, I responded, 'All set,' about a minute too late.

'I saw you had the Purple People Eater in your group,' said Howie after the round.

'I guess you're talking about Mrs. Barker?'

'Yes, Barker is like a purple dog. That's the type of women I'm terrified of marrying one day. She seems nice enough, maybe even kinda cute when she was young. Likes purple a little too much, but no big deal. She doesn't 'let herself go' as much as 'it' slips away from her over the years. I'm sure the extra 3-5 pounds per year were rationalized away, compensated with a little more make-up, a little more hairspray, not noticeable from day to day but accumulating over time. The voice gradually becomes a little louder, the laugh a little goofier. Next thing you know she looks like a caricature of her younger self, just like a sketch drawn of her years ago at the local carnival.'

'You've put a lot of thought into this.'

'These are the things that truly scare me, that keep me up at night. I always feared I would meet a perfectly normal girl who might have a quirk or two; we'd fall in love, marry, have kids, and before I could do anything about it she would morph into an unattractive, if not completely undesirable, woman. The whole purple thing with "The Barker" makes it so much worse. Did this bother Mr. Barker? Does he even realize that his wife is a freak?

Certainly she wasn't like this when he first met her; she would have been unmarryable. Does this become acceptable when you hit middle age?'

'It hasn't happened to Mrs. Sullivan.'

'Yet. Wait, who is Mrs. Sullivan?'

* * *

'Just an easy round to work out some kinks in the swing.' T.Rex spoke softly, slowly, deliberately as he fished through his bag for some balls.

T.Rex had come out to play nine by himself. It was 6:30 in the evening, and it was the first time I'd seen him without his sunglasses on. He looked more human, more vulnerable. I was the only caddie left hanging around, much to Mr. G's chagrin.

T.Rex slowly took the driver back with his short arms and swept the ball off the tee. My heart throbbed in my throat and I think I strained an eye muscle making sure I didn't lose the ball in flight. T.Rex's lack of distance certainly helped out on that one. This was the most important round of the whole summer. Not only was T.Rex the titular head of the caddie program, but he also was my ticket to the air-conditioning and steady paycheck of a bag room job.

The rumors about T.Rex seemed true. He kind of swung like a woman golfer, a good woman golfer, but a woman nonetheless. And he didn't hit it much further. I had to imagine that he was much better at one time; he had to be in order to become a pro. But lack of play and too much time spent in the pro shop must have deteriorated his skills significantly. When he stood over the ball, he concentrated so much, almost like he knew he wasn't very good, and he was afraid of others finding out.

He was dead serious as he played. He practiced his swing before and after shots. He constantly fidgeted his grip and adjusted his stance.

He attempted some light conversation on the 5th hole.

'How long you been caddying,…it's Kevin, right?' His voice cut threw the silence.

'Yes, a few weeks.'

'Do you enjoy it?'

'Yessir.'

'How far we got to the hole?'

'141,' I replied quickly.

He took out a 7-iron and put it on the green.

'Nice shot,' I said, as I had every time his play allowed me to. Otherwise, I kept quiet.

On the 6th hole he stood over his drive a bit longer than normal. He couldn't seem to get himself comfortable. He hit the ball into the fairway, but he looked concerned. He stood over the next shot even longer. He bladed the 7 iron. The ball ran its way onto the green, but it never got more than 6 feet off the ground. I handed him the putter and kept my mouth shut.

On the next hole his game self-destructed. He got off the tee okay, but he ended up in the rough. Unfortunately, he couldn't get out of the rough. He stood over the ball for an agonizing minute. He took the club back and chunked it. A huge divot emerged from the earth and the ball lurched forward 10 yards. He looked straight ahead and marched to the ball.

While I repaired the first divot, he unearthed another. This time he looked back to see if I had witnessed it. I stared at a blade of grass.

He finally made contact with the next swing, blading a 3-iron about 125 yards. I wanted to disappear. I'm sure he wanted to kill his only witness.

With his jaw jutted forward, he approached the bag to select a club. His gloved hand shook as it reached for the 6-iron. Again he stood over the ball too long, adjusted and readjusted his grip, shifted and reshifted his stance. I said a quick prayer as he took the club back. A ray of the late afternoon sun hit his iron at the apex of his swing. Then a spray of turf, a grunt and a groan. The ball barely moved.

'What the hell am I doing wrong?' he said to anyone but me.

He bunted his next shot onto the green and two-putted for a too-many-to-count.

It might have been the uphill walk to the 8th tee -- although probably not -- but beads of sweat congregated on his brow. He put a safety-swing on the ball and hit the driver about 175 yards into the fairway, normally quite embarrassing, but under these circumstances a minor victory.

The next swing, he chunked it.

He stared ahead, looking like the subject of a bad country-western song. His swing had plumb left him.

I wouldn't have been surprised if he'd packed it in after that hole. No reasonably compassionate man would have faulted him. But he marched on to the 9th. It was more of the same. Slash, chunk, dig, thwack, slap and two putts made 7.

We walked back to the pro shop without uttering a word to each other.

'Here you go. You did a really fine job.' He handed me $5. 'And I'd appreciate it, son, if you kept quiet about this round.' He held out a $20 bill.

'You don't need to…'

'Please, take it. I'd really appreciate it.'

I took the bill.

'Thanks, Kevin.' He slipped into the car and drove away.

I was glad the round was over. I didn't like being handed the hush money, but $20 was $20. I convinced myself that I'd earned it, or rather that I would earn it by keeping my mouth shut.

I quickly shoved the money into the Maxwell House can when I got ready for bed that night. That $20 put me over the $200 mark for the summer. When I turned the light off, I reran T.Rex's swing over and over again in my mind. His swing didn't seem to be much different before his melt-down than it was during it. I tapped my memory of a 3-iron he hit on the 2nd hole and compared it to the swings he took on the 8th. I focused on the hands for a while and couldn't come up with any noticeable difference. His left arm seemed straight in both swings, too.

After a hundred swings or so, I fell asleep.

Chapter 11

Two mornings later, one of the pro shop boys was sick and another was a no-show. I was one of three Spooks who Perkins, the remaining pro shop boy, rounded up to pull the 100 or so bags for Tuesday Ladies' day. I broke a sweat carrying two bags at a time to the first tee. Each bag I pulled from the top racks, which came up to my chin, was an adventure.

'Be careful there, little buddy,' said Perkins, 'you're going to hurt yourself.' With his pearly smile and Bee Gees hair, Perkins cared far too much about his appearance to be a caddie.

T.Rex looked in occasionally with his steely eyes to check on our progress. He did a slight double-take when he saw that I was one of those conscripted to help.

After we pulled all the bags, Perkins chose me to help him set up the driving range. I felt a sense of superiority as I marched past the full caddie benches toward the row of carts, which was only somewhat deflated when Howie coughed 'Proshopboy!' as I passed. This led to a chorus of similar muffled taunts including 'Brown-nose!' and "Wussboy!" from the peanut gallery.

The off-white vinyl seat felt cold against my legs as I took my first ride in a cart. I held on tightly as Perkins drove recklessly on the gravel paths, perhaps sensing that this was my maiden cart voyage. I nearly fell off a few times, but a smile was plastered on my face. We pulled around the corner near the halfway house, and Perkins slowed down as Maureen emerged. She smiled broadly. My heart raced.

'Hey, Scott,' she said to Perkins. My heart sunk. 'What you doing with little Kevin?' My heart sunk further. Little?

'Just heading to the range. Come by the pro shop when you're done today.'

'I will,' she responded and bounded back into the shack.

The work at the range was pretty mundane – setting up the practice tees, placing range balls into little wire baskets – but this line of work sure beat out a life of Spook Shoulders and blistered feet.

After another frenzied ride, Perkins stopped the cart on the first tee. I felt like John Wayne dismounting his horse as I stepped back onto terra firma in front of a jealous bench of caddies

My luck got even better when I saw Mrs. Sullivan come around the clubhouse corner about a half-hour later. She did not disappoint. My heart pounded. I needed to have her. Perkins could have Maureen.

I rushed up to Mr. G. Few things annoyed Mr. G more.

'Mr. G, if no one –'

'Did I call your number, son?'

'No, but—'

'Then get back on the bench!'

'MrG, ifnoonehasMrs.SullivanyetI'dliketohaveher!'

'Go sit—'

'I am.'

'Hi Kevin. You going to caddie for me again today?'

'I hope so, Mrs. Sullivan.' I melted.

178

Mr. G grunted.

If he had known that she was a Deal, Mr. G would have disregarded her comment and assigned her a more Senior Caddie, but a few minutes later he called out, '407!' and I was set.

I once again had a great time on the course. She seemed to enjoy my company as much as I did hers, and she appeared to like talking to me more than to the other members in her foursome. She told me what she had been up to since last I saw her, and she referred to her boys as though I had met them. When the other members made pretentious or annoying comments, she rolled her eyes at me like we had been friends for years. I didn't want the round to end. I was in bliss. Apart from the crush part, she reminded me of my mom.

At the end of the round, I wanted to kiss her, but I settled for the $12 chit she gave me.

'Hey there, Shortie!' said Perkins when I returned Mrs. Sullivan's bag to the bag room. 'Come on in here. I want you to do something for me.'

He disappeared briefly into the pro shop and returned with T.Rex.

'Take Mr. Tutlow's bag over there and see if you can put it on this top rack over here.'

I did as I was told, ignoring the onsetting hernia. The bottom of the bag banged into the rack, but I managed to secure it in its place.

'What do you think?' asked Perkins.

'Well, he is small…He may struggle a bit, but he is a hard worker. Who else do you have in mind?'

'Well, there's the McDougal kid, but he may have an attitude problem. And there's that kid they call Mouse, but he's even smaller than Shortie.'

'Hmm…' T.Rex rubbed his chin and went back into the pro shop.

My heart raced with excitement. Were they really considering me for a pro shop job? It was too good to be true.

'Okay, you're done here,' T-Rex said to me.

I returned to the caddie house and stood in line outside Mr. G's office to cash in my chit from Mrs. Sullivan.

'Hey, you little crap.' Tool bumped into me as he walked by. He grabbed the chit from my hand and held it high. 'You looking for this, Wichita Girl?'

'Give it back to me Tulis.'

'Let's see how much Wichita Girl made today. Six dollars? Seven dollars?…Holy crap! Twelve dollars!?! Who the hell is Mrs. Sullivan?

'Just give me back my chit.'

'Hey, Wichita Girl got twelve dollars from a lady named Mrs. Sullivan!'

And the cat was out of the bag. Before long, word spread like peanut butter on bread. My Deal had been discovered. My brief run at caddying success was over.

That night I sat down to dinner again with my grandparents. As my Grandma cleared our plates before serving up the cherry pie, the phone rang. My Grandpa answered. He looked puzzled. 'It's for you,' he said to me.

'Is it Mom?'

'No, it's some man.'

My body went cold. My mind immediately ran through the last couple of days to remember if I had broken any laws. Not that I could remember. For a split second I thought it might be Mr. Guelcher yelling at me for being a bad caddie.

'Hello, Kevin, this is Bob Templeton.'

Bob Templeton? Bob Templeton? Who's Bob Templeton? Oh, T.Rex, I almost said.

'Hi,' I said instead, after too long of a pause. Now I really got nervous. My grandparents stared on as eager spectators.

'I wanted to ask you if you would be interested in a job in the pro shop; you know, to work in the bag room.'

'Um, yes. I would. What would it pay?'

'It's minimum wage; $2.90 an hour.'

I quickly calculated that I would make more money without all that hard work and stress. 'When can I start?'

'Well, we had to terminate one of the boys. I don't want to go into it, but we could use you tomorrow morning if that's okay.'

'I'll see you then. Oh, what time?'

'We start at 7:00.'

7:00! I get to sleep in. 'Okay, thank you, Mr. Templeton. I'll see you tomorrow morning.'

I hung up the phone, filled with glee. Dread quickly followed as I thought about how I was going to break the news to my former caddie mates. Ambivalence set in as I realized that my days of spending time in the Caddie Yard, playing Caddie Golf, inane conversations on the caddie bench, were over.

I told my grandparents about the new job.

'That's great,' said my Grandma. 'It sounds more stable, and it'll keep you out of the sun. It's just getting so hot. Your mom will be happy too; she's been worried sick ever since you told her about that caddying thing.'

'You've been talking to her?'

'Yes, a little here and there when she's been checking in on you.'

'That's nice. I'm glad.'

'She thought that caddying seemed so dangerous, with men swinging those clubs and all those balls flying around the place. I told her it was okay, that a boy needs to experience life, get out there and breathe that fresh air.'

I weighed in at 104 before climbing into bed. I now had gotten used to seeing 3 digits smiling back at me on the scale.

I got to the country club the next morning at 6:45. I passed the caddie yard just as roll call was breaking up. I wore a golf shirt. I felt like a traitor in a sea of blue shirts. I didn't make eye contact with anyone as I searched for Mouse.

He greeted me cheerfully, 'Hey, Kev. That sucks you just missed roll call. Hurry up and put your number down, and we can play Caddie Golf. Where's your caddie shirt? Aren't you—' His eyebrows reached the sky.

I just shrugged.

'You didn't!' He was horrified. 'You've become one of Them! Oh my God, are you a Pro Shop Boy?'

'Bob Templeton called me last night.'

He laughed. 'He's Bob Templeton now? Not T.Rex?'

'They're going to pay me more money.'

'I can't believe it.'

'I won't have to trudge around the course anymore.'

His look of shock turned into a smile. 'In your defense, you were a pretty crappy caddie.' He laughed. 'Good job, Kevin. I'm happy for you. Don't forget about us over here.'

'I'd better go.'

Perkins was opening up the bag room when I got there. We took the tee time sheet and pulled each bag from one of 600 slots organized alphabetically for the most part but not always. Perkins knew every bag. I needed to keep running back to the huge peg board covering an entire wall in the back of the bag room that listed each member and slot.

'It's the brown one, Shortie; not the blue one.'

'Which Wilson is at 8:24?' I asked.

'Gene Wilson.'

I checked the bag tags. 'Is that G.B. or G.E. Wilson?'

'G.B. He plays every week with McDonald, Grassley and Owens.'

I pulled Mr. Wilson's bag and then Grassley's.

'That's Mrs. Grassley's, Shortie. Grab Mr. Grassley's. The brown one; not the yellow one.'

After pulling the bags for the morning tee times and setting up the driving range, there wasn't much left to do except watch the parade of men tee off from my new vista behind the screened door opening of the bag room.

I walked through the racks to familiarize myself with the bags. I counted 20 bag slots in each row, 30 rows. I walked up and down the aisles, mentally matching up the names with the numbered slots.

'I'm going over to pick up the range,' said Perkins. 'Come on with me, Shortie.'

He was equally as reckless a driver as the day before. Twice he drove the right side of the cart into the prickly branches of pine trees, the first time nearly knocking me out of the cart. The second time I was more prepared, but I still ended up with a head full of pine needles and a scratch on my arm. He snickered each time. I forced a laugh. I wasn't sure if he was just kidding around or being cruel.

At the range I helped him put the mesh wire top on the range cart. We hitched to the back of the cart the farm-like apparatus that flipped the balls into a set of baskets when Perkins drove up and down the hills of the range. I grazed through the trees around the perimeter of the driving range, collecting strays with a long tube device. I wished I were driving the range cart, but that would come with time. At least my new job was much better than lugging an overloaded golf bag around the course. I lifted my gaze from the bed of pine needles toward the 12th hole, which paralleled the range.

A golfer swung his 5-wood from 180 yards out. The ball rolled the entire way to the front of the green.

'Great shot, Earl!'

'Yep, I caught all of that one.'

His caddie handed him the putter and headed toward the 13th tee.

I missed the minor victories a little.

'Hey, Shortie. You finished?' Perkins aimed the range cart right at me before slamming on the brakes.

'Not really, I still have this entire row to do.'

'What's taking you so long? Hurry up.'

When Perkins finished up, he motioned me to a small shack back at the practice tees. Inside was an ancient machine that looked and sounded like a small steam engine.

'This is Big Betty,' Perkins explained. 'She's the ball washer. Be nice to her and she'll be nice to you. Feed a basket of balls into this end and then catch them in the basket on this end. Watch your fingers or she'll eat 'em up. Seriously, if it gets jammed, shut her down before putting your hand inside to shake the balls loose. Good luck, I'll be right outside if you need me.'

Betty shook violently and belched out small puffs of grey smoke when I turned her on. Through the small, dusty window I saw Perkins practicing his 7-iron. I struggled to lift the first basket to feed Betty's open mouth. Several balls fell out and scattered on the concrete floor like marbles. Betty's parts grinded so badly I assumed she would pulverize the balls rather than wash them. But she was more bark than bite, and the old lady obeyed orders with the exception of occasionally splattering me with dirty water.

After I finished with Big Betty and Perkins had worked the kinks out of his swing, we headed back to the pro shop. I got back just in time to watch Mrs. Sullivan come around the corner. All of the caddies on the bench perked up. A couple Senior Caddies jumped up to plead their cases to Mr. G.

'Settled down, boys,' he said. 'She's just practicing today.'

Nearly overnight she had gained the allure of the new girl in school. I wanted to burst through the doors of the bag room and scream:

'But I found her first! But I'm her favorite!'

Bastards. They could never understand the wonderment of her. They just saw her as an easy $12. I appreciated the whole person.

I retreated to the other end of the bag room and kicked a bag of old towels.

The first foursome of the morning was just finishing up on 18. The caddies looked tired, but they got paid and could be done for the day. My work had really just gotten started.

For each bag that came in, I had to dunk the irons into a white plastic bucket of water, scrub them dry with a towel, wipe down the woods and put the bag back into its correct slot in the bag room. By the time I finished all of the bags from a foursome, the next foursome was coming off the 18th green. Kovach was in that second group. His eyes shot wide open as he put the bags on the rack. 'What the hell happened to you?'

I smiled and kind of shrugged.

'Another one bites the dust.' He walked away, shaking his head.

Howie came through two groups later.

'Hey, pro shop boy,' he said brusquely before he dropped his bag off and disappeared.

Mouse came through a few groups later. 'Hey, Kev. How are things going? I'll be right back after I get paid.'

I dunked another set of clubs into my increasingly dirty bucket of water.

True to his word, Mouse returned. 'Kenworth is behind me. He's gotta be so pissed at me – I sanded three pins on the back nine. So how's life as a pro shop boy?'

'It's good. My shoulder feels better than yours right now. And I haven't broken a sweat.'

'Yes, but you missed some championship golf out there.'

Perkins returned from racking a bag. 'Hey, caddies aren't allowed to be in the bag room.'

'It's okay, Perkins. He'll only stay a minute.'

'Hmmm.'

'It's fine, Kev. I don't want to get you in trouble. I'll hang outside for a while.'

I finished cleaning the clubs for Mouse's foursome, and I went outside to wait for the next group. Mouse was sitting on the fence tossing tees into a range bucket.

'Sorry, Mouse. Perkins can be a hard ass at times.'

'No, it's okay. He's a jerk. No big deal.'

'So who'd you have today?'

'I had your man Mr. Morgan. I hope you're not jealous. Didn't you recognize his bag when I dropped it off?'

'I was too busy washing clubs to notice anything.'

'It was your typical round. He shot about 75.'

Tim Kenworth came around in the next group. 'Mouse, you jerk,' he said with a smile and a pretty hard punch in the shoulder. 'I handled the first two pins fine, but that third one you jammed in pretty hard. It didn't help your case that you were standing on the next tee laughing your ass off.'

'I assure you, I was laughing at you, not with you.'

'Then the next hole, I just assumed you sanded it, and the pin almost flew out of my hands, I pulled it so hard.' He dropped the bag onto the rack. 'Pro shop boy! Or is it Mr. Pro Shop Boy? So the rumors I heard are true.'

'I guess so,' I muttered.

Tim turned back to Mouse, 'I've got a Caddie Golf grudge match lined up this afternoon with the Carrito twins. Let's head over and find them. They should be off the course by now.'

'In a while, Tim. I'm going to hang out here with Wichita for a few minutes. I'll be over later.'

'Come on, man. We've got big money riding on this. Those bastards have been talking crap since Saturday that they can beat us. We've got to shut them up.'

'I'll be over in a little bit.'

'It's okay, Mouse,' I chimed in. 'I've got a lot to do around here anyway.'

'You sure?'

'Yeah, I'm fine.'

'Okay.' Mouse hopped off the fence and joined Tim in a trot to the caddie house.

I went inside and dunked another set of irons into the bucket.

Mouse stopped by the pro shop at about 5 o'clock as I was getting ready to punch out for the day.

'So how'd you do against the Carritos?'

'Kicked their butts, as expected. Took $10 from each of them. Hey, what are you doing tonight? Why don't you come on over to my house for dinner if you don't have anything else going on?'

I thought about it for a moment. My Grandma was preparing one of her special recipes, hamburger stroganoff, that night. I didn't want to disappoint her, but I also didn't feel like picking through the gristly meat.

I went to the payphone in the caddie house to call home.

'Hi, Grampa, it's Kevin.'

'Uh-huh?'

'I was wondering if it would be okay if I ate at Mouse's house tonight.'

'Well, I know your grandmother was preparing a special meal tonight, and your Mom called an hour or so ago.'

'Well, I feel bad but I thought it was nice of Mouse to offer.'

He paused. 'Okay, I'll let your grandmother know.'

'Thanks. I won't be out too late.'

I was a little nervous to eat over at Mouse's, because I never knew when my stomach would act up.

The McMurtrys lived just off West 210th Street in Fairview Park. The white clapboard house was a square, modest two-story structure standing amidst its cookie-cutter brethren along the tree-lined street. My first thought as I approached was that a fire would rip through that house in no time.

I was perplexed how they fit nine people in the house to sleep each night. Mouse had told me that the six boys grew up sharing two bedrooms, three in each. Maureen slept in a corner of the basement that was converted into a small bedroom. I'd always had my own room, and Mom and I always had enough space to stay off each other's back.

When we walked up the concrete steps of the house and into the living room, it was crawling with McMurtry boys, or more accurately, Mice. They all looked like progressively older, bigger versions of Mouse. They ranged in age from 12 (Mouse) to 22. All of the boys had gone to grade school at St. Angela's, a few blocks away, and then on to St. Ignatius High School, on the near West Side not far from downtown. Mouse would be going there in two years, assuming that he passed the entrance exam. Todd was the reigning #2 caddie, behind Kovach. Paul and Peter, were numbers 34 and 55 respectively.

'Hey, look at what the Spook brought home; another Spook!' Peter announced our arrival. Three of the boys were sitting around the living room with Mr. McMurtry, watching the Indians' game that had just started. Mr. McMurtry was holding court in his recliner; the boys were sitting on the couches and on the floor.

'Peter, how many times do I have to tell you that we don't refer to anyone as a Spook in this house,' Mouse's Dad interjected. 'Leave the caddie house banter at the country club.' Mouse's Dad looked much older than his nearly 60 years. He had deep bags under his eyes, his hair was gray, and he spoke in a subdued tone. He looked like raising six boys had been a chore.

'Everyone, this is Kevin,' announced Mouse. 'He's going to have dinner with us tonight. Where's Mom?'

'She's on the back porch with Tim and Paul.'

We walked through the living room to the back porch and found Mrs. McMurtry standing on a chair looking out the window with a pair of binoculars.

'What are you guys doing?' demanded Mouse.

'Shhhhh!' Mrs. McMurtry admonished him. 'There's a party going on at the Matthews' and we thought we saw Uncle Dan.'

'I think I see him – in the red shirt.' Peter, now with the binoculars, reported back to the other two.

'You look like a group of Peeping Toms. What are you going to do if it is him?'

'I don't know,' Mouse's Mom said matter of factly. 'But if he was in the neighborhood, he should have stopped by or at least called.' She looked at me and said warmly, 'Hi, I'm Patrick's mother.'

She then gave Mouse a hug and a kiss. 'How's my littlest angel?'

Mouse smiled but squirmed out of his mother's embrace. 'Mom, this is Kevin. Is it okay if he eats with us tonight?'

'Of course! Nice to meet you, Kevin. I was just about to put dinner on. I was worried you weren't going to be home in time, Patrick.'

Despite being in her mid-50s and having had seven children, she looked like she didn't weigh much more than 100 lbs and, while only 5'1", she seemed to have more energy than the rest of us combined.

We all sat around a circular table in the dining room. Maureen came home from the club right as we were sitting down to eat. I couldn't imagine what it was like for her to live among all those boys. It was good to see her, especially outside of work. She looked even cuter than usual.

Mrs. McMurtry served a big bowl of spaghetti and meatballs, corn and salad. As soon as she put the food down, the boys attacked it like ravenous wolves. I was afraid that I wouldn't get any food. Then again, I wasn't nuts about spaghetti and I hated meatballs, which I viewed as gristle bombs, so it wouldn't be the end of the world.

'Paul, where are you going? I just put the food on the table.'

'Need ketchup.'

'We're having spaghetti.'

'What about the corn? I need it for the corn.'

'Oh, brother. You have a problem.'

'Gotta have my ketchup.'

'Now, Wichita,' yelled Peter from the other side of the table, 'Mom's spaghetti sauce is a family tradition that has been passed down from generation to generation within the McMurtry family.'

'Yes, what is it Mom?' Paul chimed in. 'Two jars of Ragu and two jars of Prego?'

'That's right, Paul. You all seem to like it. Now shut up and eat your food.' She acted annoyed, but she clearly liked being teased by her boys.

'With the exception of spaghetti, all of the McMurtry family recipes seem to be focused around a can of Campbell's soup as its secret ingredient,' chimed in Todd, acting like the house maitre d'. 'Tuna noodle casserole? Cream of Mushroom soup. Stew? Tomato soup. Pork chops? Chicken and Rice.'

'But the best is Party Rice – two cans Consommé, one cup rice.'

'There is no dish that cannot be improved upon by the Campbell company.'

'Okay, okay,' yielded Mrs. McMurtry. 'When you boys take over the cooking, you can begin to criticize.'

'Thank YOU, Thank YOU!'

Todd began mimicking a rock concert, using a single kernel of corn as the headliner and the rest of corn on his plate as the audience. All the kids let out a small cheer.

'This next song…Thank YOU..is a special one that goes out to all of you out there who ever had love and lost it. One! Two! Three! Four!…'

'Okay, that's enough, Todd,' said Mouse's Mom, but even she was laughing. 'Kevin is going to think that this is an insane asylum.'

The volume level around the table was just one notch below a yell. Everyone was trying to make everyone else laugh. The McMurtry's were just enjoying being together.

'Kevin,' Maureen said with her beautiful green eyes. 'I heard that you got a job in the pro shop. That's great.'

'Yeah, I just started. So far, so good.'

'You're a Pro Shop Boy?' Todd called out. 'I thought you were a caddie, not a wussie.'

'Boys, leave him alone,' said Mrs. McMurtry.

'Hey, Wichita,' said Tim. 'She's defending you now, but don't sit too close to her.'

'Leave your Mom alone,' chimed in Mr. McMurtry.

'If you cross her,' Tim continued anyway, 'she immediately goes for the hair. She'll yank that right out of your head.'

'I only pull hair when you guys make me do it, when you deserve it,' she lightly protested.

I looked around the table and noticed that they all had closely-cropped hair.

'Well, I think the pro shop job is pretty cool,' said Maureen. She gave me a flirty smile and a little wink.

'Did you get enough to eat, Kevin? You hardly ate anything.'

Everyone looked at my plate. I thought I had eaten a lot considering my normally light appetite, but on the McMurtry scale I had eaten like a bird. Now that everyone was looking at me, my stomach was sure to shut down. I couldn't eat another bite.

'Come on, Kevin. Have some more.' I panicked a little. If they put more on my plate, it would just sit there and I would look like I didn't like the food.

Just before Mrs. McMurtry reached for the bowl of spaghetti to fill up my plate, I was saved by Tim. 'Brrrrrpppp.' He let out the loudest belch I had ever heard. I was a little appalled and I looked at Mouse's Mom to explode at him.

Instead, she could only muster a weak reprimand, 'Tim, not in front of company.'

'Brrrppp,' added Todd.

'Todd!'

'Oh, come on, Mom. It's only Kevin.'

'Brrrrpp.' Paul ripped one.

Everyone was laughing. Even Mouse's Dad.

'Come on, Mom. Let's hear one.' Tim turned to me. 'Mom is actually the best burper in the family.'

'Oh, I am not. Let's stop this.'

195

'Come on, Mom.'

'No.' She rose from her seat to clear the plates.

'Come on, Mom,' continued the chorus.

'Brrrrrrppppppppp.'

The table went wild. Prouder than embarrassed, Mrs. McMurtry retreated back to the kitchen after her award-winning performance.

I was oddly impressed, and more startled. My Mom would never do that.

Soon after dinner, I hopped on my bike to head home. I stared down at the spokes of my bike as I pedaled.

There was a note on the hallway table when I opened the apartment door. I read that my mom called and that I should call her tonight.

I crumpled up the note and let it drop into the trashcan.

Chapter 12

The next morning Maureen came by the pro shop before going to the halfway house. I couldn't tell if she was there to see me or Perkins.

Perkins showed me how to regrip clubs. After taking off the old grip with an exacto knife, he put a spiral layer of double-sided tape where the new grip would go. He then poured lighter fluid on the tape. The lighter fluid made the tape slippery to allow the grip to be slid on and turned the tape into a strong adhesive when it dried. He put the clubhead on the ground, lined up the grip, slipped it onto the club shaft. He moved on to the next one.

I turned to Maureen who had hoisted herself onto a work table. 'I had a great time last night. I hope you know how lucky you are to have a family like yours.'

'Yeah, they're okay.'

'Okay? They're great!'

'Yeah, I guess so. My mom isn't always like that; she was kind of embarrassing last night.'

'I now understand how nine people survive in one house. She really runs the show.'

'Yeah, we love her, but we're also a little scared of her.'

'It must be kinda weird living with a house full of boys.'

'It's okay. I don't know any other way. They kind of look out for me and they think they need to protect me, but they're also loud and kind of smelly.'

'I thought they all were great, and I'd love to have some brothers.'

'Be careful what you wish for, Kevin.'

A petulant horse fly kept dive-bombing Perkins' head. He tried to kill it with a rolled up towel, but he was unsuccessful so he grabbed a can of Raid and finally defeated his foe. He sat back down, inspected his weapon and pulled a lighter out of his pocket.

'Hey, Shortie, look at this.' An 18 inch flame fired from the can.

'That's pretty cool, Scott,' Maureen laughed.

I tried to act cool, but I couldn't manage to say anything.

'Hey, Maureen,' he continued, 'behold the fire-breathing dragon.'

She laughed and clapped.

My heart pounded.

'Look, it's like a flame-thrower.' Perkins pressed the button on the Raid can as far as it could go. The flame shot out further than he expected and lit some tee-time sheets on fire. He tried to blow the small flames out, but this only stoked and scattered them. I stood paralyzed in panic. I was going to die in this fire just like Andy Carson's little sister did.

Perkins grabbed an armful of towels to smother the flaming butterflies.

And then he knocked over the can of lighter fluid he was working with.

The lighter fluid spilled on the regripping table, and then the cap fell off when the can hit the ground. Lighter fluid poured freely on the bag room floor and then ignited immediately.

'Oh, noooo. Crap!'

'Help!'

Perkins slapped at the fire with towels, but that splattered rogue colonies of flaming lighter fluid around the room. The bulletin board went up next and then a pile of towels.

Maureen screamed.

Perkins made a couple more feeble whacks at the flames before he screamed and shot out the bag room door.

'Kevin, help me,' yelled Maureen who was furthest from the door.

I continued to stand frozen. The only movement in my body was a nervous shaking in my knees. So this was what it felt like to die in a fire, I thought.

The flames grew higher and higher and smoke filled the room. Soon the door Perkins had escaped through just seconds before was engulfed in flames. I should have had a better escape plan. I wasn't prepared enough. I ran to the other end of the bag room to see if we could escape through the other door.

'Where are you going?' yelled Maureen.

I tried to tell her my plan but I was running too fast and she couldn't hear me. I would save her. I would be the hero.

The door was locked. Why was it locked? It was never locked. I ran back to the other end, and everything was on fire. I coughed a few times and crouched to the ground where there was a little less smoke. I racked my brain for an easy way out, but I came up with no creative ideas.

'Kevin!' yelled Maureen.

Every muscle in my body tensed up. I looked at Maureen. I panicked. I lowered my head and sprinted through the flames and out the swinging doors. And kept sprinting. To the caddie yard. I jumped on my bike. My legs shook so badly I could barely pedal at first. I knew I should have stayed to see if Maureen had made it out, but my legs just kept pumping my bike pedals. I rode home as quickly as my skinny legs would go, jumped off, sprinted up to the apartment, and curled up into a ball under my window and sobbed.

The fire engine sirens started off in the distance and got closer and closer.

This couldn't be happening to me. This couldn't be happening.

The sirens finally stopped. I stayed curled up, shaking, waiting for something more to happen. I suddenly felt the strange draw to go back. But I was afraid to. Maybe it's not that bad, I tried to convince myself. They probably just put the fire out and it's no big deal. My legs were stiff when I stood up. I felt a burn on the side of my thigh and another one on my shoulder. I pedaled my bike back up the driveway of the club, where I saw black clouds of smoke billowing out of the pro shop up to the clear blue sky. It was an inferno.

I was in shock. We had burned the freaking pro shop down! Why hadn't I stopped Perkins? I wanted to reverse time. I regretted everything I ever had done that led me to this moment in time. I hated being myself. Somehow this was going to get pinned on me and I was going to rot in jail.

People scurried about everywhere. Red-orange flames danced about, swirling into a cone that reached toward the sky before releasing into the air as black smoke. Teams of firemen in full gear blasted the inferno with their hoses. A unit from neighboring Fairview Park joined them with two more trucks.

Perkins sat alone on the putting green with his hands on his head. I searched frantically for Maureen. I found her standing in shock with a blanket around her. In shock that is, until she saw me. Her eyes narrowed when she saw me, and she simply shook her head at me in disgust.

T.Rex ran around with his appendages flailing wildly. The gathering crowd stood in awe of the spectacle – some in horror, others silently calculating their insurance claims.

It was nightfall before they put the fire out completely. I was among the last to leave. I waited for the firemen to pack up their hoses. When I left, three of the walls of the pro shop still stood. Only remnants of the roof remained.

It was such a chaotic scene that no one tied me to the crime. Everyone was so focused on putting out the fire that they didn't focus on how it started.

My grandparents were at the dinner table when I got home. Tears streamed down my face as soon as they looked up at me.

'The…the pro shop,' I choked out. 'We burned it down. I almost died.'

I ran to the bathroom and vomited.

My Grandpa frowned and sighed but then he said, 'It's okay, Kevin.' He placed his hand on my shoulder, and left to let me clean myself up.

Herschel was in a full sprint. The fire seemed to validate all of my fears in life. I was right to fear fire so much. That stuff can kill you in no time. My mom was right to protect me from all the bad things. Life can be snuffed out in seconds. I vowed to redouble my efforts to protect myself from all the bad things in the world. Fire, germs, wild animals…everything!

I was shaking like a leaf when I walked back into the living room.

My Grandma put her arms around me and guided me to the couch. 'Come on in here and tell us what on earth happened.'

I told them the whole story.

'Why did you guys pull out the lighter when you were using lighter fluid?'

'I don't know. Perkins did it. It just got out of hand.'

'You're lucky you weren't killed,' said my Grandma. 'You could have been burned to death, or the smoke could have –'

'Margaret, that's enough,' my Grandpa halted her. 'Kevin, it was stupid. But kids do stupid things. That's part of being a kid. It sounds like this Perkins kid was the most at fault.'

I nodded my head up and down. 'I should have stopped him. Mom is right; I need to be more careful. Even more so than I have been. She's always worried about things hurting me, and she wasn't here to protect me. I've got to do a better job of protecting myself.'

My Grandpa stared at my Grandma, and then turned back to me.

'Kevin, I think you've been through a lot here. You came out of this okay. How about if we don't share this with your Mother?'

'I think that's a great idea,' I replied.

I slept that night out of sheer mental and physical exhaustion.

When the sun rose to start the next day, I prayed it was all just a dream. But the smoky aroma of my sneakers next to my bed struck down that hope.

I felt the obligation, the need, the curiosity, to go back to the country club. I was terrified to lift my head from my pillow, but even more ridden with angst over not knowing if I would be jailed, tarred and feathered, perhaps even drawn and quartered, or something somehow worse.

I peeled myself off of the mattress and stumbled to the bathroom. Breakfast was a non-starter, so I grabbed my three Kleenex and hopped on my bike and numbly made my way to the course.

It was about 7 am and the club was just waking up from its disaster the previous day. The search and rescue operation had turned itself over to a relief and recovery initiative. The caddie yard turned into a morgue for golf bags, an Antietam battlefield of Wilson Staffs and Pings. The hundreds of charred remains of each member's woods and irons were lined up in rows on the ground to be identified and claimed by their loved ones.

I inserted myself into the maelstrom and tried to avoid being noticed.

Everyone seemed to forget, or didn't know, that I had been in the bag room when the fire started. Rumors about the episode spread among the caddies faster than the flames themselves.

'I heard that Pyro Perkins got pissed at T.Rex and burned the place down. I never trusted that guy.'

'Well, I heard that Pyro made a plan with the members to burn the place down and collect the insurance money.'

Throughout the morning, members picked through remnants to salvage articles that survived the blaze or to make a positive identification for insurance purposes. Some fared better than others. A few bags and clubs were completely untouched, many were completely charred and ruined, almost all had at least some smoke or water damage. Some members were crushed that their beloved clubs were gone, others were happy to use the opportunity to buy a new set. Mrs. Barker looked like her dog had just died as she stood over the blackened remains of her formerly-lavender bag and clubs.

The caddies of course turned the carnage into a money-making venture. For many who were not afraid to dirty themselves and their clothes with ash and soot, the fire turned out to be a windfall. That first day after the fire was by far the most profitable day of the summer. The course was closed for the next couple of days, so most caddies didn't even bother to show up, but a group of 20 or so spent the next three days like sewer rats amidst the burnt mess, sorting through bags, cleaning up clubs, wiping down bags, consoling members, anything that needed to be done that would result in tips. I joined the group as a way to begin to put the nightmare behind me. The work kept my brain from cycling through the guilt.

About half-way through the first morning, I sat on the ground, cleaning Mr. O'Leary's Ben Hogan irons with a wooden scrub brush. I felt a sharp punch on my shoulder. I looked up into the squinty eyes of Tool.

'Hey, Pro Shop Boy,' he sneered, 'where were you when the fire started?'

'Get out of here, Tulis,' I said with my heart in my throat. I looked down at the irons and kept scrubbing.

He pushed me with his foot. 'You probably did it, you little piece of crap.'

I scrubbed harder hoping that he and everyone else would leave me alone.

The standard tip for helping out a member find his bag and clean up the clubs as best as possible was $5-10, not bad for about 20 minutes of work. On top of that, we all ended up with at least two or three sets of clubs from members who no longer wanted clubs that had the slightest bit of damage. Mr. Donnelly gave me his set of MacGregor irons. Insurance was going to get him a new set. The shafts were a little discolored but otherwise were fine. Mrs. Parkfield didn't want anything to do with her clubs after her bag melted around them, so I laid claim to her Ben Hogan woods, which weren't in bad shape after I pried off the melted head covers. I grabbed a bag that Mr. Hastings had discarded. I put in a full day and worked harder than I ever had in my life. My brain only felt modestly better.

My Grandpa met me at the door that night. 'What the hell happened to you? You look like Al Jolson.'

'Sorry, Grandpa. I'll try not to get anything dirty.'

He came back with a pile of newspapers. 'Strip to your underwear here. I'll lay down a path to the bathroom.'

After a good long hot shower, I laid out all of the money onto my bed. I unwrapped wads of dirty ones, fives, and tens and sorted them into piles. $78. I crawled under the covers, too tired and too upset to eat dinner.

I made another $55 the next day. But the following day I had trouble getting out of bed. Despite the potential financial windfall, I decided I needed a day away from the country club to hopefully begin fixing my brain. I got on my bike and turned down Detroit Avenue, not sure where I was headed. I passed by an empty Rocky River High School. A large pirate glared down from the façade of the press box. A few blocks later I passed St. Christopher's, where many of the caddies went to grade school.

It felt good to get away from things. With the glaring exception of the pro shop fire, I probably was happier over the past few months than I ever had been. My Mom seemed a world away – her love, her comfort, her friendship; but also the pain, the fears, the exhaustion. I dared to let myself entertain the thought that my own fears in life were related to spending so much of my life around her and her irrational fears. It pained me to think that. I loved her so much, she had been so good to me, all the time, but away from her, I had begun to find my own life, not completely free from my hang ups, but significantly diminished.

I followed the road across the Rocky River valley into Lakewood, where I cut up a few blocks to the lake. I rode slowly, amazed by the stately Lakewood mansions that were built in the 1920s and 30s, when land was more plentiful and heating must have been much cheaper. I reached Edgewater Park, where I caught a good view of the Terminal Tower and the rest of downtown. On my way back I cut inland toward the airport and found myself on Rocky River Drive. I rode past Our Lady of Angels church, where several caddies went to school. I continued to Lorain Road and stopped outside of a bank at Kamm's Corner.

Mom had done well at the bank she worked at. She had risen to branch manager. At first, her obsessive thoughts impacted her concentration at work. Then her fear of germs led her to wash her hands more and more. She couldn't focus on her job, and she spent most of her day going back and forth to the women's bathroom. Protecting herself and ourselves from germs became more important to her than keeping her job. Not that she thought of it that way – she was just doing what her brain told her to do. She thought she was doing the right thing for the short term.

After she lost her job just before last Christmas, she literally spent hours each day that winter and spring washing her hands. She scrubbed them for 10 minutes each time until she felt that all of the germs were washed away. That lasted her for no longer than a half-hour, until she touched anything – a newspaper, a shoe, the floor – that she wasn't absolutely sure was clean. Then she would wash again. By the end of the day her hands were beet red, the skin broken along her knuckle line. Eventually, the cracked skin refused to heal and became infected. Her doctor insisted she needed help.

But right now I realized that I needed help. I didn't know how to get back home.

I stopped at a 7-Eleven for directions, and the man behind the counter had never heard of Rocky River. Herschel briefly nibbled on the idea that I had wandered across state lines, or into some Twilight Zone universe, and that I would never again find home. I pedaled to a gas station, the lighthouses of the 20th century. The attendant looked at me like I'd just robbed a bank, but he reluctantly gave me directions that led me back home to my grandparents.

My adventure helped to put the awfulness of the Pro Shop Fire behind me, but I had no idea what was next for me. Surely I had lost my job in the pro shop. I had turned my back on caddying. I fell asleep without coming up with any new options.

Chapter 13

By the weekend a semblance of normalcy returned to the club with a full slate of tee-times for Saturday morning. Only a few charred bags remained in the caddie yard mortuary. An unsightly mobile office trailer stood in for the pro shop. I saw a completely new kid that T.Rex had recruited standing in the doorway. I didn't dare ask T.Rex to get my job back. I avoided him at all costs. I feared the confrontation.

Mr. G held the first roll call since the fire, and I stood against the fence, feeling uncomfortable in my caddie shirt that I had donned once again. The muscles in my arms and legs twitched, maybe due to the early morning chill.

'I hear that when Pyro Perkins realized what he had just done,' said a caddie next to me to his friend, 'he become paralyzed with fear, screaming like a school girl until Mr. G rushed in to knock him out of his shock and saved his life.'

After Mr. G ran through the numbers, I joined the rush of stragglers to get my number added to the bottom of the list.

'407.'

Mr. G looked up, held my gaze for a couple of seconds and wrote my number down.

I found Mouse after roll call sitting on one of the picnic tables.

'How are you doing, Kev?' he said as I sat down.

'I'm fine. It's weird to be back.'

'My sister's pretty mad at you. She told me you just left her in the burning pro shop.'

'I tried helping her, Mouse. I really did. I ran to the back door to find a way out for us. But it was locked. I tried yelling to her, but it was pretty crazy in there. And then I just panicked.'

'I told her she should be mad at Pyro. He's the one who burned the place down.'

'Tell her I'm sorry, if you get a chance.'

'I'll try.'

By late morning I was out on the links again, caddying for Mr. Wagner, who was a 17 handicap, despite missing a right arm. He swung the club 'right-handed,' like most golfers, using only his left arm. To putt he turned around and addressed the ball from the 'left-handed' side. He cocked his wrist early in the swing, which let him get more torque, but otherwise his swing was pretty smooth. He was able to hit the ball about 200 yards off the tee.

He was a lanky man in his mid-50's or so. A stiff Westwood cap covered his bushy, brown hair. Between shots, he kept his remaining arm busy puffing on a chain of cigarettes.

On the first green I instinctively tried to hand him his putter into his phantom hand while he gave me his wedge. He didn't seem to notice. I'm sure it wasn't the first time.

On the next hole we stood together killing time until it was his turn to hit his approach shot.

'That was some fire last week, huh?' he said to me.

'Um, yes...did your clubs make it through; you know, were they burned up?'

'No, luckily I was in a member-guest tournament the week before, so I had them in my trunk. I just lost an extra putter that was in there. I tell you, though, those kids should be taken out back and shot. I hear one of them already had a criminal record, and they're thinking of pressing charges.' My stomach dropped. 'I understand another one wasn't even from here. They sent him back home to Oklahoma or Texas or something.'

My stomach plummeted. 'Interesting.'

He hit his shot into the left trap.

'Too much right hand.' He handed the club back to me. 'So, where do you go to school?'

'Um, I'm not from here. I'm visiting my grandparents for the summer.'

He squinted at me. 'Where you visiting from?'

'A...um... Michigan.'

I followed up my round with a late afternoon round of caddying for Mrs. Thomas again. Having been elbowed out of the Mrs. Sullivan sweepstakes, Mrs. Thomas became my new Mrs. Sullivan, minus the crush and the big tips.

There wasn't any competition for her from the other caddies, because technically she was a Screw. But she was my Screw, dammit. She couldn't replace Mrs. Sullivan, but she helped to ease the pain.

At the turn she handed me a huge handful of ginger snaps.

'I remember how much you like these. Try not to eat them all at the same time.'

It felt good to be back in a routine.

After the round, I checked out the first tee to see if I could go out again. It was pretty slow. Mr. G was over at the caddie house. I walked up to the starter's desk, where a small group of caddies had gathered.

Todd McMurtry and another Senior Caddie tried to see who could balance the most golf tees on a Spook's head. Todd was leading with nine. Kovach then demonstrated the art of putting a fly on a leash. He had pulled a long piece of hair from Alice Cooper's head. Then he caught one of the many flies that hovered around the first tee desk. While Todd McMurtry held the fly by one wing, Kovach used the strand of hair to delicately tie a double knot around the fly's head. He held the end of the hair and let the fly go. It flew around in circles, tethered to Kovach's finger tips for about a minute before the knot unraveled and set the fly free.

The caddies then turned their attention to the intercom that was connected to the loud speaker in the caddie yard. While pretending to hold down the Talk button, Todd, Kovach and the Carrito brothers mimicked Mr. G's peppy "coooome-a-runnin'!" cadence and announced other inane things into the microphone.

"Now batting for the Indians, Boooooog Powelllllll!," followed by laughs from everyone.

I was scared that this was a dangerous game that could get us in trouble, but I laughed along. I wanted to be part of the group.

"Attention, K-Mart shoppers, there's a blue light special on Screws at the first tee," More chuckles.

"Mr. G, coooome-a-runnin'!" Belly-aching laughs all around.

After a few others took their turns, I stepped up the intercom. 'Breaker 1-9, report to the first tee, 10-4.'

Everyone just stared at me.

'Go back to the caddie bench, Pro Shop Boy,' Kovach said to me dismissively.

As I walked away, Pablo Carrito walked up to the intercom. 'Mrs. G, coooome-a-crawlin',' he announced in a poor impersonation of Mr.G.

This time, we heard the strange echo of Pablo's voice in the caddie yard. Without Pablo noticing, Kovach had pressed the Talk button. Seconds later, Mr. G appeared around the corner of the Caddie House. His face was beet red and steam was coming out of his ears. We scurried like a bunch of cockroaches.

"75! Was that you!?!" Mr. G yelled at Pablo. "75! Start counting the trees on your way out of here! I want you off the property. You are fired!"

Pablo sprinted down the driveway until he was too far for Mr. G to chase him. He recovered from his panic, and he was kind of laughing as he caught his breath.

It wasn't even me who'd been caught, and I was shaking. I was afraid Mr. G would finger me as a co-conspirator.

The next day was an unusually cool, rainy day, so I was sitting in the Caddie House with a handful of other kids when Pablo Carrito shuffled across the floor and into Mr. G's office. I overheard him mumble a poorly-rehearsed, half-hearted apology.

'Son, I don't know what to do with you,' replied Mr. G. 'I try so hard to turn you boys into men, and some of you thank me by turning into wiseacres instead.'

'I don't need you, son,' his voice continued from his office. 'I don't need any of this. I could be sitting on a beach in Florida instead of taking guff from you. And what would happen to you boys? They'd replace you with carts. I'm going to give you another chance, 75. Why? I don't know – you seem to give me more pain than you're worth over the years. But you're a good caddie and, from what I've seen, a hard worker. I'm going to give you another chance, but I'm going to keep a close eye on you. You slip up at all, AT ALL, and you'll be counting the trees for good. FOR GOOD. You got that?'

'Yes, thank you, Mr. G.' He walked out and smirked when he passed me.

Later that day, the unthinkable happened. I actually was standing next to his dark brown leather bag. 'BOOTH' was actually scribbled in Mr. G's awful handwriting on my caddie card. I was the only caddie left when Mr. Booth came around the corner, so Mr. G had no choice but to assign me to him.

'Now, 407, are you up to this? That bag is awful heavy,' advised Mr. G. 'I can always tell Mr. Booth that we're out of caddies, and he can take a cart.'

'I'll be fine, Mr. G. I can do it.'

'Now remember that Mr. Booth requires the highest level of attention. Wash his club heads after each shot. Replace every divot. And wash his ball on every green. Have you got a wet towel?'

'Yes, I do.'

'Most importantly, keep your eyes on the golf balls. I don't want to hear about you losing even one ball out there. Are you sure you can do this?'

'Yes.' My stomach tightened up.

'And one final thing, 407; don't embarrass the caddie program.'

With those inspiring final words rattling in my brain, I met Mr. Booth on the tee. Despite my nerves, I was excited to prove that I could do the job, even if I wasn't completely sure that I could. In the past two months I had become a much better caddie, but I was pretty sure I wasn't yet in the Booth category.

Booth looked like he'd just arrived off the boat from County Kerry. He was short and stocky, with thick orange hair, and plump, rosy cheeks; like a pumpkin atop a bigger pumpkin. He was a good golfer, about a 5 handicap, putting him on the border of being among the best golfers in the club, which he desperately wanted to be, but not quite. Mouse had told me that Mr. Booth had inherited his father's bottling business, which he had turned into one of Cleveland's largest private employers. I only knew all these members as golfers who wore goofy pants and shoes and struggled to hit the ball around the course. It was tough for me to picture any of them out in the real world as successful businessmen.

The first few holes went very well. I didn't screw up once. There was no member-caddie banter with Mr. Booth; he was all business. As he stepped up to each shot, he asked, 'How far to the hole?'

I answered immediately, since I knew the question was coming each time. One time I told him the yardage as soon as he walked up, before he had the chance to ask the question. He didn't seem to like that.

'What's the wind doing?'

'Moving a little left to right.'

Without looking at me or saying another word, he selected his club and addressed the ball. The routine never changed.

I realized on the sixth hole that Mr. Booth was putting together a nice little round. He sank a long putt for birdie that put him at 1-under for the round. His demeanor became a bit friendlier as well. As he walked off the sixth green he handed me his putter,

'Thanks...what did you say your name was? Kevin?'

'Yes. Kevin'

'Thanks, Kevin.'

On the next hole, he even said, 'Thanks, Kevin,' after I replaced a divot for him. This was downright chatty for him.

I almost messed up our newly found friendship on the 8th hole when I had a little bit of trouble finding his drive that he hit into the rough. My eyes frantically darted from blade of grass to blade of grass, but the Titleist failed to appear. A white mushroom teased me for a moment. It took about 30 seconds of searching before I found it a little to the right of where I originally was looking, not a major screw-up, but enough to plant a seed of doubt in Mr. Booth's mind that maybe I was really a Spook in caddie's clothing.

At the halfway house, I saw Maureen for the first time since the fire.

'Hi, Kevin,' she said quietly. After a long pause, 'What can I get you?'

'I'll have a Coke, please.'

She turned to get it, and I tried to find a way to tell her how sorry I was.

She came back, put the cup on the counter, and turned to take an order from one of the members inside.

I didn't say a word.

Mr. Booth continued to play really well. He still was 1-under at the turn. He gave up a stroke with a bogie on the 10th, but made it up with a birdie on the 12th. This was the best round of golf that I had ever witnessed in person.

As we made our way down the long par-5 fairway of 13, Mr. Booth said softly to me, 'I don't mean to jinx myself, but I've never broken par before in my life.'

I said nothing in response. I didn't want to put a hex on him.

Mr. Booth was starting to show some signs of pressure. He laughed when someone in the foursome made a joke, but it was unquestionably a nervous laugh. Inside, he seemed to be bubbling with excitement.

By the 15th hole, still at 1-under, he stopped talking to everyone else in the foursome and only spoke to me; I became his good luck charm.

'Has anyone snagged you up for the club championship yet, Kevin?' he asked as we walked the 16th fairway en route to his monster drive in the middle of the fairway.

The thought of me, Spook number 407, caddying for Mr. Booth, the biggest Deal at Westwood in the club championship was as far-fetched and comical as me running off and eloping with Mrs. Sullivan. The Senior Caddies had been jockeying all summer to caddie for Mr. Booth in the club championship. Caddies weren't allowed to carry doubles because of the championship's match play format. Mr. Booth paid his caddie in the club championship as though it were a doubles loop. If I had ever even voiced a desire around the caddie yard to caddie for Mr. Booth in the club championship, the Senior Caddies would have hung me from a tree by my underwear for my stupidity.

'No, not yet.' Or ever, I thought.

'Well, let's talk about it after this round.'

'Okay,' I said, as though offers like this come my way every day.

He hit a great second shot within 10 feet of the pin. He gave me a sly wink when I handed him his putter. He sank the putt for birdie.

And then came the 17th hole.

Number 17 is a relatively short par 3, about 135 yards, but there was a small lake in front and to the right side of the green, with only a few feet of safety between the green and the edge of the water. Standing over his ball on the tee, Mr. Booth was two under par and almost assured of breaking par for the first time. Maybe he had too many thoughts going through his head, because he hit his pitching wedge fat. Really fat. The ball and the divot flew through the air and both sailed into the lake. The Titleist splashed in the water like a torpedo detonating, as if to taunt Mr. Booth and push him over the edge. He stood there stunned, silent. He walked over to me and took another ball out of his bag.

He teed the new ball up and stood over it. He took a deep breath. If he hit it on the green and one-putted, he could still manage a 4 and would lose only one stroke to par. He swung the club and made good contact, too good. The ball easily cleared the water and ended up in the sand trap beyond the green. An up and down from there would leave him with a 5 on the hole, bringing him to even par for the round. Who knows? He could still birdie the last hole to bring him his first ever round under par. After the others in the foursome hit their tee shots, we all walked in silence down the path to the green. The crunch of spikes on the gravel echoed against the canopy of the trees.

Mr. Booth's ball sat in the middle of the trap with a reasonably good lie. He entered the trap to address the ball. The water was now beyond the putting surface and wrapped around the green to where I was standing, waiting to rake the trap. As he began his swing, I don't think he even had thought about the water, but as he reached the top of his swing, a ray of sunlight momentarily emerged from the

219

clouds and cast a glimmering ray of sunlight off of the still water. Whether the light reminded him of the danger that lurked behind the green or merely distracted him, it doesn't matter. He lifted his head and body ever so slightly as he came through the ball. The Titleist shot out of the trap at 100 mph, never reaching an altitude above 2 feet. It skipped a couple of times on the water's surface before slowing, submerging and descending slowly to the bottom of the pond.

Mr. Booth stood there staring at the pond in utter indignation. His face turned beet red, his fists were clenched, and he was trembling with anger. I thought he was going to explode, not figuratively, but literally explode – blood and flesh flying everywhere. I wouldn't have been surprised if he did. Actually, I was surprised when he did not. No one else in the foursome knew what to say. No one dared look at him. I had the opposite reaction. I couldn't take my eyes off of him. I've never seen more hate in a man's eyes. He hated himself, he hated me, he hated his foursome, he hated his life – everything that had ever happened to him that had brought him to this moment.

He took his anger out on his sand wedge. He walked out of the sand trap and slammed the club head onto the turf three times, making three huge divots. He then threw the club as hard as he could into the ground. Unfortunately, he threw it so hard that it bounced up off the ground, hit a down slope, flipped over twice and fell into the murky pond.

He looked at me, still angry, but now startled on top of that. He paused for a moment. 'Son, go see if you can retrieve it.'

Unsure, I pulled his 2-iron out of his bag, walked over to the pond, and felt around for the sand wedge. Within minutes, Mr. Booth was doing the same. We had both seen exactly where it went in, and it was only about five feet from the bank, but the water wasn't clear enough for us to see the club.

'We need to find that club. My wife's father gave it to me for Christmas last year.' His anger was still there, but it was quickly being overtaken by frustration and concern.

We kept searching in vain.

'This isn't working. You're going to need to go in after it,' he said authoritatively.

I looked at him to see if he was serious. He was.

'Mr. Booth, um, I'm not sure...'

'Come on, it's five feet from the edge; it can't be more than a couple of feet deep.'

Herschel rustled awake. My desire to impress Mr. Booth was coming into direct conflict with my intense aversion to water. I was also hesitant to retrieve a club that he'd thrown in rage. I had some dignity.

I made a lame attempt to explain. 'Mr. Booth, I'm not so great with water. I don't even know how to swim.'

'Come on, son. You don't need to swim. It's only a couple of feet deep. You've got shorts on. Just take your shoes and socks off and go in. I'm sure we'll be able to find it.'

'I really don't think I'll be able to find it…' I started to panic a little.

'Are you going to make me go in after it?' he asked me incredulously. His anger resurged.

My absent response implied that I hoped he would.

'Jesus Christ!'

He stared at me and shook his head as he quickly and deliberately took off his shoes and socks and rolled up the legs of his golf trousers. The rest of the foursome had putted out and were viewing the spectacle in muted delight.

Mr. Booth gingerly put one foot into the water. It disappeared under the murkiness, but it barely reached his ankle. A bit more confidently he put the other foot in. He reached around the bottom with his feet, attempting to locate the club, but to no avail. Recognizing that the club was out a few feet, he stepped further out. One careful step – the pond was only a couple inches deeper. Two steps – a couple of inches deeper. Three steps – a couple inches more. On the fourth step he dropped like a rock.

'Holy crap! He's up to his mouth!' Mr. Crawford called out.

'Someone help him!' cried Mr. Daulton, nearly doubling over in laughter.

'Ahwww!!!' was all Mr. Booth could manage as he struggled to keep his face above the water.

Amidst the chaos, I extended the 2-iron to Mr. Booth's bobbing figure. Mr. Booth desperately grabbed onto the club head and slowly climbed back up the underwater ledge that he had fallen off of. He emerged from the pond a sogging, dripping, muddy wreck. His shirt and pants were absolutely soaked. His psyche self-destructed before my eyes. His anger had succumbed to humiliation and depression.

With his clothes drenched, sticking to his skin underneath, he was too pathetic a figure to laugh at anymore. The other golfers were unsure what to say or what to do. One by one, they turned and made their way to the 18th tee.

Maybe it was a drop of pond water, but I was pretty sure that I saw a tear fall out of the corner of Mr. Booth's eye as he stood there wondering what to do next. I handed him my golf towel. 'You okay?' I couldn't help but to feel responsible for his misfortune. My fear of water kept me from being the one standing there as a water-logged mess. Then again, it kept me from drowning as well. After all, he was the idiot who threw the club in the first place.

'Yes, I'm okay,' he seethed under his breath.

He tried to save face by walking to the next tee and teeing up a ball. But with his sopping clothes hanging on his body, he made a horrible swing on the ball and launched it into the trees. No one yelled 'Jack Martin.'

He played out the hole in silence, staring straight ahead. There was no more talk of breaking par.

After the round, he handed me $15 and leaned in toward my ear. 'You will never caddie for me again,' he whispered through clenched teeth. He turned and retreated to the men's locker room, still dripping water from his clothes as he walked.

As I returned his clubs to the bag trailer, it hit me that we never did find his sand wedge. And I would have to find another member for the club championship. But at least I didn't have to get wet.

Chapter 14

After roll call the next day, Mr. G announced that five caddies, including Tim Kenworth and me, were promoted to A Caddies. Mouse had made it 3 weeks earlier. For the rest of the summer I was number 256. 407, I hardly knew you. It meant an extra $2 per round, and more importantly no more running for carts.

I felt like I deserved the extra money, because the weather had turned oppressively hot. Carrying a 30-pound bag 18 holes took its toll under those conditions.

I was sitting at one of the picnic tables with Tim, Buddha and Alice Cooper when Kenny Carrito slid into the seat next to me.

'So have you guys heard what's going down? We're organizing a strike next Tuesday,' began Kenny.

'Yeah, we heard something about it,' replied Tim for the rest of us.

'We all know caddies are treated like dirt and we get paid like crap,' Kenny continued. 'We sit around for hours without making any money, and then make a few measly bucks for more than 4 hours of work. It sucks.

'I don't know...what would Mr. G do?' I weakly offered.

Kenny turned to me and looked intently into my eyes. 'These members are treating us like slaves. It's all 'yessir' and 'no sir' and then we carry their bags around for hours. And the food here sucks. Those hot dogs are made out of real dogs.'

I noticed Pablo making the pitch to another group of boys across the caddie yard.

'So what would be the goal?' challenged Tim.

'The goal? The goal is more money. I hear that caddies on the East Side make almost twice as much as we do here. And Rickles told me his cousin came to visit a couple of weeks ago, and they make three times what we make in this dump. It's slavery.'

'You think it'll work?' asked Alice.

'Something has to. These members don't get it. You know what Pablo did last week? He had Five-Bills Wills two days in a row. Can you believe Mr. G did that to him? Two days in a row with that Screw. When Wills paid him the second day, Pablo handed the $5 back to him and said, "Here, sir, you seem to need this money more than me," and just walked back to the caddie house. Wills just stood there shocked; it was classic. But that's not going to change anything. We need to do more.'

'Wouldn't they just replace us with carts?' I offered.

'You believe that crap? You're pathetic. The old man just says that to scare us. Mr. G's not looking out for us. He's looking out for the members. They're the ones that pay him. It's bull. And you think any of the members care about us? They just care about what next new expensive car they're gonna buy, or whether they're going to buy a bigger house. And they just stick their noses in the air like they're better than us. So what do you guys say? You in?'

'Sure, we're in,' responded Tim with a grin, 'whatever you guys want to do, we'll support you.'

'Awesome,' replied Kenny. 'I knew I could count on you.' He shook hands with Tim and went over to another group.

226

'Are you crazy?' I said to Tim. 'Mr. G will kill us if he finds out about this'

'C'mon. We are paid like crap. Besides, we could all use a day off. Nothing's going to happen to us.'

'What do you think, Buddha?' asked Alice.

All eyes turned toward the end of the bench to Buddha's calm silence. His 30 seconds or so of silence provided the inspired answer others were looking for. For me this just confirmed my suspicion that Buddha didn't have much working upstairs.

'Kevin!' Mouse called to me as he ran toward the picnic table. 'Come here.'

I got up and jogged toward him. 'Come follow me,' he pleaded. 'You've got to see the steamer that Howie just took.' He was summoning me into the bathroom.

'The what?'

'The steamer. You know, a dump, a crap.'

'Why on earth would I want to see that?'

'It's huge. Trust me. Just come in.'

'Ah, I don't think so.'

'Come on.' Mouse had a magical power that enabled him to get me to do just about anything.

I trailed Mouse, a few steps behind, into the bathroom. Howie Weston was standing in one of the stalls. He pointed down into the toilet.

'Look at that! Look at that!'

I looked into the toilet. It indeed was large.

'Interesting.'

'No,' urged Howie, pointing his finger inches from the toilet water. 'Look how huge that is, and look at that color.'

To appease him and to increase my chances of getting out of there quickly, I took another step in and looked a bit closer into the bowl.

Just then, Howie quickly reached into the water and snatched the log out of the bowl.

I screamed and every muscle in my body lurched back to escape from the stall. As Howie began to chase me with it, I knocked over Mouse and fled the bathroom as fast as I could. I kept running, screaming bloody murder across the caddie yard with Howie in hot pursuit. I thought I was being attacked by a madman.

As I continued running, my mind was trying to sort out what was happening. Why would Howie do something so gross as to pick up a turd in his hand? Why was Mouse laughing so hard when I knocked him over?

As I sorted things out, I was 95% sure that it wasn't actually a real turd, but that lingering 5% made me keep running until Howie stopped chasing me. I looked back and Mouse and Howie were collapsed on the ground laughing.

After they recovered from their laughing fit, they told me that about a half hour earlier Mouse had been looking for his bagged lunch on a shelf in the caddie house when he came across an abandoned bag with a banana in it so old it had turned completely black. Knowing that Howie would enjoy the find, Mouse showed the turd-esque banana to him first. It was Howie's idea to put it into the toilet.

Now that I was in on the trick, we spent the next few hours performing the trick on any new unsuspecting soul who showed up in the caddie yard and who was sufficiently intrigued to go into the bathroom to look at Howie's dump. A surprising number obliged, which said something either about Mouse's powers of persuasion or about the average teenager's fascination with feces. I don't think I have ever laughed so hard in my life. Reactions ranged from 396's violently running away screaming 'No! My shirt! It's new! My shirt, it's new! To Alice Cooper not moving an inch and matter of factly commenting, 'Hey, man, why'd you just pick up that turd?'

I decided to stay in bed the morning of the caddie strike, with the idea that I would skip out on Ladies' Day and get a loop in during the afternoon. It was a compromise I made with myself to support my fellow laborers while still making some money and avoiding Mr. G's wrath.

Mouse was way too loyal to Mr. G to consider participating in the strike. He later told me that caddie turn-out was a little light and the last few foursomes needed to ride carts, but there was none of the chaos that Pablo and Kenny had hoped for. Mr. G and the members seemed oblivious to the fact that any walk-out had been organized.

When I rode my bike through the gates at about noon, Pablo and Kenny Carrito were hiding in the bushes on either side, monitoring the strike.

'Hey, Wichita!' One of them yelled at me. 'You traitor!'

I put my head down and pedaled.

With caddies crossing the picket lines, Pablo and Kenny decided to take their grievances directly to the members.

Word began trickling in that they had started to flag down each car that entered the gates. They accosted each driver, shouting, 'We caddies are underpaid. We're going to quit unless something drastic happens!'

Mr. G's first reaction was confusion. 'No, of course my caddies aren't planning to all quit,' I heard him tell a frightened member.

His next was disbelief. 'None of my boys would do a thing like that.'

After more reports came in, he hopped into a cart to see what was going on. Sure enough, he saw the Carrito twins flagging down a Lincoln Continental being driven by Mrs. Henderson, an 80 year-old widow. The sight of an angry Mr. G approaching the scene in his cart was enough to convince them to abandon their revolutionary plans. They took off running.

'You boys are FIRED…FIRED…FIRED! And don't bother trying to come back,' he yelled at the fleeing twins. He turned to Mrs. Henderson, 'I'm sorry, Ma'am.'

Safely off Westwood grounds, the Carrito twins yelled back at Mr. G, 'Westwood sucks! Caddying sucks!'

They kept that up for 10 more minutes or so, yelling at cars that entered the gates, until they finally lost interest and went home. I guess the Carritos were never cut out for caddying. This time, they didn't beg for their jobs back. The revolution had been suppressed.

I caddied for Mr. Morgan that afternoon. He wasn't his normal friendly self on the first tee, and he barely talked to me on the first four holes. I, of course, blamed myself – I must have screwed up something or maybe he's just tired of me. On the fifth hole he got a little upset when I had trouble finding his second shot in the rough.

On the next few fairways he talked fairly quietly with Mr. Bennett. I caught only glimpses of the conversation. I picked up key words like 'first wife,' 'kids,' 'houses,' and 'money.' I was able to fill in the color.

He chopped his way around the course for what I could only guess was an 85. We finished up the round with his handing me $7 as he mumbled something that sounded like, 'Thanks, son,' and headed to the clubhouse.

The magic seemed to be gone.

Chapter 15

'Yeeeeeerrrrrr Out!'

Boston's Rick Burleson slid awkwardly into second and twisted his ankle. He lay in the dirt for a minute or two before limping his way out of the game. Our seats at the Indians' game were so good that we could hear the umpire's every call, which was saying something, considering the cavernous expanses of Municipal Stadium. The stadium had been built near downtown on the shores of Lake Erie for the city's failed attempt to attract the 1932 Olympics.

My reaction when we got inside was 'It's that new?' The place was a dump. Faded gray paint chips fell from the ceiling; rusting I-beams obstructed views; huge yellowing porcelain troughs served as urinals. The wooden fold-down seats were ridiculously uncomfortable and had no less than 15 coats of old paint topped off with a demi-glaze of perma-grime.

The Indians shared the stadium with the Browns. With a capacity of over 80,000, it was far too immense for the intimate pastime of baseball. No more than 8,000 were in attendance that Tuesday night. I felt like I should have introduced myself to the few dedicated souls seated near us. And we were in the good seats. Out in the nether regions of the outfield, there was no sign of human life form.

Mr. G had offered us the seats while we were hanging around the first tee waiting for another loop.

'Boys, Mr. Booth just gave me four box seats for the Tribe game tonight. They're his company's seats, tenth row, first base side.' Mouse and I jumped at the chance. I had never been to a professional sporting event before, and I had been following the Indians' dismal season all summer.

'You know, boys,' harkened Mr. G with a sparkle in his eye, 'I remember one weekend back in the 50's when the Yankees were in town. Al Lopez, was the Indians' manager at the time. Well, he brought out Yogi Berra and Phil Rizzuto to play at Westwood. I caddied for both of them, even though I was a die-hard Tribe fan. Not bad golfers. They gave me $20 plus two tickets to the game that night.'

That was at least the third time I had heard Mr. G tell that story, but I was glad to hear it again this time.

We needed a ride down to the stadium, so Mouse gave two seats to his brother Paul, who had just gotten his driver's license. He brought along Rickles.

We got to our seats just as the Indians' pitcher finished up his warm-ups in the top of the first.

'Okay, who's going for the first brewski run?' asked Rickles.

'Um, I'll just take a Coke,' I parried nervously.

'No way, skirt-boy. You're having a brewski.'

'How are we gonna get beer? We're not old enough to drink.'

'They serve anyone at the stadium. As long as you're old enough to walk, you're old enough to drink at the stadium.'

'I'll take one,' said Mouse.

'Me too,' said Paul, 'and get some foot longs too. Mouse, give Rickles some cash.'

It wasn't that I didn't want to try my first beer. I was intrigued by what it would taste like, what it would feel like to be drunk. But I was terrified of getting caught, and drinking so openly in public, especially so obviously underage, seemed like a recipe for disaster.

To take my mind off of my impending arrest and inevitable strip search, I focused on the game. 'Who's pitching?'

'Wayne Garland,' said Mouse. 'This guy has killed the organization.'

'You ain't kidding. We're paying him millions – and look at this guy,' chimed in Paul. 'Even I could hit him.'

Just then, the lead-off man hit a shot up the middle. The crowd began booing.

'Garland, you stink!'

'Give back some of that money, Wayne!'

With the sparse crowd, each yell pierced clearly through the night air.

After two more hits and Boston's first run, Rickles returned with our vittles.

'Aw, man. I wanted ketchup on mine, not mustard,' complained Paul.

'Are you kidding?' said Mouse. 'The mustard here is the best in history. Kevin, you've got to try this mustard.'

'Ketchup is the greatest invention in history,' asserted Paul.

We all pondered that for a moment.

'So, better than the airplane?'

'Yes.'

'Better than the printing press?'

'Definitely.'

'Better than the wheel.'

He paused. 'Yes.'

'You're an idiot.'

'I'm going up and wiping this crap off and putting on some ketchup.'

I looked around, slouched down and sneaked my first sip out of the 24-ounce beer cup. It tasted terrible. At first. But after a few more swigs, it started to go down more smoothly. The foot long was the best hot dog I'd ever had. The bun was stale, but the brown mustard indeed was heavenly, like no mustard I'd ever had before.

Garland finally retired the side, but not before Butch Hobson and Fred Lynn crossed the plate for Boston to give them a 2-0 lead. Cleveland sent up Rick Manning, Duane Kuiper and Bobby Bonds in the top of the first to face Dennis Eckersley. The former Indian summarily dismissed them in order.

I was a quarter done with my beer, and I didn't understand why I felt a little light-headed; surely I couldn't be tipsy after only six ounces. I began to relax and was less afraid of being arrested by the stadium cops. I sat back and began to appreciate a bit of the elusive charm of the old place. When the Indians started a mini-rally in the bottom of the second, a guy sitting a mile away in the bleachers thumped an Indian war-drum. I followed the lead of Mouse and

Paul who grabbed two empty seats behind them and banged them down in unison with the drum. It didn't help. Tom Veryzer grounded into a double play to end the inning.

'So Wichita, how's caddying been treating you?' asked Paul.

'It's okay. It was a little tough going at first, but I'm getting the hang of it a little better.'

'I hear Booth wants you to caddie for him in the club championship,' he said with a laugh.

'Yeah, I heard you pushed him in the lake,' said Rickles. 'Good going.'

'Who is going to caddie for him?'

'I don't know. All of the Senior Caddies are getting snagged by other members. I heard the other day that Todd is caddying for Finnegan, and Kovach is caddying for Holland.'

'I hear the Wichita Kid wants to caddie for Sloan in the club championship.'

'CRACK.' Dwight Evans sliced a ball high up in the air in foul territory. As it reached its apex, it began curving into the stands in our direction. Half way down, it looked like it was laser-guided to zero in right at me. I always wondered what I would do if a big league ball headed my way. I had imagined making a brilliant, barehanded grab that would win me the favor of the admiring crowd. Now that I was in the actual situation, with the ball gaining increasing acceleration, I abandoned all hopes of bravery and cowered out of the way. I would have had to fight Rickles, who was standing next to me and elbowing everyone out of the way to get his hands on the ball.

'SLAP!' The hard leather of the ball smacked Rickles directly in the palms of his cupped hands and skipped two rows back. It rattled around the seats before coming to rest next to an old woman, who calmly reached down to pick up her souvenir.

'Oh, crap,' Rickles yelled as he inspected his stinging hands.

'Rickles, you shoulda had that. What happened?'

'I think my hand is broken,' he whined.

'How did you not catch that one, Rickles?'

'I think my hand might actually be broken.'

'Wichita, that actually was hit right at you. Did you even make a play on it?'

'Yeah, I was right there. Rickles just out-jumped me.' I felt a little cowardly, but since I'd escaped physical pain, I felt smart more than anything. Why was it such a big deal to catch a foul ball – especially when you could just walk into a store and buy one?

Rickles went up to find some ice for his hand and came back with another round of beers.

'This should ease the pain.'

Boston was in the middle of another rally. Rice doubled and Yastrzemski homered. The Bosox were up 6-0. Garland was long gone, replaced by Dan Spillner.

'So I heard Tool got Sloaned the other day,' said Rickles.

I sipped my beer.

'Man, if that weirdo ever did that to me, I'd punch the crap out of him,' said Paul. 'I'd kill him.'

'Did he really get Sloaned?' asked Mouse.

'That's what I heard,' said Rickles.

'I swear, I've never actually talked to anyone who got Sloaned. It's always some Spook you hear of, or some guy who doesn't caddie anymore. It's always second-hand; I wonder if it's all bull.'

'Kev, you caddied for Sloan a few weeks ago. He do anything to you?'

'No.'

The bat cracked the ball and Buddy Bell muffed the routine grounder.

'Bell, you suck!' yelled Rickles.

I was off the witness stand.

We left the game before it ended with the Indians losing by 2 runs. When I got up for the first time, I stumbled over one of the seats.

Outside the stadium a limo sat idling just outside of Gate B. Paul dared his younger brother to open the back limo door and climb in. Mouse was always quick to try to gain the respect of his brothers, so he easily accepted the dare. The beer he'd had didn't hurt either.

With us trailing slightly behind, Mouse casually walked up to the limo and opened the door. As he began to sit down, he feigned surprise and said to the occupant, 'Oh, I'm sorry, I thought this was mine.'

He jumped out, slammed the door shut and looked at us like he had seen a ghost.

'It's Rick Burleson. Oh, my God, it's Rick freakin' Burleson! He got hurt earlier in the game, so he must be just leaving the park on his own. His ankle looked all wrapped up.'

'Well…go get his autograph!' ordered Paul after he regained his breath from laughter.

Mouse took a deep breath and opened the limo door again.

'Excuse me, Rick, I mean, Mr. Burleson—'

'Get the hell out of here, you little brat!'

Mouse jumped back and slammed the door. We all ran about a 100 yards before collapsing in laughter.

By the time we reached the car, the alcohol had fully saturated my bloodstream, and my body was feeling numb. I slumped down in the velvet back seat of the Cutlass and closed my eyes. My last conscious thought before passing out was: How on earth did Mouse recognize what Rick Burleson looked like?

'Wichita, wake up! We're home.'

'Wichita! Wichita!'

'Wake up, you little drunk. Get the hell out of the car.'

In a fog, I stumbled toward Mouse's house, where I had arranged to spend the night. I braced myself against the wall as I made my way down the long main hallway, putting more and more of my weight against the wall with each step. Suddenly my reliable wall gave way. The basement door flung open with a bang. My shoulder hit the first wooden step, followed by my face, then my hips. My feet cart-wheeled into the air, which only increased my velocity toward the basement floor.

'Kevin, where'd you go,' cried out Mouse from the first floor.

'Mouse, what was that?' I heard Maureen call out.

'I'm just down here,' I replied casually.

'Down there? Why the heck are you down there?'

'I was just getting up.'

I checked myself out. Nothing seemed broken. Mouse and Maureen helped me off the basement floor.

'I've got him,' said Maureen to Mouse when we reached the top of the steps.

Maureen put her arm around my waist and led me to the couch in the living room. She stroked my hair after she put a blanket over me.

I looked straight into her green eyes. 'Maureen, I'm so sorry for what happened in the pro shop fire.' I slurred a little more than I had hoped. 'I tried to find a way out for us, I really did, but when the back door was locked, I panicked. I'm so sorry.'

'It's okay, Kevin. Mouse already explained it, and I've thought a lot about it. I forgive you.' She gave me a soft kiss on the forehead. 'Good night.'

I kept my eyes closed and fell asleep in seconds.

I awoke the next day flat on my back, arms crossed on my chest like a corpse that had been prepped for a wake. If only I felt that good. My head felt like it would explode with every heartbeat. My

241

mouth tasted like someone had inserted a dead rodent in it during the night. I tried to figure out what terrible thing I had done to my body. The world was spinning, and I immediately needed to throw up. The bushes in front of Mouse's house would have to do.

Throwing up was second nature to me, but this was different. This was a gut-wrenching, full-body, toes-through-your-throat heave. And, after all remaining beer, bile and footlong remnants had been expelled, came the dry heaves. And more dry heaves. And more dry heaves. I replayed the night in my mind to be sure I hadn't been hit by a bus.

Despite all that, I feel pretty good. Because Maureen had forgiven me.

'How was the game last night, dear?' My Grandma intercepted me as I tried to shuffle by the kitchen. 'It was a good thing you made plans to stay at your friend's house last night with the game going into extra innings.'

'Looks like it was quite an ending,' my Grandpa said as he studied the Plain Dealer. 'That Buddy Bell is some player.'

'Yes, quite an ending.'

The front page featured a picture of a triumphant Buddy Bell crossing the plate.

'Can I make you some breakfast?'

'I'm fine. Maybe some juice, thanks.'

'Thanks.' I sipped the juice. 'I think I'm going to crawl back into bed.'

'Are you feeling alright?'

'I'm fine. Just a little tired.'

I slept until noon and lay in bed listening to silence until 1:00. I pulled myself together, had some water to rehydrate myself and headed to the course. I picked up a nine-holer for Mr. and Mrs. Keegan in a cart. The first time I tried to run, I became short of breath and got a side-splitter in my ribs. I didn't try anything but a short jog the rest of the way. I barely spoke a word the entire round. I was very happy when the round was over. I had made it through the afternoon. I was only hours away from bedtime and a new day.

Mr. Morgan called to me as I walked back to the caddie yard.

'Kevin, how are you doing today? Did you just finish up a round?'

'Yes, with Mr. and Mrs....Yep, just finished up.'

He was dressed for dinner in blue slacks and a yellow sport coat.

'I think I mentioned it to you, but I'm going to make a run at the club championship this year.'

'No, I don't think you told me that.'

'Didn't I? I thought I mentioned it our last time out. Anyway, it's been a few years, but I thought what the heck.'

'Great.'

'So has anyone snagged you yet.'

'For what?'

'The club championship. You want to caddie for me in it?'

'Sure,' I was downright giddy.

'Great. I told you you've been my good luck charm this year. The qualifier is next Saturday. I don't know what time we go off, but the tee times will come out on Wednesday. It should be between 8:00 and 8:30. Sound good?'

'Sounds great.'

'Okay, I'll see you then,' he turned toward the clubhouse to catch up with his wife.

I couldn't believe what had just happened. I was sure that no one would believe me. It gave me a burst of energy. I rode home, choked down a couple forkfuls of food and crawled into bed. Not such a bad day after all.

Chapter 16

It was about 5:30 on a Saturday evening. I already had done a loop that morning and had spent the hot afternoon playing Caddie Golf with Howie. God, it was hot. He and I decided to go over to the first tee to see if we could pick up a quick nine hole round, which would not only put some money in our pockets but also meant that we would be the first caddies out the next day. He hung around the tee for a half hour, and just when we had decided to give up, Mr. Henson and his gang came around the corner of the club house.

'This is going to be great,' said Howie. 'I caddie for these guys all the time.'

'Howie!' said Henson. 'You got me this afternoon?'

'I don't think either of us have a choice.' Henson smiled at that. He looked like he had been a linebacker in high school.

I was assigned to Mr. Wilson, who looked like he did all of Henson's homework for him in high school.

'Okay, Wichita,' said Howie as the players warmed up on the tee. '2-dollar Nassau, auto-presses, full handicaps, camels and snakes, bingos on the par threes.'

'Howie, what the heck are you talking about?'

Howie stared at me in pity. 'Okay, we'll play something simple – something your feeble Oklahoman mind can understand.'

'Kansas.'

'How do you play that?'

'I'm from Kansas, not Okla—'

'Same difference. Let's bet $1 a hole. You have your member, Wilson. And I'll take Henson, against him. Wilson's a 15 handicap. Henson's a 17. So I get strokes on number 8 and 15. You can press at any time when you're down.'

'I guess that's okay. I can't lose much money, can I?'

'No, a couple of bucks either way. If you've got any questions, I'll teach you as you go along.'

From the first tee shots I feared I had made a sucker's bet with Howie. Mr. Henson used all of his 250 lbs to crush the ball 290 yards. Mr. Wilson hit his barely 230. I felt better on the second shot when Mr. Wilson hit his ball 200 yards and Mr. Henson hit his 20, into a sand trap. Mr. Henson's ugly swing didn't work well in the sand. Mr. Wilson ended up taking the hole.

Howie and I made our way to the forecaddie spot on the second hole.

'Did you see Henson in that sand trap back there?' said Howie. 'I told him he looked like a beached whale.'

'You said that to him!?!' I replied.

'Sure, we always joke like that with each other.'

Mr. Wilson teed off, safely in the fairway. Mr. Henson teed his up.

Mr. Henson popped his ball up in the air short of where we stood about 140 yards away. 'I got it!' yelled Howie as he charged in on the ball. Like Rick Burleson, he waved off the would-be infielders as he got under the ball. He raised his imaginary glove and at the last second let the ball land safely behind him. Mr. Henson subtly flipped him the bird, but he was laughing.

On the next hole Mr. Henson cranked his ball deep into the gully on the right. Howie dutifully ran down the steep, wooded hill to find the ball. He emerged a few minutes later out of breath and motioned to the golfers, who had just left the tee, that the ball was out of bounds. Mr. Henson had to borrow a ball from Mr. Wilson and go back to the tee for what would be his third shot.

'What happened there, Howie?' he muttered when he finally caught up to the group. 'My balls do not go out of bounds.'

'I saw it land on the other side of the creek, but when I got down there I couldn't find it. The weeds are real thick down there.'

'You should always keep a spare, son. You should have known better.'

Mr. Henson's erratic game was working in my favor. After three holes, I was up $2.

'Press,' said Howie as we reached the 4th tee.

'What's that mean again?'

'Basically, we have another bet starting now for $1 a hole. Another way of looking at it is that we are playing each hole now for $2. With the way Henson is playing, that's good news for you.'

Mr. Henson's awful play continued for the next few holes.

He pulled his drive on the 5th deep into the trees.

Howie called out 'Jack Martin,' but it did no good. Rather than try to punch out on his second shot, he decided to pound the ball through the grove of trees and pray that it didn't hit anything. He took out his 5 wood and swung as hard as he could. He smacked the ball well, but it hit the center of a tree trunk 15 feet in front of us, and came back at him traveling 100 mph. With his hands gripping the club up near his head on the follow through, he instinctively caught the ball an inch from his face. The whole thing happened in about 0.2 seconds.

'Oh my God,' he said in shock, 'that almost killed me. Oh my God, that's the best catch I've ever made.'

On the next hole, Mr. Henson popped his tee shot nearly straight in the air. As he followed through, he began to sprint as fast as he could to the front of the tee. Forty feet later, with his free hand extended, still in a full sprint, he caught the ball as it fell out of the sky.

'Now that is the best catch I've ever made.'

'You have the golf game of a cartoon character,' remarked Mr. Wilson.

Mr. Henson looked at Howie, 'Did you see that? Why aren't you more excited?'

Howie hesitated at first, but then confessed, 'Because you're playing like, well, Elmer Fudd. Please don't tell Mr. G. I'm sure that he would fire me – again – if he found out, but Wichita here and I are betting on you two, and I'm losing my shirt.'

Mr. Henson smiled broadly. 'So how far down are we?'

'I'm 4-Down on the main bet, 3-Down on the press.'

'You've only pressed once, huh? I thought you'd have more confidence in me. Well, press him again, Howie!' he said grandly as he stepped up to the tee, 'I'm feeling a comeback settling in.'

'Press!'

Mr. Henson stepped up, spanked his drive down the middle of the fairway and slapped Howie five.

'Why do I feel like this isn't the first time you two have done this routine?' I muttered.

For the next three holes, Mr. Henson was a new golfer -- a good golfer. He at least temporarily lost the extra hitch in his swing and actually gained some touch around the green. I suddenly found myself down $2.

'Hey, guys,' Henson said as he looked up at the sky, 'this is too much fun to quit now. We had only planned on playing nine, but is everyone up for another nine?'

'Sounds good to me,' Howie chimed in.

Being on the western side of the Eastern time zone, Cleveland doesn't begin to get dark until just after 9:00 in the summer. I really didn't think we could finish in time, but I didn't really have much choice. I had to get my mind readjusted to walking nine more holes.

'Um, Howie, this is getting a little out of hand. Can we, like, cancel the betting, and I'll just pay you the $2?' I pleaded as Mr. Wilson and Mr. Henson stopped off into the halfway house.

'Hmmm, let me think about that, Wichita...No. What you can do is press the bets if you want.'

'I think $3 a hole is enough.'

The competition was more balanced on the back nine. Mr. Wilson only lost two more holes by the 16th, so I found myself down $8 to Howie, but the sky had gotten darker and darker.

I gave Mr. Wilson his driver and walked ahead of the group to forecaddie on the 16th. Mr. Wilson stepped to the tee and slapped his drive over my head and into the woods. I ran deep into the trees and finally found it next to the trunk of a tree. I stood there all alone in the silence of the woods with my conscience. I stared at the white golf ball against the dark bark of the tree, deciding what to do next.

Could I do it? Heck, Howie's been cheating all round. Mr. Wilson might even expect it from me. I chose to cross over to the Dark Side. A rush of adrenaline darted through my limbs as I dropped the towel, then reached down and picked up the Top Flite. I didn't move it very far; I couldn't wait to get rid of the hot potato before anyone caught me. He still had a difficult shot, but I did save him a stroke.

My heart was pounding when Mr. Wilson reached the ball. Was I too obvious? Would they report me to Mr. G? Would I be fired? Would I ever find another job again?

If Mr. Wilson had any inkling, he didn't let on. For all he knew, his ball had landed right where it was.

'Ooo, boy. This isn't good.' He tested the lie and surveyed the line to the green.

I wanted to yell, 'Well, you're still in the trees, but if I hadn't helped you out, you'd still be up against that tree.' He knocked the ball into the fairway and saved his par. The crime wasn't worth the angst, especially if I wasn't going to get credit for it.

By the 18th hole, the twilight had faded and it was getting very difficult to see. The lights of the clubhouse cast a glow in the distance.

Mr. Wilson teed off. None of us saw it.

'Where'd it go?' asked Mr. Henson.

'I don't know, but it sounded good.'

'It sounded good. What, do you buy your clubs at Radio Shack?'

'Well it is pretty dark.'

After a short search we miraculously found both of their drives in the fairway, and we made our way to the green.

With the crickets chirping and the cool air forming dew on the grass, Mr. Henson stood over a 15-foot putt to win the hole. He rolled it in.

'Draino!' he yelled. 'Take that, Wichita!' My nickname had just made its inevitable jump to the member ranks.

I had just lost $14 to Howie. It was almost 10pm. I was tired and dejected, despite the extra tip Mr. Wilson gave me.

I went right to bed when I got home. I lay with the window open, listening to the sounds of the night. I flipped my body with my head at the foot of the bed so that I could see the streetlights and breath the cool night air. Each breath made me feel like I was part of the mysterious activity of the night. Headlights occasionally pushed their way through the tree branches. Who was in the car? Where were they going? A train sounded its horn as it cut its path through the suburbs. In the distance a siren blared.

* * *

The next morning, either the alarm didn't go off or I hit the snooze too many times, but I didn't wake up until 6:20. If I missed 6:30 roll call, my number would go down to the bottom of the list. Instead of being the first one out, I would have to wait around for hours. I threw my clothes on, ran downstairs, hopped onto my bike and pedaled as fast as I could.

When I got to the caddie house, I jumped off my bike, not even bothering to lock it up, and frantically ran through the caddie house. When I emerged into the sunlit caddie yard, Mr. G was at the podium and all the caddies were lined up against the fence. There was absolute silence and everyone turned to stare at me. It felt like a dream that I once had in which a crowd of people were all gossiping about me and immediately shut up when I walked into the room. I felt exposed, like I forgot to put my pants on or something.

'407,' said Mr. G softly.

'Yes, Mr. G. I'm sorry I'm a couple minutes late. Can I still get my number down? Please?'

'407, I just got done telling everyone.' He went on to explain to me briefly what had happened.

I stood there stunned.

'I'm sorry.' He picked up his clipboard and walked back into the caddie house. 'God dammit,' he said to no one in particular.

Through my teary eyes, I looked back at the boys lined up against the fence, still utterly silent. All of them stunned. Many of them had tears running down their faces. As they all continued to stare at me, I turned and in a daze walked back through the caddie house, got back on my bike and rode home, crying all the way.

The skid marks from the car's tires stretched for 20 feet along Detroit Road. No one knew at what point along those 20 feet the car hit Howie, but his body ended up on the sidewalk 40 feet from the car. His bike was a mangled pile of metal. They said he died instantly, as though that was supposed to make us feel better.

Howie's death crushed me emotionally and physically. I lay in my bed most of the day crying. I felt like I had the flu. My body shook; it felt brittle, like an arm or leg could break off at any moment. My entire reality had changed. Could it be possible that someone could be gone so quickly? I didn't deal very well with change, and this was the ultimate change. All my Mom's worrying about something bad happening, maybe she was right. This is what she was protecting me from, or better yet, what she was protecting herself from.

I had only known Howie for a couple of months, but I had seen him just about every day. For Christ sakes, I was the last one to see him alive. He spoke his final words to me.

I called up Mouse that night in the hopes that it would make me feel a little better. He was morose, but calm.

'What are people saying around the caddie yard?' I asked.

'It sucks. Everyone liked Howie. He was a good kid. Everyone is just bummed out.'

'I've never had anyone close to me die before. I've never felt like this.'

'Me neither. My neighbor across the street died of a heart attack while he was raking leaves a couple years ago. It was really weird. His body was just lying out there in the grass before someone finally called for an ambulance.'

The funeral was two days later. I rode to St. Christopher's on my bike, perhaps as a tribute to Howie, but also because I wanted to be alone. My Grandma tried to insist that she'd drive me there since I was in a sport coat and tie, but I won out in the end. The church was absolutely packed. About half of the attendees were from his grade school class; he obviously was as popular at school as he was in the caddie yard. The other half came from the caddie ranks.

Seeing the caddies in their street clothes, it hit me that these were their clothes, this was who they were. When they were at Westwood, it was just their summer job, a sidelight to the rest of their lives.

My eyes drifted during the funeral to the cavernous expanse of St. Christopher's Church. I tried to take my mind off the casket by visualizing a golfer hitting a ball from the back of the church toward the altar. How far would the ball ricochet against the marble? I could see the ball traveling through the air in my mind, could see the angle of the golf ball careening. I had seen thousands of golf strokes in the last couple of months. I was in another world. If I stood on the altar, what club would I need to hit the ball out of the stained-glass window high up on the wall. I mentally swung a 7-iron. Nope. Not enough loft. 8-iron? Not quite enough lift. It would need to be a 9-iron. In my mind, I moved around the church hitting balls at various targets or avoiding other impediments. That settled me down a bit. By the time we were ready to file out of the church, the tension in my body, in my stomach, had eased a bit.

'Let's go to Dunkin' Donuts to try to grab something to eat,' Mouse said to me as we walked into the bright sunlight.

'I'm not in the mood to have a donut.'

'So get something else.'

'What? Like a cup of coffee?'

'Where else we gonna go?'

'Fine. I'll sit with you.'

Mouse ordered us four chocolate-covered donuts and a large milk.

'How you doing?'

'I feel like crap. How about you?' I responded.

'About the same.'

'It was a nice service.'

'Yeah, it was. I was thinking about my neighbor, the one I told you about who died raking his leaves?'

'Yeah?'

'When he died, I read his death thingy in the paper, what do you call it?'

'An obituary?'

'Yeah. It talked about what a great guy he was, how much he was loved in the community. But the thing was, he was a jerk. He was always yelling at us to stay off his lawn. If a ball ever landed in his yard, he would take it and not give it back. It seems like whenever people die, people make them out to be saints or heroes or something. Why can't we be honest and just say what kind of person they really were?'

'So what should they have said about Howie?' I asked.

'Oh, I think everything they said was dead on. No, he was a great, great guy. He made me laugh more than anyone I've ever known. But I think it would have been more genuine if they also included that...that he picked his nose too much or that his hair was way too red.'

'That he had intestinal issues,' I added. We both laughed. It felt good to laugh again.

He took a bite of his donut. 'I don't know. It's a crappy, crappy thing to happen. I feel terrible for his family, I really do. I'm just shocked that he's gone. Holy crap.' He paused. 'At the same time, the last couple of days I've thought about how well I knew Howie. I had only met him a couple of months ago. I don't know, maybe it's the only thing I could think of that could make me feel better.'

I pondered this for a moment. I had never really had much of a conversation with Howie beyond caddying and the physics of a

Caddie Golf shot. I had never been to his house; I didn't know his parents; I had never even seen him outside of caddying. I didn't know what he wanted to do with his life. What goals, what dreams had his accident snuffed out? I didn't know what made him really happy, what made him scared.

I thought of Mouse too. Some of those same things could be said about my friendship with him. I knew a little about Mouse's family, and we had spent a lot of time together, but I didn't know a ton about him. The one thing I was sure about Mouse was that he was a good friend. Certainly, he was the best friend that I ever had.

'Yeah,' I responded. 'I kind of see what you mean. But Howie really was someone special. I think he's the first person to teach me not to take life too seriously. I'll always remember him for that. He truly was an idiot. A wonderful idiot.' I choked up a little, but tried to transition it into a laugh.

Mouse laughed, let out a sigh and took another bite of his donut. 'Here,' he tossed one in front of me, 'eat one of these.'

'I'm not that hungry. Thanks.'

'Come on, I know you're sad, but you've got to eat something. You're skinnier than a golf club. Eat. I never see you eat. What's wrong with you?'

I desperately wanted to tell him about my stomach, but I was terrified to. I had never told anyone, other than my Mom.

'Mouse,' I began, and then stopped.

'What? Is there something wrong with you?'

257

'Well, I've never told anyone this, but I've got this thing with my stomach.' Each word came out easier than the prior one. 'When I get nervous or upset about anything, I can't eat. Or I throw up.'

'That's a little weird,' he said matter of factly.

'I've been like this as long as I can remember. It sucks. It really sucks. I always have to watch what I'm eating or if I'm going to make a fool out of myself by throwing up, like, in front of a lot of people'

'That's no big deal,' he said. 'When I get nervous, my palms sweat a lot. I was playing a basketball game last year, and when the game got tight, I had trouble holding onto the ball because it was this slippery leather ball and my hands were all slippery. I get it.'

It wasn't the same thing, but I didn't say that to Mouse. It felt great telling someone for the first time. It made it so much less of a monumental issue that I was afraid people would persecute me for.

I hopped back on my bike to ride home. I pedaled slowly with my head down, thinking about Howie. Suddenly my bike slammed into the rear bumper of a parked car. I flew over the handlebars and landed safely on the trunk of the car. What an idiot. Luckily my bike was unharmed. I hoped that Howie saw that from heaven. It would have made him laugh.

My Grandma was in the kitchen finishing up lunch. 'How was the service?' she softly asked.

'Fine.'

'I'm just cleaning up here. Can I make you a fried bologna sandwich?'

258

I pondered the offer for a moment. People actually fried bologna? Shockingly, a fried bologna sandwich seemed perfect for the occasion. For the first time in a few days, my stomach was surprisingly settled.

'Sure. I'll have one.'

'I used to always make these for your Mom.'

She threw a pat of butter into a frying pan along with four slices of bologna, which transformed into little sombreros when they cooked. She put them on a single slice of white bread and rolled it up. It was delicious, kind of like a buttery hot dog, and it had the same strange soothing effect on my stomach.

Later that afternoon, I rode over to Westwood to see if there was anything going on. It was cool and windy. A thunderstorm had rolled in off Lake Erie about an hour before and cleared most everyone off the course. I wandered over to the first tee to see if there was anyone still around.

The area around the first tee was empty except for a sole, familiar figure practicing on the putting green.

'Hey, Kevin! How's my old friend?' Mrs. Sullivan said as she waved me over.

'Okay, I guess...Actually, I've been better.'

'Why? What's going on?'

'I don't know if you heard, but a friend of mine, Howie...' tears began welling up in my eyes and my voice shook, 'Howie was killed a couple of days ago. He was hit by a car.'

'Oh, Kevin, I'm so sorry. I heard some women talking about that in the locker room, but I didn't get any of the details. That's horrible. I didn't know you were friends with him.'

'Yeah, I obviously didn't know him until this summer, but we hung around a lot since I got here. He was the funniest kid I ever met.'

As I told Mrs. Sullivan more about Howie, about playing Caddie Golf with him, about caddying with him the night before his death, I began to feel a little back to my normal self. I began to see the light at the end of the tunnel, that my life might return to normal. As we talked, we took turns hitting putts with her club, handing it back and forth.

'My brother died of cancer last year.' She took a deep breath. 'He started having these sharp pains in the side of his stomach. By the time he took it seriously and had it checked out, the cancer had spread from his kidney to several other organs. He went from being a seemingly healthy, fit 40 year-old to being dead in less than six weeks.'

'Oh my God, that's terrible.'

'I had never had someone close die suddenly like that before -- you know, I had grandparents die of old age and such – but never...,' she paused, 'never suddenly like that. It hit me – all of us – very hard. Trust me that everything is going to be okay. It's not easy to hear, but death is a part of life.'

Just as she finished her sentence, Mrs. Sullivan holed out a 40-foot putt. She gave me a warm smile as it dropped into the cup. Then she looked me in the eyes and said, 'It's going to be okay.'

I smiled, thanked her and walked away. It was the last real conversation I would have with her all summer. Although I had surrendered her to the Senior Caddies earlier in the summer, she was there when I needed her.

Chapter 17

The qualifying round of the club championship was like any other Saturday morning. Mr. Morgan played with his regular cronies. Even though he had to play from the blue championship tees, he outdrove them on every hole.

The lowest 8 scores on the day played their way into the tournament brackets. I figured he would need a score no higher than 76 to make it in. He started out a bit rusty but made two up-and-downs from off the green on the first two holes to save par. Overall, he seemed pretty relaxed and put together his typically steady, if somewhat boring, 38 on the front nine. The back nine was much of the same – hit it on or near the green in regulation, try to make par. He dropped three bogies onto the scorecard on the back nine, and he stepped up to the 18th needing to make par to come in at 76, which would leave him on the bubble of making it to the next round. He hit his drive straight down the middle, stiffed a 5-iron to within 15 feet, and sank the putt for a birdie and a 75.

A small crowd gathered outside of the former pro shop as T.Rex posted the scores on a large poster board.

'How'd we do out there today?' T.Rex said to the group. I kept my head down so that he wouldn't notice me.

'Not bad for an old man,' said Mr. Morgan as he handed the scorecard to T.Rex.

'What'd you shoot?' asked Booth with a gin and tonic in hand.

'What did I have, Kevin? 75?'

'Yes, 75.'

'75?' Booth shot a look over to Mr. Holland, who was one of the top golfers at Westwood.

'From the blue tees?' blurted Holland.

Mr. Morgan nodded and walked over to his bag.

'75,' Booth repeated to Holland or to no one in particular.

'How did that guy post a 75?' said Holland. 'My wife hits it further than that old coot does. He's gotta be like a 12 or 14 handicap.'

'He's a 7,' T.Rex chimed in without looking at them. T.Rex pulled out his magic marker and scrolled Mr. Morgan's 75 in an upper grouping just below Booth's 76 and Holland's 73.

'I wouldn't worry,' Booth recovered. 'If he's in the hunt, Walter's true colors will show. He's never really rebounded from those collapses several years ago. Five times he had the lead going into the final holes, and he lost the match every time. Especially at his age now, I don't see him as much of a threat.'

'75,' Holland repeated.

* * *

It was an uncharacteristically chilly day for early August, in the high 60's, sunny with cumulous clouds above. The format for the remainder of the club championship was match play, rather than stroke play, which meant the goal was to win more holes head-to-head than your opponent. The total number of strokes was irrelevant. If Mr. Morgan lost the first hole by 3 strokes, for example, tied the second hole and then won the third by one stroke, the match would be even.

With the 7th seeding in the tournament, we were matched against Mr. Finnegan, who carried a 1-handicap and had won two of the last three club championships. He ran a few successful Ford dealerships in the area. I had seen him a couple of times on TV touting his low, low, looowww prices. His hair was as perfect as it appeared on TV. A gale-force wind would be no match for his Teflon dome.

'So you're going to tee it up one last time, huh, Walter?' Mr. Finnegan said as he greeted Mr. Morgan on the tee. He wore a red-striped shirt and brown Sansabelts.

'Hopefully, not the last time,' Mr. Morgan replied with a coy smile.

'Indeed. Well I'm honored as always to be playing with the great Walter Morgan.'

'Thanks, Gary.'

Mouse's big brother Todd caddied for Mr. Finnegan. He glanced down and acknowledged me, 'Wichita.'

I nodded.

Since Finnegan had the lower handicap, he was the first to tee up the ball in our twosome. He worked quickly, no practice swing. He took one brief look down the fairway and put his short, compact swing on the ball, which started out low and seemed to rise half-way through its flight as though it hit a second booster.

'Nice ball, Gary,' said Mr. Morgan. He remained a bit subdued.

265

Mr. Morgan teed up his ball and took an extra deep breath before addressing it. His swing was deliberate, less fluid than normal, and he pushed the drive deep into the right rough. My stomach sank a half-inch, and the four of us silently marched off the tee.

Mr. Finnegan handed Todd his driver, and with military efficiency Todd cleaned it off, put the headcover back on and returned the club to the bag. I had never seen him or any Senior Caddie carry singles before.

Match play had a different feel to it. Aside from it being unusual to be in a two-some on a busy Saturday morning, the intensity was palpable. There was no chit-chat, either with Mr. Morgan or with Todd. Each player stood in the way of the other player's aspirations to advance to the next round.

I panicked for a few seconds when I couldn't find the ball at first, but I finally found it buried in a patch of crabgrass near of grove of young elms that separated the first hole from the second. Mr. Morgan pulled out his Cobra Baffler and whacked away at the ball. It lamely made its way to the edge of the fairway. He managed an uninspired bogey 6 to Mr. Finnegan's par 5. We were 1-Down after 1 hole.

Both men teed off on the next hole. Mr. Finnegan hit his ball into the middle of the fairway. Mr. Morgan sliced it again into the right rough. Mr. Finnegan marched off the tee. Mr. Morgan stared at the ground as he walked.

'Looks like the old man's out of his league, Wichita' said Todd from under his tattered Indians cap as he walked away. 'It's too bad, too. I like Mr. Morgan.'

Mr. Morgan had a good lie, but a tree stood in his path to the green.

'Do you think I can make it over that tree?'

'Do you think you can get it up that quick?'

'That's what I'm asking you.'

'I don't know, it's pretty tall. I don't think it's worth the risk.'

'I think I can.' He pulled out a 5-iron.

The ball rocketed up toward the birch. Its initial trajectory made it look like it would clear the tree, but it lost velocity too quickly and clipped a branch near the top, caromed to the left and fell on the edge of the fairway. He didn't look at me when he handed the club back.

Mr. Morgan parred the third hole, but Mr. Finnegan birdied it. 3-Down after 3. I began to wonder whether he was out of his league.

Hole 4 – par three over a ravine. Mr. Finnegan put his ball in the middle of the green. Mr. Morgan matched him with a shot that sailed directly over Finnegan's ball and dead-stopped ten feet beyond as though the green were made of velcro. He pursed his lips and gave his fist a slight pump.

The pin was on the left side of the green, so both had 30+ foot putts. Mr. Finnegan lagged his putt perfectly, leaving himself with a tap-in par. Mr. Morgan took an extra minute to line up his putt.

'Kevin, how many inches do you see on the break?'

I surveyed the undulations of the green. 'About five to the left.'

He stepped up and hit what looked like the perfect putt. It broke exactly as I had envisioned and headed toward the cup. But it broke an extra inch in the last foot and slid by the hole; and didn't stop.

'Sit down! Sit down!'

The ball hit a slight down slope and finally rested ten feet past the hole. He missed the come-backer. 4-Down after 4.

'Kevin, I'm tense. Have you ever seen me this tense? I'm tense.'

I shook my head.

'This isn't much fun,' he continued. 'Let's stop caring so much and have some fun.'

'Sounds like a good plan.'

Mr. Finnegan had other plans. He and Mr. Morgan tied the next hole with a pair of bogeys. Mr. Finnegan drained a 15-footer on Hole 6 to match Mr. Morgan's par on #6.

'He can't keep this up, can he?' Mr. Morgan mumbled to me as we walked down the path to the 7th tee.

On the par 5 7th, Mr. Morgan found himself in a greenside sand trap while Mr. Finnegan was on safely in three. We were staring 5-Down in the face.

I handed Mr. Morgan his sand wedge as he entered the bunker. He adjusted his stance so that the club didn't hit any branches on the backswing. He finally settled in. Adjusted his feet. Brought the club back. Checked the pin. You could have heard a pine needle drop.

He took the club back a final time…

'CAW! CAW!'

An large crow swooped down across the green.

Miraculously Mr. Morgan stopped his swing and doubled up laughing.

After we had a good laugh, he regained his composure and, still smiling, addressed the ball.

A cloud of sand and ball blasted out of the trap. The sand fell gently onto the green, while the ball continued to float through the air. It zeroed in closer and closer to the pin until it slam-dunked into the hole.

We both screamed. I expected the crowd to erupt like a PGA tournament, but it was just the four of us; even Mr. Holland had to admire the shot.

'Now that's fun,' Mr. Morgan yelled to me.

Mr. Finnegan gave his long putt a run but didn't come close, and we left the green 3-Down through 7.

As Finnegan climbed the tee on 8, a stiff breeze kicked up and a tuft of hair on the right side of his head improbably blew out of place. He tightened up a bit on his drive and blocked it to the right toward the country club pool. It landed between two mounds in the right rough, commonly known as Dolly Parton's Grave. His next shot didn't quite clear the second breast, shot up in the air and landed on the edge of the fairway quite a distance from the green. He bogeyed and Mr. Morgan took the hole. They tied the 9th and we finished the front nine 2-down.

'How you feeling?' he asked me as he handed me a Pepsi at the turn.

'Good, I think we're doing real good,' I responded, meaning we no longer were in jeopardy of embarrassing ourselves.

'I think so too. Let's keep it together on the back nine and I think we can win this one.'

I took a quick swig of Pepsi.

They tied the 10th. Mr. Morgan took the 11th by sinking a 30-foot putt, and I started to believe that we had a chance, but he gave it right back on the 12th by missing a 3-foot putt. We were back to 2-down heading into the long par-5 13th. Perhaps Mr. Finnegan wanted to take advantage of his superiority off the tee to try to put Mr. Morgan away. He indeed hit it far, but with a little too much right hand, and he pulled it into the pine trees on the left side. Morgan stepped up and hit it into the fairway. I didn't even look over the fence for the Sambuca Woman. I had no time for her today. Four shots later, we were only down 1. They played the next three holes even.

'Just two more holes to go, Walter. You're up again.'

Mr. Morgan hit his 9-iron cleanly onto the 17th green. Mr. Finnegan followed suit, but was a little further away. Mr. Morgan routinely two-putted, while Mr. Finnegan missed his second putt to drop the hole.

'We're all even coming into the final hole. Perhaps I underestimated you, Walter.'

'Perhaps.' He tried to contain a smile as he pulled his driver out of the bag.

Both men hit it into the fairway. Mr. Morgan was about 160 yards away. Mr. Finnegan was about 20 yards beyond him. The pin was in the back left corner of the green, which was well-protected by traps.

Mr. Morgan paused for a moment with his eyes on the green and his right hand holding his 5- and 6-irons. I was ready to burst waiting for him to solicit my input. He silently pulled out his 6-iron and hit it safely onto the fat part of the green. I would have told him to hit the 5.

With Mr. Morgan safely on the green, Mr. Finnegan squared up to fire at the pin with a 9-iron. He blasted the ball high up into the air. It looked like it might never come down as it drifted directly in line with the pin.

'Get up,' urged Mr. Finnegan.

'Be enough,' coaxed Todd.

It eventually landed hard on the upslope just short of the apron. It bounced a couple feet in the air and landed on the edge. It sat there for a moment before it slowly took a revolution backwards, gained some steam down the slope and rolled into the trap.

Mr. Finnegan slumped his shoulders and slammed the club into the ground.

'Crap,' said Todd.

Mr. Finnegan couldn't convert the sandie. Mr. Morgan took the hole and the match.

* * *

The second round was the next day, and the brackets matched us up with Mr. Holland. He had only won one club championship a few years back, but with a 5 handicap was always in the hunt. He was a hefty man with a mustache and slicked-back hair. The bags under his eyes rivaled the size of his enormous golf bag, which was carried by Kovach. I stood at attention on the first tee. I tried to take up as much space as possible, but I was half the size of Kovach – actually closer to a third.

Mr. Holland was the first to tee up the ball in our twosome. His self-taught swing was swaying but consistent. He launched the ball high in the air toward the right side of the fairway. Mr. Morgan matched him with a drive down the left side of the fairway. They both hit the green in three, but Mr. Holland lipped out his par putt.

'It never broke,' he pleaded to Kovach.

Kovach let him vent for a few seconds and then exchanged his putter for his driver. 'We'll get 'em on the next one.'

But they didn't. Mr. Holland and Mr. Morgan matched each other on the next 6 holes. Mr. Morgan broke the stalemate by taking number 8 and hitting an amazing chip on 9 to go 3-Up at the turn. Holland played fairly well, but Morgan just played better.

He picked up two more holes on 11 and 13. After 14 it was all over; Mr. Morgan was up 5 with 4 holes to go. He crushed him.

Rather than play out the remaining holes, they headed back to the clubhouse. 'I think I just got my butt kicked.' Holland extended his hand to Mr. Morgan.

Kovach was not so cordial. He threw the bag onto his shoulder and stormed back to the clubhouse, muttering to himself.

The next thing to do was to wait out the result of the other match between Booth and Constable. Tool carried Booth's bag – a pair for the ages. Number 14 had Constable. Constable was an enigmatic sort. He played very rarely, at least at Westwood, barely spoke to anyone on the course and carried a 2 handicap. He also tipped incredibly well. He was known to pay $20 per round for his bag, whether it was singles or doubles. No one was quite sure what he did for a living, but it was assumed that he was pretty rich. Any loop with Constable had a mysterious quality to it. He never signed up for a tee time and whenever he showed up to play, word spread around the caddie yard immediately, and the jockeying to get him began.

Mr. Morgan and I waited silently next to the former pro shop for them to appear on the 18th. A small group including Mr. G and T.Rex, gathered to the side of the green. When the bobbing heads of the golfers emerged across the green horizon of the 18th fairway, I looked for any sign to tip off who was winning. Both 14 and Tool had their heads down as they chugged up the fairway 180 or so yards from the green. Booth and Constable both walked confidently. Constable was the first to stop walking. He picked up some blades of grass and tossed them into the air. He saluted the pin as he handled his irons. Finally, he selected his club. The ball landed in the thick rough a few feet off the fringe.

Booth was about 10 yards closer. He already had his club and wasted no time tomahawking the ball. It landed short but took a hard bounce and rolled up nicely onto the green. T.Rex provided a polite clap.

Constable fought the ball out of the thick rough, but not close enough. He two-putted for bogey. Booth two-putted for par.

It would be Mr. Morgan and Mr. Booth, Tool and me, the following Saturday for the club championship. My heart sank.

Tool knocked me with his shoulder as he walked by the following Tuesday morning. I took two steps back to keep from falling down.

'Oh sorry, Wichita Girl, I didn't see you there.' He shoved me again. 'You think that old fart you're caddying for has any chance against Booth on Saturday?'

I didn't answer. I was terrified.

He pushed me again and walked away.

Mouse and I were assigned to the same foursome of women starting their round off the 10th tee. Tool was in the group behind us.

'Why does Tool hate me so much?' I asked Mouse. 'I've never done anything to him, and he goes out of his way to scare me and make me miserable. I'm really sick of it.'

'I don't know what his deal is. He's definitely a jerk, but for some reason he's singled you out. The way I look at it, you can either let it bother you, or you can fix his bags.'

'You didn't.'

'Absolutely, while he was busy pushing you around, I was busy unclipping his straps.'

'But, Mouse, that's just going to get him madder at me. He's going to kill me. I'll be lucky to be alive for Saturday's match.'

'Don't worry. I'll take all the heat. He can't touch me. My brothers would kill him. We should be safely on the tee when the bags go smashing on the ground.'

'I feel sick.'

'I tell you what, think of it as a memorial to Howie. This is exactly the smart ass stuff that he would have done if Tool bothered him.'

'I miss him.' I choked back tears.

'I do too.'

As our women teed off, I kept my eyes on the ball while my ears focused for the impending sound of metal on concrete. But nothing came. I didn't dare look back at Tool. We made our way down the 10th fairway. Still nothing.

Forecaddying on the 11th, which paralleled the 10th, gave us a chance to view the situation. Tool made no sign that anything had happened.

'Do you think he figured it out and unfixed them?'

'Relax, sometimes it takes a hole or two.'

'He's going to kill me.'

Three holes later, still nothing.

'I can't take it any longer. Are those bag tag straps made of steel?'

'This is weird. Maybe he's smart enough to have figured it out. Probably not.'

'I doubt it, but maybe he did. I'm dead. This is the worst. Now he's going to think I fixed his bags and we won't even have the pleasure of witnessing it. Have I mentioned I'm dead?'

'Don't worry.'

By the 18th hole I had accepted defeat and moved on from thinking about Tool for the meantime. While the foursome putted out, I held the pin on the edge of the green. I looked back to see Tool 150 yards out at the edge of the sloping gully. Just as I put the pin back, his woman duffed her shot. Tool put the two bags on his shoulders. On his second step down the hill, both bags went. They slammed to the turf and Tool grabbed the empty straps. The clubs in both bags shot down the hill like snakes. The woods took the early lead out of the gate, but their headcovers slowed them down. The long irons took over and were the first to reach the bottom of the gully. It was a yard sale. Tool stood paralyzed with the empty bags at his sides. I race-walked off the green.

'The eagle has landed,' I mumbled to Mouse when I reached the next tee.

'No,' he said with a smile.

'Yep, down the hill.'

'No.'

'Yep.'

'Excellent.'

'I'm dead.'

For the next nine holes I focused on avoiding getting anywhere near Tool's group. When their hole paralleled ours, I stayed in the far side of the rough. When they reached a green behind us, I was quick to forecaddie. I didn't dare look their way.

After the round, I high-tailed it to the caddie yard. I had hoped to get paid and ride home before Tool finished up.

'Kev, I don't know what you're worried about,' said Mouse. 'I told you I'll take the heat.'

'I don't think I'll wait to find out if he buys that. Maybe he won't be as pissed off tomorrow. I'll catch you later.'

No such luck. I bumped right into Tool's chest as I left the caddie house to hop on my bike.

'So you think you're pretty funny, don't ya, Wichita Wuss?'

'Hey, it was all my doing,' Mouse jumped in. 'Kevin had nothing to do with it.'

'This is between me and him, Mouse,' Tool pushed Mouse away. 'Get out of my way.' He pushed his chest up against me. 'I'm tired of your crap, Wichita. You hear me? And I'm tired of your friends jumping in to protect you.'

I moved back a step. He moved his chest forward.

'Listen, Tool. What's your problem with me? What did I ever do to you?'

'What did you ever do to me? You've been a pain in my ass all summer.'

'What do you mean? You've been a jerk to me all summer.' My blood started to boil. 'You made me look like a fool when I Spooked. You shoved my face into the toilet. You shoved me into a bush. You fixed my bags. You've been bullying me all summer. Why?'

'Because you're a little wuss. I don't like you.' He pushed me again with his chest.

'Well I've had enough,' my voice began rising. 'Leave me alone!'

'Or what?' He shoved me again. 'Huh? You're gonna puke again? You're going to go home crying to your mommy and daddy?'

That flipped a switch inside of me.

'I said leave me alone!' I pushed him with all my might and released a flurry of punches to his face. I was a man possessed. Spit and snot flew out of my mouth and nose. Tears streamed out of my eyes. He put up his arms to protect himself, but he stumbled backwards. I kept punching and screaming 'Leave me alone!' until I was out of breath and out of energy. I looked up and Tool's lip was bleeding.

'What the hell's wrong with you, you freak?' he said as he pressed the back of his hand to his bleeding lip. 'My lip is bleeding.' He showed me his hand. 'Look what you did to me. I ought to kill you.'

I was still trying to catch my breath.

'Go…ahead…I don't…I don't care…anymore.'

Mouse was standing next to me speechless.

I stumbled over to my bike and hopped on. My legs were shaking and soon my whole body was. Tears streamed down my face as I pedaled home.

I took a few minutes to pull myself together before I opened the door to the apartment, but I was emotionally drained.

My Grandma met me at the door. 'Kevin, your Mom called. Wait – are you okay?'

'I'm fine, I just got roughed up a little playing basketball.'

'Well your Mom called. I don't know if it's a sign that things have gotten better or worse, but she wants you to come visit her.'

'When?'

'Tomorrow morning. We booked you on a flight to Wichita at 8:00. I started packing some of your things because I didn't know when you would be home, but you can finish up.'

'But…how long will I be gone?…I have the club championship on Saturday.'

'Well, that may have to wait. I don't know how long we'll be out there, but I can't imagine it'll be before Saturday.'

'But Mr. Morgan…wait, you guys are going too?'

'Yes, now go pack your things.'

'How did she sound? Is she doing okay? Did she say what she needed?'

'I don't know.'

Chapter 18

The taxi pulled up to the hospital in Wichita at about noon. It was my first time ever in a cab. The hospital seemed like a world away from Westwood. I felt like I was living in someone else's body for a day.

The red brick structure looked more like a college campus than a loony bin. It actually was pretty, with rolling lawns and stately oak trees. I hadn't eaten since dinner, and I felt dizzy climbing the entrance steps. My Grandpa gave the nurse at the front desk my mother's name. I analyzed her face for any sign of sympathy or concern, but she was a stone wall. After a brief, silent wait, another nurse led us down a burnt-red carpeted hall to Mom's room.

Mom sat feet-up watching TV when I peeked one eye around the door of her room. Her hair was a little longer and a bit grayer. Her hazel eyes were as piercing as ever. She had lost a little bit of weight in her angular face, but she was always pretty thin. I observed for a few more seconds before I revealed the rest of myself.

'Sweet bugs! You made it. I was so worried.' She hit a button, and Bob Barker disappeared from the TV screen. Mom shuffled over in her pink slippers. 'Oh my god, come here!' she said as she grabbed me tightly. Finally she pulled away. 'Kevin, I hardly recognize you. You look like you've grown 3 inches. Look at you, how much do you weigh?'

'I don't know, I know I was putting on some weight, but—'

She pulled me over to the bathroom and put me on the scale.

'112! That's with your shoes on, but still!' she said.

'Oh my gosh, I didn't know I had put on that much. I guess I haven't weighed myself in a couple weeks.'

I stepped off the scale. 'You look good too, Mom.' She did, but I noticed her hands were completely covered with gauze and bandages.

She held them up. 'It's okay; I just had kind-of a relapse. I'm doing a lot better. You should have seen me three weeks ago. I went into a bathroom, touched a toilet seat, and I didn't wash my hands for six hours. I eventually had to because I had to eat, but six hours.'

'I'm proud of you, Mom. I really am. So what happened then?' I nodded toward her hands.

'Oh, this is nothing. A week ago, there was a guy whose hand I touched when I was getting change in the gift shop they have here. I noticed that he had a band-aid on. That freaked me out…ooh, it freaked me out so much. I tried to be strong and ignore it, but who knows what diseases he has? I told myself I'd protect myself just this one time, so I came back and scrubbed my hands clean. You know the drill; I kept scrubbing. I scrubbed a little too much, and then I was afraid I had missed some spots. They put these bandages on to, you know, prevent some sort of infection. They're coming off tomorrow, and at least now I know I can do it – even if I do have some hiccups along the road. I think part of my problem recently is that I miss you so much, Sweetie. I'm so glad we're together again.'

'I miss you too, Mom. I can't believe I'm actually here. It's so good seeing you.'

'It's been pretty lonely here.' Her voice cracked, and a tear ran down her cheek when she turned her head. 'I thought it was the right decision to send you off for the summer. I mean, what other choice did we really have? But now that's all behind us. With you back here with me, and me checking out tomorrow, I figure we can make it back to Salina by late afternoon—'

'What?!? Mom, hold on. We're going back to Salina? Tomorrow?'

'Well, yes, Sweet Bugs.' She looked at me confusedly.

'I'm much better than I was, and school starts soon. Why'd you think I had you fly here?'

'I thought…I thought I was just visiting. I don't know what I thought.' The pit in my stomach grew deeper. I stared out the window.

'I hope the place in Salina is okay,' she continued. 'I've had Mr. Robbins, the apartment manager, check in on it every couple weeks or so to be sure no one has stolen our things. We're going to have a lot of cleaning to do.'

'What are you going to do? For a job?' I asked, still staring out the window.

'I don't know. Maybe the bank will give me my job back, or any job, but we're running out of money, and me being in this place isn't helping out much. I'll find something; I have to. We'll be okay. We're together. We'll be okay. This place has helped me a lot. I can get back on track. Once we get back to Salina we'll start figuring it out. I can find a doctor there.'

'What about going back to Cleveland?'

'Cleveland?' She burst out with a laugh. 'Yes, we could both move in with your grandparents.' She shivered.

'Mom, I think you should know that they're here.'

'What do you mean?'

'They're here.'

Her eyes shot wide open. 'You mean here, in Wichita? What are they doing…'

'I mean here, outside the door.'

My grandparents tip-toed into the room with unconvincing smiles. Mom looked over and didn't move a muscle. They stopped about half-way. 'Hi, darling, it's so good to see you. It's been way too long.'

Mom still didn't say a word. After a couple of seconds, she got up and ran to the bathroom.

She emerged a few minutes later.

She took a deep breath. 'Hi, Mom. Hi, Dad.' She walked over to them and gave them cordial hugs. 'I'm sorry. I was surprised, very surprised to see you. You look good.'

'So do you, honey.'

'I don't know about that.'

A long pause.

'So.'

'So.'

'So, what are you guys doing here?' my Mom asked.

'We came to visit you.'

'Well…why?'

My Grandma took a deep breath. 'We wanted to make sure Kevin made it here okay. And we wanted to see you; to make sure you're okay.'

'Well, I'm okay. I'm doing great.'

'I can see that,' she looked down at my Mom's hands.

My Mom shot her a look and turned back toward her chair. She slumped in it, exhausted.

'Thank you both for taking Kevin for the summer. I couldn't – I don't know what I would have done.'

'It was no trouble at all. It was a pleasure.'

'But,' she continued with her voice raised a few decibels, 'Kevin and I need to get out of here and get on with our lives. This has been a good break, but I can take over things again.'

'Are you really fine?' asked my Grandma.

'Yes!' Mom said louder. 'I've been taking care of him, of us, his whole life. I'm sorry that I had to lean on you guys once. Once! But I can take it from here, thank you. We're going to go back to Salina tomorrow. That's my decision.'

'We just want what's best for Kevin.'

'I'm what's best for Kevin. What, you think you can just start taking over when he's 12 and decide what's best for him, for us?' She was screaming now. 'You weren't there 12 years ago, and all of a sudden you're here now?'

'Sarah, don't talk to your mother in that tone,' piped in my Grandpa.

Mom looked at him with a mixture of shock, distain and outrage. She opened her mouth, but she turned away instead.

'You never let us be there 12 years ago,' my Grandma's voice was shaking but relatively calm.

Mom spun around. Tears streamed down her face. 'You didn't approve!'

My grandparents let her continue.

'I was your perfect little girl who messed up once in her life, and you didn't know how to handle it.'

'We were nothing but supportive,' said my Grandpa.

'You were nothing. You didn't come visit. You barely called. You weren't there.'

'You told us not to.'

'Good parents come anyway.' She lowered her voice and sounded out each syllable, 'Good parents come anyway.'

My Mom continued to sob quietly for a few minutes. Otherwise, there was silence.

'Sarah, we're sorry,' my Grandpa said. 'We truly are. We thought we were doing the right thing by adhering to your wishes. We didn't know what to do. I admit it, we were surprised. But we tried to be there for you. I, I guess, it's our fault for not doing a good enough job.' He walked over to her with his head down and tentatively put his hand on her shoulder.

'Thank you,' she whispered through the tears.

My Grandma finally walked over and joined him. I kept my distance.

After a while, Mom stood up. 'I appreciate you being here now,' she said quietly. 'But Kevin and I need to get on with our lives in Salina.'

'If that's what you need to do, we'll support you all the way,' my Grandma said as she walked up and hugged my Mom. 'We love you, Sarah. I'm sorry we ever let things get in the way of us. If you need to go, that's fine. We can even spend some time with you there if you want us. If you need money, we can help out.'

I stood there shocked at what was happening.

'What about me?' I erupted. 'Did anyone think about what I wanted to do? I can't go back to Salina. I won't go back to Salina.' They all turned to face me. 'Does anyone ever think about me? For the first time in my life, I've started to feel happy. I like Cleveland. I like caddying. I'm comfortable there.'

'Kevin, you'll be fine back home in Salina, once you get adjusted,' said my Mom.

'No! I can't go through it again. It was hard as heck at first for me, but now I want to stay! I've made friends there, something I don't have in Salina. I don't throw up anymore; well, not as much anyway. I can't go back to Salina. There's nothing for me there. I hate it there compared to Cleveland. It's all just going to be the same way it's always been in Salina – miserable! You say that you're better, Mom, that you're going to get better? How?!? Look at your hands.' She kept staring at me. 'You're no better off than when I left. I can't go back to that life. I can't keep moving when you decide the apartment isn't clean anymore. I can't keep changing my pants because you're afraid I sat in something when we went out to eat because you were too busy cleaning some invisible spot on the floor so that you didn't have time to go the store and get groceries.' I was out of breath. 'I can't go back there. I'm not happy there. Please don't make me go back there. I can't go back to that life. It's not fair!'

My mother slumped back down into her chair and began to cry, her face in her bandaged hands.

She looked up at me and finally spoke, 'I always was a nervous kid – whether it was that my food somehow was poisoned, or my fear of dogs. Do you understand how afraid of dogs I was?' She looked briefly over to my grandparents. 'The reason I read so much as a girl was because I was afraid that a loose dog in the neighborhood would attack me, and I thought I might be safe if I stayed indoors.' She turned back to me. 'I hid most of it from everyone. I didn't let anyone know how scared I was. I knew that it wasn't normal, so I didn't talk to anyone about it. When I went away to college, it got worse. Living in the dorms, so closely with so many other girls, there was nowhere to hide, except further inside myself. I know that I started to cut myself off from you guys even more then – I apologize – but I closed myself off from everyone. That's when the fear of germs and the hand-washing really started. I could function obviously, at school, at work, I don't want you to think that this has always been so debilitating, but it was always a struggle.'

She paused briefly. We waited quietly for her to continue.

'When I found out I was pregnant with Kevin, I lost control.' She looked at me intently. 'Don't take this the wrong way, Sweetie, but I thought I had ruined my life. I quickly came to realize that you are the most important, greatest gift a person could ever ask for, but back then I thought I'd ruined my life. Before that I never thought I had the power to ruin my life; I was always pretty straight-laced. But I had screwed up pretty bad; and I became intent on making sure that something never happened again – that nothing bad would ever happen to me and my wonderful baby. I feel like I need to do everything I can to protect you, me, us, from anything bad that can happen. And I thought I had the power to control that. But the harder I try to protect you, the more things I find that can hurt you. I need to protect you and me all the time – all the time – from germs, fire, traffic, anything that can kill you. Everything I do to protect you I do so that I won't ever lose you. I…I guess I never thought enough about how much it was taking out of you.'

'It's not your fault, Mom.'

Chapter 19

My grandparents and Mom dropped me off at the first tee just 10 minutes before the 11:00 tee time. We'd taken the first flight out of Wichita, and I really didn't think we were going to make it.

'Bill, you're going to kill all of us!' my Grandma screamed.

'We'll be fine. We have to get the boy to his match,' he pressed the pedal and grinned.

We reached the country club as the members were assembling on the first tee.

'I was starting to think you weren't going to make it,' Mr. Morgan greeted me with a smile. 'Where have you been? You had me nervous.'

'I had some family things to take care of. I'm sooo sorry.'

'256! Where have you been?' Mr. G scurried up to me. 'Hurry it up, son. I was just about to give your bag to Kovach.'

Mouse met me as I walked over to the water fountain to wet my towel. 'Where the heck have you been? You just disappeared. Did the Tool thing scare you that much?'

'No, I had to go back to Kansas to see my Mom.'

'Everything all right?'

'Yeah, it's fine.' I barely paid attention to Mouse, partially because I was so frazzled about the match and partially because I was overhearing Kovach and two other Senior Caddies who were hanging around Mr. G's desk.

'I can't believe we're going to have a Spook and Tool caddying in the club championship. What a disgrace,' said Kovach.

'It's a farce.'

'That's what you get when you have a jerk and an old fart making it to the finals.'

I joined the rest of the twosome on the tee, where things were intense but less crazy.

Mr. Booth walked by me on his way to his bag.

'Good luck, Mr. Booth,' I offered.

'Thanks, son…' he glanced my way and his smile slid away from his face. I had seen him at his worst, submerged to his mouth in muddy water, and I'm sure he had no interest in dredging up the incident.

He grabbed his driver from Tool and fled to the other side of the tee.

'Good luck, loser,' Tool mumbled to me.

I didn't respond.

About 15 members had gathered near the first tee to walk along with the match. Another dozen assembled in carts. Mrs. Morgan was there – hair pulled back tight, golf skirt revealing tan legs. She looked about 20 years or so younger than her husband. Mr. Finnegan, Mr. Holland and some of Mr. Morgan's cronies joined the crowd. Most were wearing their golf shoes, presumably so they would be ready in case the coach called them off the bench.

'Gentlemen,' began a nervous T.Rex as he flailed his short arms, 'I wish you both luck in this match to decide this year's Westwood club championship. We will play 18 holes in match play format. Standard USGA rules apply. I will serve as referee if any rules, questions or issues arise. We flipped a coin earlier to decide who would tee off first, and Mr. Booth won that. So without further ado, Mr. Booth, you have the tee.'

The pumpkin-headed Booth approached the tee. He wasted no time, no practice swing, as he took his Hogan driver back and launched his ball deep down the fairway. A few members clapped lightly.

Mr. Morgan stood over his ball a little longer than usual, but when he brought the club back it was as smooth as ever. The persimmon driver struck the ball cleanly. The tee popped up end over end straight up to waist level before landing softly on the tee box. A perfect drive.

It wasn't until we started down the fairway, out from under the lofty trees that I noticed how hot the day was. The grass was so dried out it crunched under my feet. Mr. Booth already had circles of sweat marks on the back and armpits of his light blue golf shirt. His red hair looked on fire. Mr. Morgan was dressed in a white shirt and fire engine red pants. He was sweating too, but at least he looked more comfortable. He showed no outward sign of nerves or pressure.

We arrived at Mr. Morgan's shot first. He was still 220 yards away. He pulled out his 3-iron and landed it on the runway in front of the green. Mr. Booth was 205 away. He shielded his eyes as he stared at the pin. He juggled the heads of his 3-iron and 6-iron. He decided to go for it and pulled out the 3. His ball started out a little right, but faded onto the green.

'Good shot, Alex,' applauded Mr. Morgan calmly, almost cheerily. He walked over to me and pulled out his 8-iron. 'Let's run this one up there close.'

And that's what he did. He hit the 8-foot putt to match Mr. Booth's tap-in birdie. Classic Morgan. I felt good.

On the next hole, classic Morgan wasn't enough. Mr. Booth blasted his drive past Mr. Morgan's and left himself with a 9-iron onto the green. Mr. Morgan's chip wasn't close enough. They both 2-putted. Mr. Booth had won his first hole.

It was strange caddying in this environment, with spectators along for the ride. I felt like an extra on a movie set. I was in every scene but no one really noticed me unless I obviously messed up.

The third hole was the only hole Mr. Booth allowed Tool to forecaddie on, since the threat of the gulley was so ominous.

'Your man's dead, Wichita,' said Tool. 'He's out of his league and everyone knows he'll collapse if he ever gets any kind of lead. That's why he hasn't played in the club championship for like a decade. He's the biggest choker out here.'

'We'll see,' I replied.

'And you didn't really hurt me last week,' he said unconvincingly. 'You know I could kick your ass.'

I looked him straight in the eye. 'Tool, do whatever you want. I'm done worrying about you.' And I was. I picked up the golf bag and walked away.

Both golfers hit their drives safely and put their second shots on. Mr. Morgan marked his ball and handed it to me. 'What do you think?'

I surveyed the 25 feet between his spot and the hole. 'Looks like it breaks about six inches to the right.'

'That much? I was going to play it on the left edge.' I handed back his ball.

'Never leave a birdie putt short. Right, Kevin?'

'Right.'

The ball started off at the hole and then slid four inches to the right of the cup.

'That's good,' called Mr. Booth.

'Thanks.' Mr. Morgan picked up for par.

'Shoulda listened to you,' he said as he handed the putter back to me.

Booth hit his 15 foot putt for a birdie and a 2-hole lead.

Mr. Morgan looked concerned as he approached the 4th tee. He stared out at the par-3 hole and walked over to me.

'What do you think? 4-iron or 3-iron?'

'The pin looks a little up. I think the 4-iron would be enough.'

'4-iron it is.'

He seemed to make good contact, but he pushed it right. It splashed into the sand trap short of the green.

'Goddamnit!' he said; I wasn't sure if at himself or at me. He slammed the 4-iron back into the bag and fumbled around for the sand wedge.

Mr. Booth took the hole for a 3-hole lead after four holes. They tied the next two holes and then Mr. Booth hit his ball into the trees on the 7th hole. Mr. Morgan and I stood together on the fairway as we waited for Mr. Booth to hit out of trouble.

'So how is your mom doing?' he asked.

'Fine, why?'

'Isn't that why you went back home this week?'

'Yeah. It is. She's doing fine. It's -- it's been a little tough.'

'Well, let me know if there's anything I can do; if you ever, you know, if you ever want to talk about it.'

I paused. 'Thanks.'

Mr. Morgan parred the hole. Mr. Booth double-bogied it. We had fought our way back to 1-down.

Mr. Booth hit his drive on the 8th hole far, but too far left, into the pine trees. Tool had no idea where the ball landed, so we walked over to help them search for it. The pines were spaced closely together, and the rough was unusually high amidst the pine needles. No one saw it land. It could be anywhere.

T.Rex checked his watch several times as we combed through the underbrush.

'Mr. Booth,' he finally announced. 'We've been looking for 10 minutes now, we're going to need to wrap this up if we can't –'

'Here it is,' yelled Tool. He stood proudly over the ball. It sat up in the rough along the tree line with a clear line to the pin.

'Looks like they found it,' said Mr. Morgan.

'That can't be the ball,' I protested to him, 'His ball was nowhere near that point.'

'Maybe it kicked right,' Mr. Morgan tried to reason.

I groaned.

I stepped on something hard. I stopped cold. I lifted my foot, and a Titleist stared up at me.

Mr. Morgan reached down and picked it up. He looked at it and turned it toward me to show me Booth's markings.

I wanted to blow a fuse.

'He...they can't...'

He sighed. 'Kevin, if they want it that bad. They can have it.'

'But, they...'

'It's okay, Kevin. Everything's going to be okay.'

Even with Tool's help, Mr. Booth lost the hole. He then missed a short putt to lose the 9th. He stomped off the green.

'That's a lot of work to be all tied up,' Mr. Morgan said while wiping his brow as we walked off the 9th green. 'I feel like I've been through a war.'

The crowd grew even more, to about 50 or so, as we started the back 9. A group of caddies joined from the caddie yard, including Mouse. Three familiar faces appeared in the back of the crowd. My Mom gave me a subtle wave as we made eye contact. I gave up an embarrassed but appreciative smile.

Mr. Morgan found himself on the 10th green in two while Mr. Booth had hit his second shot into the deep, greenside sand trap. His ball was a fried egg, with a side order of high bunker lip. He took one look at his ball buried in the sand and slumped his shoulders. He swung hard with his sand wedge, and a huge cloud of sand emerged from the trap and settled softly onto the green. But no ball. He stared at the sand in disbelief. He took a deep breath. He attacked the ball again. It plopped out of the trap but trickled down the lip and back in. His face reddened. On his third try, the ball rolled onto the front of the green. When he emerged from the trap, he was sweating like Nixon and swearing like LBJ.

Mr. Booth picked up the ball and conceded the hole. For the first time in the match, Mr. Morgan had the lead. Mr. Morgan won the next hole, and miraculously we were up 2 holes with only 7 holes left.

Mr. Morgan looked relaxed as he put his next drive into the fairway.

We stood where his ball landed while we waited for Mr. Booth to select a club to hit his ball out of the rough.

'We're moving here,' I said quietly.

'Huh?' Mr. Morgan looked my way. 'What do you mean?'

'We're moving to Cleveland. My Mom and me.'

'You are?' He let the clubhead hit the ground. 'That's great.'

'We're going to live with my grandparents, at least at first. It'll be tight, but we'll work it out.' I kept my gaze toward the green. 'My Mom is going to see some specialists over at the Cleveland Clinic, doctors who can help her stop being afraid of everything all the time.'

We watched as Mr. Booth silently chose his club and hit his ball onto the edge of the green.

'That's really great, Kevin. I'm really glad to hear that.'

'Knock it on the green.'

He did.

Each was about 25 feet from the hole. Mr. Booth was the first to putt – a curling downhill lag. My heart skipped a beat as it kissed the edge of the hole, but it just slid by and kept rolling about 10 past. He held the putter like a hammer and looked ready to explode. Mr. Morgan didn't give his putt a chance; he left it 2 feet out to the right, but he tapped in for par. Booth approached his ball and hovered over the come-backer. His putt again lipped out.

'Jesus Chr—' Mr. Booth knocked the ball off the green with the back of his putter. He stormed off the green like a bull. He threw his putter at the bag as Tool replaced the pin. Mr. Booth was now down 3 holes with 6 holes left to play.

Mr. Morgan handed me his putter. 'I may win this damn thing after all,' he said under his breath. That made me nervous.

Mr. Morgan tied Booth on the next two holes, but he didn't look comfortable. He stood over the ball longer than usual, and he kept checking and rechecking his grip. Nevertheless we were up 3 holes with 4 to play.

But on the 15th tee, he cranked his drive deep out of bounds on the right side of the hole. The ball sailed high over the trees and landed in a backyard. He suddenly looked terrified. He dug into the bag and pulled out a second ball. It too sailed out of bounds to the right.

'Give me the 3-wood,' he said quietly.

I took the driver out of his hands.

He hit his third ball into the trees on the right, but at least it was in bounds. He looked like he was going to puke.

Mr. Morgan took two shots to get out of the trees. Mr. Booth hit his second shot onto the green.

'You can have the hole, Alex,' conceded Mr. Morgan. We moved to the 16th; 2 holes up with 3 to go.

Mr. Booth hit first. He pounded his drive into the left side of the fairway. Mr. Morgan stepped up and again launched his ball right. He took a couple of practice swings as the rest of the group left the tee.

'What am I doing wrong?' he said to himself. A band of sweat formed on his forehead.

As I walked down the fairway, I tried to replay the vision of my composite golf swing that had put me to sleep so many nights and compared it to Mr. Morgan's swing the last few holes, but I couldn't pinpoint the problem. He wasn't making any obvious mistakes, like lifting his head or anything.

We found his ball in a grove of trees on the right.

'I may have an opening through those two trees right there,' he said. 'But let's just hit it left into the fairway. You agree?'

'I agree, let's get back into the fairway.'

He pulled out a 3-iron. The ball went 45-degrees right, hit an oak tree square on the trunk and landed 10 yards behind us. He slumped his shoulders.

'What the hell am I doing wrong?'

I replayed his last swing in my head.

'It seems like you're not pausing at the top of your swing like you usually do,' I offered. 'You usually pause there, just for a half second, but I don't think you've been doing it on the last few holes. I think you're rushing your downswing, and you're not getting your wrists through it.'

He took a couple of practice swings. 'Well, let's try it. We've already lost this hole, so let's give it a shot.'

We walked back to his ball and he put a controlled swing on it. His shot didn't go far, but at least it went straight.

'Maybe that's it. We've got to figure this out or I'm going to lose another one of these.' He looked pale.

Booth, with no pressure on him, landed his ball in the center of the green. He 2-putted for par. After losing the hole, we were up only 1 hole with 2 holes to go.

We approached the 17th tee. My experience with Booth on that hole a few weeks earlier was a distant memory for us both at this point. The hole was playing 130 yards today.

Booth took a huge divot with his 9-iron. The ball landed on the green like a slice of bologna hitting a deli counter.

'What club do you think?' Mr. Morgan asked, looking at me needily.

'Let's go with the 8-iron,' I responded. 'And remember to pause at the top for a sec. Don't rush the downswing.'

He looked at me straight in the eye. 'Okay.' I had become his sensei.

He took an extra practice swing; checked his grip a couple of times, and then slowly pulled the club back. He made solid contact. The ball started to leak a bit to the right but it held its course and landed on the right side of the green. He gave my shoulder a squeeze as he handed the club back to me.

Mr. Morgan was first to putt. I lined it up. Dead straight. He left no doubt that this birdie putt would not be left short. But he pushed it to the right; the ball never even threatened the cup, and it rolled 15 feet past the hole.

'Walter,' he held the shaft to his forehead. 'What are you doing?' He marked his ball and cursed under his breath.

Booth rolled his putt from 20 feet to within 2 feet of the cup. He tapped in for par.

Mr. Morgan furrowed his brow as he lined up his putt. He took back the putter and decelerated as he came through. The ball headed right for the cup but stopped a full rotation short.

'You woman!' Mr. Morgan grunted.

'That's good,' offered Booth.

As Tool returned the pin to the cup, he looked my way and smirked. We were all tied up going into 18.

Mr. Morgan was physically exhausted – the heat had taken its toll on him – and emotionally spent. His face looked drained.

'Just one more hole to go,' I said as I took the head cover off the driver. 'Remember to pause at the top. Don't rush things.'

He nodded and turned to watch Booth tee off.

Booth crushed his ball but it hooked left toward the trees.

'Jack Martin!' Booth called out along with a few spectators, but it kicked left into the trees.

He slammed the club head into the tee box.

Booth's poor drive breathed a little life back into Mr. Morgan. He stepped up to the tee and put a big swing on the ball. It leaked to the right but landed safely out of trouble. He walked over to his bag and handed me the driver.

'I'll go to my ball,' he said. 'You follow that little son of a bitch, and make sure he doesn't pull any shenanigans. Don't let his hand go near his pocket.'

Tool and I race-walked down the cart path to reach the trees. I had a line on where it hit, but didn't see where it went after it kicked left. Tool focused more on the perimeter. I searched deeper in the trees. The gallery joined the search party. We scoured the deep rough and checked under each tree branch.

'Here it is!' Tool and I yelled simultaneously, even though we were staring down at two different places. Tool looked at me like I'd trumped his full house with a 4 of a kind. He dropped his towel and picked up the second ball he had dropped. I pointed everyone to Booth's ball that was leaning up against the trunk of a pine tree.

'Christ,' muttered a deflated Booth. He took out a few clubs and checked his swing options. He finally pulled out his putter and turned it around to hit the ball left-handed. He whacked at the ball like a machete and slapped it about 30 feet out of trouble.

The door was wide open for Mr. Morgan.

'How far we got?' he asked.

'Well, that tree back there is 192 yards from the green and we're 17 yards from that, so we have 175 to the green.'

'How the heck do you know that tree is 192 yards from the green?'

'I counted it off one time.'

He smiled. 'Good job. So what club?'

'4-iron,' I responded firmly.

He took the club from my hands and addressed the ball. Then, he looked up at me. 'Aren't you going to say anything else?'

'What? Oh, yes, pause at the top.' He looked down again at the ball. 'And have fun,' I added. A smile crept across his cheeks as he settled in over the ball.

He hit the ball well, but it took a bad bounce on the green and shot into the trap to the right of the green. The crowd groaned.

'Oh, no.' said Mr. Morgan. The open door was slammed shut.

'You were robbed,' I responded.

With that, momentum shifted back over to Booth. He had about 150 yards to the green. He wasted no time pulling out an 8-iron and hitting his ball 15 feet from the pin. A beautiful shot. The gallery couldn't help but to applaud. I almost applauded. Mr. Morgan said nothing.

As I ran through the possible outcomes, I noticed Tool negotiating the steep slope of the 18th fairway with choppy little steps. I thought of when I fixed his bags a few days earlier and smiled. If Booth missed his putt and Mr. Morgan could get up and down from the trap, we would move to the first hole for a sudden-death playoff. I sized up Booth's putt with every closer step I took, willing it to be further away from the pin than it appeared.

We reached Mr. Morgan's ball in the sand. Pretty good lie. Big embankment, but he had enough room to get his shot over the embankment and onto the green without a problem.

I handed him his sand wedge, and he carefully stepped to his ball. I picked up a rake. He twisted his feet in the sand to secure his stance. He adjusted his grip. He looked at the pin. He readjusted his grip. He looked at the pin. He paused and bounced a little at the knees. Finally, he took the club back and swung hard through the ball. A mammoth mass of sand flew into the air, and the ball squirted out. A brief gust of wind blew the sand back into his face. He twisted out of the way, blinded. The ball headed directly toward the hole. It landed about a foot beyond the pin. It stopped. Then spun backwards, and rolled right into the hole.

The gallery erupted. A rush of excitement ran through my body. I launched the rake straight into the air, unconcerned that it might impale me. It was the best shot I ever saw. A second rush surged through me when it dawned on me that we had just won. I launched myself into the air. I looked over at Mr. Morgan. He held his arms high in the air. His fists clenched. He was beaming. Mrs. Morgan broke free from the gallery and hugged him.

I looked over at Tool. He looked like he'd just lost his puppy; no, like someone had just killed his puppy.

Booth slowly walked over to the cup, peered down and then trudged silently to the clubhouse, as if in a daze.

I walked over to Mr. Morgan, and he gave me a hug and thanked me. But quickly he had to field the onslaught of his fellow members who had witnessed the spectacle. I picked up the bag and made my way to the nearby bag rack.

My Mom and grandparents quickly joined me. They were glowing. Mouse stopped by with a handshake and a pat on the back. But eventually the excitement died down and I was just another caddie waiting to get paid.

Mr. Morgan emerged from the crowd.

'Kevin, I assume this is your mother I've heard so much about, and your grandparents.'

I introduced everyone. I was glad that my Mom's bandages were off. I hoped he wouldn't notice the residual scabs.

'Well, Kevin is a wonderful young man. I couldn't have done it without him.'

'Thanks, we're very proud of him.'

'And for your great work, I wanted you to have this.' He handed me a personal check.

I took a quick look, saw a 5 and a zero, and shoved it into my pocket. $50 was a pretty good pay day. A couple more rounds and I would hit my goal for the summer. 'Thanks, Mr. Morgan. I really enjoyed it.'

'And we'll still see you around here some more; summer's not quite over.' He looked quickly at my Mom and back at me. 'And I understand that we'll be seeing you long term around here.'

My Mom averted her eyes.

My Grandpa interjected, 'Yes, looks like Kevin and his mom will be living here for a while.' He placed his hand on my head and then on my shoulder.

'Well, good to meet you. If you'll excuse me, I need to go buy drinks for the entire men's grille.' He took a couple of steps and spun back around, 'Hey, Kevin. There's a dinner tonight, an awards ceremony, at the club. How'd you like to come join Mrs. Morgan and me?'

He caught me off guard. 'Um, sure. That'd be great.'

'Meet us in the front lobby at 6:00.'

'Okay.'

'We'll see you then.'

My grandparents, Mom and I made our way to the Oldsmobile. I reached into my pocket to get a good look at the check. I stopped dead.

'There's another zero.'

'What?'

'There's another zero. It's not $50. It's $500.'

'He gave you $500?'

'Looks like it.' I checked the writing below the number. 'Five hundred and no/100s.'

'He gave you $500? You're sure it's not a mistake'

'Doesn't look like it.' I handed it to Mom

'What, is this guy made of money or something?' asked my Grandma.

'For carrying a bag?' My Grandpa looked like he was questioning his career choices.

'Holy cow, $500.'

'You must have done one great job.'

'We're proud of you, Kevin.'

Later that evening I sat in an old sportcoat that was too small for me and a tie I'd borrowed from my Grandpa at a white table-clothed table with Mr. and Mrs. Morgan, Mr. and Mrs. Finnegan and Mr. and Mrs. Holland. Needless to say, I was the odd-man out in many ways. There were about 100 people in the dining room with a dais set up in the front. I felt like everyone was observing my every move, when most likely no one noticed me. I was conspicuously younger than everyone else. And my stomach was conspicuously acting up on me.

'Are you comfortable, Kevin?' asked Mrs. Morgan next to me. She wore a red cocktail dress that sufficiently revealed her finer features.

'Yes, this is really nice.'

'Well, eat as much as you want. You deserve it.'

'Thanks.'

I picked through my salad -- worthless food, not enough calories. T.Rex took to the podium as they served our dinners – steak, roasted potatoes, and cooked carrots. I removed the fat from my strip steak as T.Rex handed out the awards for the higher-handicap flights that also had competed. My stomach still wasn't welcoming, but with everyone's attention focused on the awkward acceptance speeches up front, I managed to calm down enough to eat half of my steak and potatoes. I actually was pretty full when T.Rex began to introduce Mr. Morgan.

'When this tournament began,' started T.Rex, 'few would have listed Walter Morgan as the favorite to win. We consider Walter as a valuable member of this club. A kind person; a friend to many, many of us. We also remember Walter as quite a player in his day.' T.Rex cracked a smile, and the room filled with polite chuckles. 'Well today was Walter's day. Walter was a great player back in his prime, but he never was able to pull out a win. Now he will always be remembered as a champion. So without further ado, let me congratulate and introduce Walter Morgan.'

The room erupted with applause. Mr. Morgan snaked his way among the tables to the podium. He took out a pair of reading glasses and extracted a folded-up piece of paper from his burnt-orange sport coat.

'Thank you,' he began. 'Thank you, all. It makes me proud to stand up here. I kept telling myself all last night and all this morning that it didn't matter to me if I won today or not. That my life would be the same no matter what happened. I can assure you all tonight that that was a load of bunk. I was just telling myself that to calm myself down. This…this feels great. It indeed hurt to come in second place all those times, all those years ago, so much so that I dropped out of competing. I'm glad I came back. I should have come back earlier. You should never run away from your defeats.

'There are a couple of people whom I would like to thank. First, my wife, Jessica. You encouraged me to make a run at the championship again. Thank you; you're quite a gal. Secondly, I invited a young man tonight to join me at this dinner.' My heart sped up. 'Kevin Campbell, my caddie, is a great little guy. He helped me keep things together today and throughout the tournament. Come on up here, Kevin.' My blood went cold. I didn't move.

'Come on, son,' I heard behind me. A hand gently prodded me.

My worst nightmare. I was caught completely off-guard. All eyes were on me, and potentially soon, the contents of my stomach. I quickly swallowed several times to keep my steak and potatoes down. I slowly stood up. I walked like a zombie past each table. Each step threatened to detonate the TNT in my gut. My face went numb and then my entire body. I was a bag of nerves when I reached the front.

Mr. Morgan shook my hand in front of the podium and said, 'Why don't you tell everyone what you said to me on the course, Kevin, when it looked like I was going to fall apart again?'

Terror! What was he thinking? I looked out at the sea of faces smiling back at me. I looked behind me for help, but Mr. Morgan had taken two steps back. He too smiled and waited for my words.

And then, I leaned toward the microphone and said, 'Well, I noticed that he, um Mr. Morgan, wasn't pausing at the top of his swing like he usually does. I just told him to, you know, pause.' The crowd erupted in applause.

'Yes, Kevin, has been my good luck charm all summer. Thanks for all your work, Kevin. And thank you all for your support.'

I had done it. I didn't freeze. I didn't projectile vomit. I didn't make a fool of myself. It may have seemed like a small victory for someone else, but it was a huge victory for me. I had been put in the worst situation I could imagine – a full stomach and a full crowd – and I emerged unscathed. To me it was bigger than winning any club championship.

'Nice job, Kevin,' Mrs. Morgan whispered to me upon my return to the table.

She had no idea.

After dinner, I stopped off at the caddie house to pick up my sweatshirt that I left a couple of days ago. The sun was about to set and the caddie house was empty. My sweatshirt was hanging on the hook where I had left it. Suddenly I heard soft footsteps outside.

'Kevin,' said Maureen as she peaked around the door. 'You scared me. I was looking for Mouse, but it didn't look like anyone was here.' She walked toward me. 'What are you doing in here so late?'

'I'm just picking up my sweatshirt.'

'I'm glad to see you.' She tilted her head and put her hand on my arm. 'I saw that you guys won. I was on the 18th hole when he hit the shot.'

She paused and moved in closer. My heart was beating in my throat. My stomach began to swirl.

'Kevin, I swear you've grown four inches this summer.'

'You think? I don't know.' I focused on controlling my stomach.

She pushed some hair out of my eyes. 'And your hair has gotten blonder.'

'Maybe,' I stammered.

'You just look older than when I first met you.'

'It's been kind of a crazy summer.'

'It sure has been. A lot has happened.'

'Maureen, again I'm sorry—'

She moved in closer and said, 'It's fine.'

She leaned in and gave me a soft, wet kiss. After a few seconds she pulled away and looked into my eyes, smiling. I pulled her back to me and kissed her a second time. My first two kisses.

'I've got to go, Kevin. I'll see you around.'

'When?'

'Around.' She smiled and walked out.

I waited in the dark by myself for a minute or two. Happy. Excited. Proud of myself. I hadn't thrown up then either.

What a day.

Epilogue

About ten years later, I saw Mouse. I had only seen him a few times since that summer of caddying. I wish it had been under better circumstances.

'It's good to see you, Kevin. I'm really sorry. I know how much he meant to you.' He gave me a long, firm handshake.

I looked down at him. He had grown a little, but not much. 'Thanks, it's good to see you too.' I stood in my navy blue suit near the large flower arrangement in the room full of faces I mostly didn't recognize.

'You know, with you gone, I ended up caddying for Mr. Morgan a lot. He used to keep me up to date on what was going on with you. You ended up working for him at his law firm, didn't you?'

'Yeah," I replied. 'He got me a job in the mailroom. I worked there all through high school, until the summer after I graduated from Rocky River.'

'I kept on caddying through high school. I went to Ignatius, of course, as though I had a choice. And then the summer after I started at Bowling Green, they changed the rules and let college kids caddie. I moved up into 'management' and helped run the first tee with the new caddie master. I also supervised the kids in the bag room. It was pretty fun.'

'What year did Mr. G end up leaving?' I asked him.

'He ran things for a couple of years after you left. When they fired T.Rex, they decided it was probably a good idea to put some new life in the caddie program. He stayed around for a few more years, mostly as a golf course ranger. It was probably the best thing. I think the job was getting to be too much for him. You could tell the caddies were starting to lose respect for him just a little bit.'

'How about the other guys?'

'You remember Tool?' Mouse asked.

'Yeah. How could I forget?'

'About a year or two after the summer you were there, he lit a pack of firecrackers off at the range. He took a cigarette, took off the filter, lit one end and used it as a delayed fuse. He came back to the caddie house to watch it eventually blow. The pack started going off when Mrs. Dresser was in her backswing. She fell to the ground. I think she thought she got shot. Everyone was running around trying to figure out what was going on. Mr. G fired him on the spot. He went to high school at St. Ed's, and I never saw him again.'

We both laughed and then went silent for a moment.

'I think about Howie a lot,' I said.

'Yeah, me too. He was a great guy.'

'He still makes me laugh, whenever I think of him. I'll always remember him.'

'Me too,' replied Mouse. He glanced over at the casket. 'Never leave a birdie putt short.'

'What's that?'

'Never leave a birdie putt short. Mr. Morgan used to always say that whenever he had a chance for a birdie.'

'Oh, yeah…yeah, I do remember that.'

'To this day I say those words to myself whenever I stand over a birdie putt,' Mouse continued. 'Not that I get that chance often. Never leave a birdie putt short. Those are good words to live by. It always makes me think of him and smile. Now that I think of it though, I may have dropped in an extra birdie putt or two over the years that I would have left short, but I've three-putted more goddamn birdie opportunities in my life because of those words of Mr. Morgan's.'

We laughed again.

'So what are you doing now?' he asked.

'I finished up law school at Case two years ago. Mr. Morgan helped me get a job again with his old law firm. He had retired by then. It's going pretty well. I'm working my butt off, and the work's not all that exciting, but it's okay. I have an apartment down in Lakewood that I rarely see. How about you?'

'I'm selling welding materials. Sell 'em to auto shop companies, construction firms, even some high schools for shop class. Been doing it for five years or so. It's fine. Been keeping my eyes open for anything better, but it's fine for now. Pays the bills.'

He briefly scanned the room. 'And how's your Mom doing?'

'Great,' I paused. 'Really great. She got a job with National City soon after we moved here. She's been there ever since. She works downtown. She still lives a few blocks away from my grandparents.'

'That's great. I'm glad to hear it.'

Another short pause.

'And what's Maureen up to? I haven't seen her in years.'

He smiled and squinted a bit. 'She's good. Really good. She graduated from Dayton and has been working for an accounting firm. She travels a lot, but she's happy. You should think of giving her a call.'

'That's a good idea. Maybe I will. And we should get together sometime too, Mouse. It's been too long.'

'I agree, maybe we should.'

'Maybe we will.'

He shook my hand.

Author's Notes

I caddied at Westwood Country Club from 1979 through 1987. My summers there shaped who I am as much as any school I attended. This book started out as an attempt to compress all of the stories from my eight years there into a single narrative. The majority of the situations actually occurred, but not necessarily to the same characters in the book. The caddies and members in the book are fictional, but most were inspired by actual Westwood caddies and members. All names and descriptions have been changed.

There are many people whom I would like to thank for supporting me throughout the process of writing this book. The first is my brother in law Dan Coyle. Dan is a best-selling author, who is infinitely better at writing than I, but he was nothing but encouraging throughout the process. He read multiple drafts, reworked plot concepts and put me in contact with his industry contacts. He is a true friend.

Next is my older brother, Fritz, who used his superior legal skills to proof read multiple drafts. If his editing skills are any indication, he is an outstanding lawyer. Fritz was a caddie several years before I started, which was just one of the many ways he has charted the path that I have followed in life.

Joe Pahl has been my best friend since grade school. He was the inspiration for the character of Mouse. Joe also caddied at Westwood, and he has put up with my reliving caddies stories for years. Joe is like a brother to me.

My group of friends from college – Jeff West, Jeff Guelcher, Anthony Profaci, Todd Burnette, Brad Shaw, Joe Felber, Greg Ahearn and Carl Loschert -- are the funniest crew of idiots I have ever met. They honed my sense of humor over the years and provided source material for a few of the scenes. They are friends for life.

Thanks to my parents, who have always been loving and supportive and who trudged down to the Cleveland Public Library to find a book for me on Westwood history.

Mark Guerrera is a friend in Arlington and a fellow Georgetown grad. Mark was a caddie growing up in Connecticut. I told him about the book I was working on two years ago, and he told me I needed to finish it. With his encouragement, I did.

Finally, the most supportive person throughout this process and throughout my life has been my wife, Laura. She is the most giving, loving and kind person I have ever met. Laura has patiently allowed me to find the time to put into this project over the years, and she was an invaluable sounding board for storylines in the book.

About the Author

Rob Fisher was born and raised in Fairview Park, OH, a suburb of Cleveland. He lives in Arlington, VA, with his wife, Laura, and their three children. Rob has an undergraduate degree from Georgetown University and a graduate degree from the University of Michigan. This is his first novel.

Connect with Me

Friend me on Facebook: http://facebook.com/ rob.fisher2

Made in the USA
Middletown, DE
28 September 2018